beachside kisses with my enemy

A SWEET ROMANTIC COMEDY

KRISTIN CANARY

To the guy who's shared countless small quiet moments with me.
I love you.

author's note and content warnings

Hi, friend! Thanks so much for picking up this book. This book does NOT contain sex or swearing, and it *does* end with a happily ever after! It is Book 2 in the Hallmark Beach series but can stand alone. However, you may find it more enjoyable if you begin with Book 1.

While I do intend for my books to make you LOL and swoon, sometimes characters do deal with things that might be triggering to you. Here are some things you'll find in this book:

- Death of one or more parents (past event)
- Parental abandonment (past event, but still affecting the present)
- Very brief mention of miscarriage
- Mention of an emotionally abusive marriage (past)

Also, fair warning: This book will make you hungry. Hehe. Happy reading, and welcome back to Hallmark Beach!

Kristin

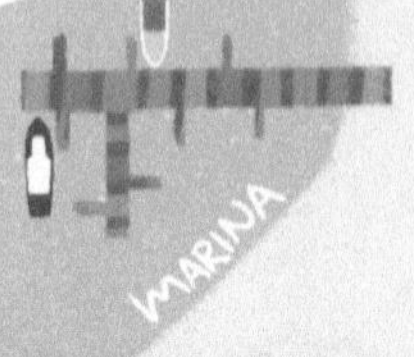

HALLMARK BEACH
hallmark beach
MARINA
THE PURPLE SEASHELL
1
Olive Paradise
2
THE BLUESTOCKING BOOKSHOP
3
RAINBOW ICE
4
The Green Robin
5
Just Peachy Boutique
6
The Pink Rose
7
MAIN ST.
THE BLACK HOLE
8
Blackberry muffin
9
AL'S GROCERY
10
The White Mocha
11
Something Blue
12
Red Sauce Pizza
13
The golden highlight
14
HIGHWAY 1
LEGEND
1: The Purple Seashell
2: Olive Paradise
3: The Bluestocking Bookshop
4: Rainbow Ice
5: The Green Robin
6: Just Peachy Boutique
7: The Pink Rose
8: The Black Hole
9: The Blackberry Muffin
10: Al's Grocery
11: The White Mocha
12: Something Blue
13: Red Sauce Pizza
14: The Golden Highlight

one

I've heard it said that life is a series of moments.

All moments encompass the same amount of time, and yet, not all moments are created equal. Most pass inconsequentially. You won't remember them. They might build toward some bigger thing, but they aren't the bigger thing itself.

This is not one of those moments.

I inhale and exhale a final breath, adjust my tie, and exit the manager's office at the back of Paprika, a five-star, urban-chic restaurant that serves a bunch of fancy dishes I'd never normally eat. But I cooked them, back when I was just a lowly chef's apprentice straight out of grad school. That was before Dale saw my potential and plucked me from the program, placing me on the path to management.

Sometimes, I really miss those days of anonymity in the kitchen. Not that it was stress-free. Let's just say that working with food is easier than working with people. But if being the manager of one of the most popular restaurants in Los Angeles is what I have to do to make my dream come true—to get back into the kitchen, and with my own recipes—then so be it.

Doesn't mean I have to like it.

Even now, as I walk onto the restaurant floor with purpose —the scrape of silverware hitting platters, the boisterous laughter of foreign businessmen, the soft hum of jazz music floating—I'm flagged down by the hostess. She knows I've got a meeting with Dale and that I'm not to be disturbed if she can help it.

I'd say it's good to be needed, but when it's a twenty-four-seven situation, it gets a little exhausting.

I glance at my watch as I stop at the hostess station. "What's up, Denise?" Turning my back to the customers who are hanging out in the lobby, I face my very pregnant lead hostess. "I only have a moment."

"I know, and I'm so sorry, Blake. Mr. Moffitt." Denise looks like she's going to cry, and that's no small thing given she's usually tough as nails. Maybe it's the hormones. She told us all the other day that she sobbed at some commercial featuring puppies, and that her husband was concerned for her well-being. Still, I don't like the idea of my people being so stressed that they're crying. *I* might work eighty-hour weeks and let the pressures of this job get to me from time to time, but that's not what I want for them.

"It's fine." My voice is gruff and short, but thankfully, Denise doesn't seem to notice. "Now how can I help?"

She grips the deluxe hostess stand—which looks more like a secretarial desk you'd find in a fancy law office, given its size and the fact it's made of the finest oak—and keeps her eyes focused on something behind me. "Somehow we're double booked. The gentlemen by the door have a party of twelve, and the women over there want a twelve-top for their bachelorette party. Both of them have reservations for the same table. And the men have been...testy."

I jerk my head up and glance back. I've seen enough to know that the men are *those* kind—the ones in suits who think the importance of their jobs and the size of their bank accounts entitle them to treat "the help" poorly. Pursing my lips together, I glance back at Denise. Study her closely. "Did they threaten you?"

She rubs her finger against the corner of her right eye and blinks. "Nothing I can't handle." Denise straightens. "Sorry for getting emotional."

"Hey, if I need to throw them out..."

Denise glares at me. "I'm not letting you do that. Not tonight, with Dale here."

I shrug. "Dale supports how I run this place." Not that he knows about every jerk I toss out of here. Maybe he wouldn't be okay with the effect on the bottom line. But he cares about his employees. He's a decent guy.

I wouldn't be potentially staking my future on him if he weren't.

My stomach twists at the idea of said future. But I have to deal with this problem before I can contemplate what Dale's going to say to me tonight. Why he sent me that email this afternoon. "How are wait times looking?" I ask.

"An hour at least. Probably closer to ninety minutes. Another eight-top just got seated."

Not unusual for a Saturday night in the city. Personally, I don't get it—I mean, our food is good and service impeccable, but is any food worth waiting two hours for? I rub the bridge of my nose and think. "Here's what we're going to do. I'll appeal to their sense of chivalry—whether they have one or not—and comp them fifty percent off their meals. Let's clear a spot at the bar and give them a free round as well."

Denise nods along with my plan. "Great idea. But I'll handle it. You go."

I narrow my eyes at her. "You sure?"

"Yes. I know this meeting is important."

She may not know *why* it's important—because I haven't told a soul about the fact that I finally submitted to Dale the business proposal I've been tweaking for the last three years— but Denise is perceptive. It wouldn't surprise me if she somehow knew my dream of opening my own restaurant, or that I finally got up the courage to ask my boss and mentor to become an investor.

"All right." I point toward one of our nearby busboys. "But if you need backup, Trent can assist."

Denise lifts her chin. "I've got this." Then she flicks on a smile and approaches the gentlemen—though I hesitate to call them that, honestly. The lead guy, with his pomaded head and Ray-Bans tucked into the collar of his expensive shirt, curls a lip at her. But thankfully, he listens. Finally, he nods, gives another dude a fist bump, and directs the group to follow Denise to the bar.

Phew. Another crisis averted.

My phone buzzes in my pocket and I pull it out. My chef's asking me a question about the special tonight, and my thumbs fly as I answer him and stride as quickly as I can across the floor to the back corner where Dale is tucked into a booth we usually save for VIPs.

He sets down his menu—as if he doesn't know every single item on it—and glances up at me, his bald head catching the light of the glass wall sconce behind him. His tan leathery skin nearly glows against the stark white of his modern-fit dress shirt, under which strain the muscles he works daily at honing. Dale Gunderson may be fifty-four (and more than twenty years my senior), but he's fitter and more stylish than I'll ever be. Definitely richer too.

Dad would have approved of my choice of mentor.

"You're late." The edges of Dale's voice tease, and the corners of his eyes crinkle.

I stuff my phone away and slide across from him. "Your restaurant is going to be the death of me."

Laughing, he snaps, and Beth—one of our best servers—appears with a bottle of wine and two glasses.

"Oh, none for me, thanks," I say. "I'm still on the clock."

"Nonsense." Dale waves away my protest while Beth pours the red liquid into the glasses and disappears. He lifts his glass and swirls the wine, then looks me in the eye. "We're celebrating tonight, after all."

I stiffen. "We are?" All I know is what his email said: *Read your proposal. Let's do dinner and discuss.*

It was very Dale-like—direct and to the point. And yet, mysterious, keeping vital information close to the chest.

"Well..." He draws out the word like silly putty. "There are obviously details to work out, but I've always known you had something special, Blake. I was just waiting for you to realize it too."

My jaw drops and my chest aches. Words I've waited my whole life to hear—though from a different source that I'll never hear it from now—and yet, there's a flicker of apprehension too. "Thank you, Dale. I don't know what to say." Leaving the glass of wine alone, I fold my hands on the table and lean forward. "So, you liked the proposal?"

"It needs work." He takes a sip, then snaps again at Beth, who brings out two sizzling steaks. Despite owning thirty restaurants across L.A., Dale's not much for fancy food either. Quality food, yes. But give him a hunk of perfectly grilled meat and veggies heaped with butter, and Dale Gunderson is a happy man.

I thank Beth as she and her assistant Shelby bring out the shared sides of asparagus, mashed potatoes, and house-made sourdough. On the outside, I'm calm and collected. On the inside, my mind is roiling.

Finally, the food is all in front of us, and Dale lifts his knife and fork to his steak as if he didn't just drop a bomb into my carefully laid plans.

Because I'd hoped this would go differently—that Dale would jump at the chance to invest in a restaurant that's basically an expansion of the food truck I opened in college as a side gig. Not tell me it *needs work*, whatever that means.

I reach for my fork, but don't lift it, instead running my finger across the cool silver neck. "So, um, what work do you think it needs?" Man, could I sound any less professional? At least my voice didn't crack like a pre-pubescent ninny. But the uncertainty in it definitely shouldn't belong to a guy who has his MBA from UCLA.

Dale lifts an eyebrow as he pushes a slice of steak into his mouth, groaning at the taste. "That's good. You really should try it."

I'm not exactly hungry right now—not with my future in the balance—but I want Dale to take me seriously, to know he can count on me to be steady, so I cut off a piece of steak and follow his example. The crisp, buttered edges of the cooked meat melt against my tongue, and something in me relaxes.

That's what good food does.

And maybe Dale knows me better than I think he does, because a tiny smile flits across his lips. He reaches for his cloth napkin and pats his mouth. "The proposal was good, Blake. I like the basic ideas. The city isn't overrun with restaurants specializing in grilled cheese, so the market research section was spot on. However, I think we need to push it more upscale than you proposed."

"Really? More upscale, like this?" I glance around and hold in a shudder. Paprika is nice and everything, but a little fancy for my tastes. And these aren't exactly the kinds of customers I pictured serving when I created my recipes. To be honest, I pictured the people in my hometown of Hallmark Beach, four hours north of here. I've spent the last twelve years since leaving there—first for college in Phoenix and then for grad school in L.A.—perfecting my recipes, always wondering what residents like my sister Marilee and Alberta Jenkins and Burt Reynolds (not the actor) would think of them.

Can't help but wondering what *she* would think of them too.

"She" being Lucy Reynolds, the girl who got away.

Rather, the girl I left.

Two weeks ago, on the first weekend of April, I finally got the chance to cook for my hometown. In a bizarre twist of events, I landed back there for a last-minute wedding thrown by one of my sister's friends. They needed a caterer, and even though I hadn't returned to Hallmark Beach since my parents' funeral six years ago, my sister was desperate.

I'd already failed her more times than I can count. I didn't want to do it again. So I begged Dale for the time away, dusted off the truck I hadn't used in three years since I started managing Paprika, and fired up the grill.

I was only in town for six hours, but it was heaven.

All but the interaction—or non-interaction, really—with Lucy, who shot me glares all night from afar. Not that I blame her, especially after what happened the last time I saw her. Still, she never seemed like the kind of woman to hold a grudge.

She didn't even hold a grudge when I spent a year flirting with her and then left for college—just acted normal whenever I'd come home for the summer. After that, it was me who pulled away, who held her at arm's length, and for good reason.

Part of me wishes I'd had a chance to clear the air with her a few weeks ago. The other part is kind of glad she hates me.

"It doesn't have to be quite *this* upscale, per se." Dale's voice breaks into my thoughts, and I blink to refocus and remember what we were talking about. "But we also don't want to run a fast-food joint that feels accessible to just anyone." He says "fast-food joint" like it's a dirty word as he scoops a heap of mashed potatoes onto his plate. "We want gourmet, dressed-up food. Like your mama made it, but put a tuxedo on it, you get me?"

I get what he's saying, yes. But it's not what *I* pictured for my restaurant. Still, all businesses have to compromise a bit, right? And I don't have a lot of other contacts begging to invest. I've got a small nest egg tucked away, but Dale's my best shot at getting the right location and exposure for success.

And if there's anything I know, it's that this restaurant *has* to be successful.

"I can work with that." I sit back in my seat. "What did you think about the recipes I submitted? Will they work?"

"Yes, absolutely. But I want more."

"More?" I blink.

"More." Dale shovels in a bite of potatoes and studies me. After swallowing, he continues. "I know you pictured a limited menu of four or five sandwiches, and while that might work for a food truck, it won't work for a real restaurant like the one I'm picturing. While there's merit to doing something and doing it well, I just don't think that's the brand we want for you or this place."

Though I understand it, branding was always the thing I hated talking about in grad school. Honestly, most of grad school wasn't my cup of tea. But I knew that to find the sort of success Dad always wanted for me, I needed to understand the ins and outs of business.

Even branding.

Too bad I can't just be myself. That's never been enough, though, so not sure why I'd think things would change now.

"And what brand is that?" I ask as I take another bite of my steak.

He studies me again, and I start to squirm under his assessment. Finally, he speaks. "You've got the potential to go the distance here, Blake. To not only create a dining experience that will be scalable and unique, but to have wealth and fame like you never dreamed of. I know you're all about the cooking—and I know you've missed it since coming to work for me as manager—but you could be so much more. We're talking Michelin stars. We're talking franchises. We're talking brand endorsement deals." Dale taps his plate with his fork. "We're talking celebrity chef status. I've got a buddy at a local TV network, and they've been looking for the next best thing. I want to put you on his radar."

My head is spinning. Dale's vision for me is so much larger than the one I have for myself. But it's still fully in line with my goals. Even Dad—if he were here—wouldn't be able to laugh at my chosen career as too "unstable" if I was a celebrity chef, now could he?

But wow. It's still a lot. I grab up my glass of water and chug half of it down. What Dale is saying...it sounds too good to be true. But it still will require more of me. More recipes. More creativity.

I don't want to throw away this opportunity, but I also don't want to lie to my mentor. "I love where you're going with this, and I understand the vision. I *want* to get you more recipes. But I'm just not sure how I'm supposed to find adequate time or energy to do that, and at the same time, continue to run a top-notch restaurant for you here."

Dale steeples his fingers, nods. "Do you think you could train a replacement manager over the next month?"

"What? Why?"

"Just as you said. You don't have the space for it. So, make the space for it."

I blink at him. The man's gone mad. Is he really telling me to quit my job? "I wouldn't even know what that looked like." What would I even do? Just sit around my kitchen in the cramped apartment I share with three other dudes and "dream up" recipes? I don't think so.

"How did you go about creating the original recipes in your proposal?"

"Trial and error, mostly. When I opened the food truck, I started with a basic grilled cheese." Just like my mom taught me, back when I was in elementary school and cooking became the thing we did together. My escape from the world, from the pressures Dad put on my grades and the sports he wanted me to play, all ways to ensure I made a different sort of escape—one from Hallmark Beach someday.

An escape he never made, to his everlasting regret.

"And how did you expand from there?" Dale asks.

"Customers would ask for variations and tweaks to the original, and that sparked my creativity, I guess. Allowed me to let loose in the kitchen."

"That's what you need to do, then. First, train a replacement—my nephew has been looking for a job, so this is a great opportunity. Then, reopen the food truck. Take the summer and give yourself room to create, room to dream again."

Room to dream...what would that be like? "To what end?"

"So by the end of summer, you're ready to start hiring staff and get things under way with the restaurant. I've already got the perfect location in mind. Checked with my realtor, and the lease will be available come August. We can take over and launch by the new year—maybe even sooner, depending."

Whoa. This is exactly what I've wanted for years, but after

thousands of moments of no movement, time is moving at a rapid-fire pace. "Um, I—"

"Blake." Dale locks me in with his gaze once more, his eyes cutting me with their intensity. "I can tell you're freaking out a bit. Don't even try to protest it. I know you." Then his expression softens a bit. "This is what we've been working toward. It's why I took you from the kitchen in the first place and made you manager. You needed to know everything there was to know about running a restaurant—for *this* moment in time. I see greatness in you, but you've got to see it in yourself too."

"Thank you." My mouth is dry, but my water cup is empty now. I'd snap at Beth like Dale did, but what for him is simple efficiency and command would feel like rudeness from me. "I am really grateful for this opportunity. I don't want to mess it up."

"And you won't." He cocks his head. "You know, sometimes a change of scenery can inspire creativity and greatness. You didn't really tell me much about your trip back home a few weeks ago, but when you returned, something in you seemed...I don't know. Lighter, maybe?"

He's not wrong. At first, I dreaded going back to Hallmark Beach, especially with the way I'd left after the funeral. After my conversation—or rather, disagreement—with Lucy. After the way, in my own grief and determination to not let Dad down (even in death), I abandoned my sister.

But two weeks ago, Marilee—and almost everyone else I encountered—treated me better than I deserved.

Everyone except Lucy.

She gave me death glares from across the vineyard where the wedding was held.

But everyone else was friendly and polite, not telling me—to my face at least—what a lousy brother I'd been. My sister even told me her roommates were moving out at the end of this month, so that by May first, my old room at the family home will always be available whenever I want to visit.

Maybe Dale is on to something. Because if anything, being back in Hallmark Beach recently was more than penance. It was an escape from the big city—from the pressures I live with every day. Pressures that have become normal, yes, but still burdensome at times.

I mean, I'm still determined to reach my dreams.

But wouldn't it be nice to reach for them *and* be somewhere that feels a little more like *me* than L.A. does? Dale's offering me that chance. To spend a summer in Hallmark Beach. To create again. To cook again.

To reconnect with my sister. To be a better brother—the chance to turn around my one regret.

Well, the only regret I would ever consider doing something about anyway. The other one...yeah. Best to leave that in the past.

"You're right, as you always are, Dale." And maybe it would be more prudent to get all the details down in writing, to hash everything out now, but in the six years I've known him, Dale has always looked out for me.

I trust him. And if he thinks this is what I need to do to make it in the big leagues, then this is what I'm gonna do.

I offer him my hand across the table. "And you've got yourself a deal."

two

LUCY

One month later...

After working in a restaurant for nearly thirteen years, lots of things don't faze me anymore.

Strange food orders.

Spilled drinks.

Hangry customers.

But a child running out of the restroom screaming "I peed in the sink!" at the top of his lungs?

That one's new.

His mother, a woman who looks around my twenty-eight years, races out after the boy, who looks to be around three or four. "No, he didn't! I swear," she screams as she chases her child around the tables. He's one fast little dude.

The other customers inside The Green Robin—an adorable restaurant with pink walls and lime-colored furniture that's also my home away from home—keep their eyes on the mother and son as they weave through the tables and out onto the back patio. Unfortunately, there are far too few of them here for a

Friday night, but it's only the third week of May, so I'm hoping things will pick up with the coming start of the Hallmark Beach summer season around Memorial Day weekend.

Jenny, one of my teenage waitresses, looks at me with wide eyes. "What do we do, Lucy?"

Laughing at her horror, I shake my head. "First, I'm going to help that poor mama out. And if he did really pee in the sink, then we're gonna clean it up."

Jenny wrinkles her nose. "Not it."

"Me either!" And that would be Sam, the hostess with a nose ring and spiked purple hair.

"Me three." Tiny Taylor—a forty-eight-year-old beast of a man with a droopy mustache—leans out of the kitchen door, his chef's hat askew. Steam billows from behind him.

If I was acting in my normal capacity as a server, I'd probably pipe up and say the same thing. But three weeks ago, owner Winona Lambert left me in charge of The Green Robin until the end of the summer so she could take her daughter on a once-in-a-lifetime graduation trip through Europe. She trusted me enough to leave things in my hands, and I refuse to fail her.

Especially since I know just how special a trip like that is.

"You guys hold down the fort in here." I put on an exaggerated brave face. "I'll be back."

As I walk through the restaurant toward the back patio, I greet guests and ask them how their dinner is. Our regulars already came through, and given the eight o'clock hour and the fact that we don't usually get people pulling off the Pacific Coast Highway this late for dinner, these guests must be staying at our town's singular inn, The Purple Seashell, owned by my Aunt Janine.

Most of the guests smile and mumble that their dinner's delicious—something I don't doubt, since Tiny makes a mean burger—although one older gentleman complains that his non-grilled onions are too crunchy. Instead of getting upset over the sheer ridiculousness of the complaint, I just wave to Jenny, who rushes over. "Can you bring this table a complimentary piece of fudge cake, Jen?" I turn to the guy, whose bushy eyebrows arc. "It's the best thing on the menu. Trust me."

He beams and rushes to nod. I leave Jenny to deal with him and exit onto the deck, scanning the few occupied tables until I find the small family of four in question. A breeze off the ocean just beyond the boardwalk nips at me, and I tug closed my black blazer, which I'm wearing over my normal uniform of a T-shirt, jeans, and white KEDS sneakers. The jacket is my attempt to look more professional. More like a manager.

Pretty sure I'm not fooling anybody, though.

The woman is feeding a little girl in a high chair, while the man with her listens to the little boy chatter as he stuffs his face with French fries. I head that direction, and the mom looks up, then buries her face in her hands. "Are you here to kick us out?"

"Of course not." I squat beside the kid and hold up my fist. "Hey, little man. You like your food?"

"Mmm hmm." The kid presses his own fist against mine and then pushes another fry into his mouth. "This playth ith ama-thing."

"Georgie, don't talk with your mouth full," Mom says.

"It's okay." I wave my hand in the air. "I do it all the time."

The kid snort-laughs.

Then I tilt my head. "This place *is* amazing. Did you know I've worked here since I was sixteen? That's more than twelve years. Crazy, huh?"

"Whoa. You're like, really old."

His dad rolls his eyes and ruffles the kid's hair. "Nothing like a kid to make you feel good about yourself, right?"

"Totally." I stand up. "Are you folks having a nice meal?"

"We are," the woman rushes to say. "I'm so sorry about

disturbing the peace inside. But just so you know, Georgie didn't pee in the sink. He peed in the urinal in the family restroom. He just thought it looked like a big sink." Her cheeks are tinged pink.

Okay, now *that's* funny. "I've never thought of it like that, but that is a really good point, Georgie. Thank you for bringing that to our attention."

Georgie nods, as solemn as if he's been bestowed a medal of honor. "You're welcome."

I tap my knuckle against the green tabletop. "Anything else I can get y'all?" I don't care how long I've lived on the West Coast. I'm a Texan through and through and will hold a death grip on my *y'all* until I draw my last breath.

"We're so good, thank you," the woman says.

"All right, then." Turning, I head back inside, where a classic rock station plays lightly overhead—song forty-two out of the sixty in this particular rotation, if I'm not mistaken. The smell of meat and cooked onions permeates the air. All of this is the norm.

But what's not normal—at least, around this time last year— is that not a single new customer has arrived recently, which might mean we need to cut servers and close up early. Again.

The Green Robin has seen lean times before, but the responsibility for them has never been on my shoulders. I'm still not sure why Winona chose me to watch over her baby for three whole months since I never went to college and I don't have any sort of business experience. But I do love this place, and this whole town. That's basically all I've got to recommend me. She thought it was enough, though, and I'm not going to waste my energy entertaining my doubts.

As Mama always said, if you ignore your negative feelings, eventually they'll go away. That philosophy has worked for me so far in life, so I think I'll just keep right on going.

Maybe I need to sit down and brainstorm ways to bring in new business. Tiny might have some ideas for new menu items that could entice people to come inside. I pivot toward the kitchen door to ask him, but before I can get there, Chloe Kensington breezes in.

Outside of this town, she's known as the princess of the small European country of Kentonia—but here, she's simply Hallmark Beach's newest resident along with her boyfriend, Frederick Shaw, who used to be her bodyguard and now works as a cellar rat out at the Loveland family vineyard.

Tia, one of Chloe's bodyguards, slips into the restaurant after the princess and does a casual sweep of the restaurant before settling against the wall, arms crossed over her chest. She's a lot less friendly than Chloe's other bodyguard, Les, but she takes her job of keeping the princess safe seriously, so I'm all for it.

Not that she really needs to be kept safe here in Hallmark Beach. But it was the concession Chloe made to her parents for staying in America, so I'm all for that too, since Chloe's become one of my closest friends.

She waves to me, a wide grin splitting her lovely face, her perfect blonde curls bouncing. "Evening!" Her British-like accent is as charming as the way she leans in to offer me a kiss on the cheek by way of greeting. "Do you have a moment to chat?"

"For you? Duh." I link my arm through hers and make eye contact with Sam, who nods. She's got things covered out here.

We walk down the hall to Winona's tiny office, which I've taken over for the time being. My boss would probably faint at the messy pile of papers—fine, *piles*, plural—on the desk and the three empty coffee mugs I haven't had the chance to return to the kitchen. But I'm of the opinion that what she doesn't know won't hurt her.

Chloe's absolutely stunning in a red jumper-pantsuit-thingy, and despite all the royal pomp she grew up with, she doesn't bat an eye when I have to move my old ratty backpack from the chair on this side of the desk so she can sit down.

Instead of going around to the other side, I push aside a few restaurant magazines and sit on the edge of the desk, facing her. "What's up?"

Chloe and I have only known each other for a few months—since she escaped to Hallmark Beach in the middle of March so she could plan a secret wedding for her princely brother and his bride—but I feel like she's been my friend my entire life. Then again, this whole town has embraced her as one of their own, and I don't blame them one bit. When she decided to stay and take over Rhonda Howard's wedding and events shop, Something Blue, I cried happy tears.

She taps her manicured nails on the arm of the wooden chair. "Alberta Jenkins informed me today that Rhonda was supposed to be in charge of the town's Independence Day festival. And now that I've purchased her store and she's moved away, apparently it's on me."

I whistle. "Yikes." That Alberta Jenkins—owner of Al's Grocery and the head of our town council—sure knows how to drop a bomb. "Has anything been done yet?"

"Apparently the very basics. A fireworks vendor was booked a year ago, and the council has booked a few musical groups to play during the netball tourney."

"Netball? You mean volleyball?"

"Right, yes. Anyway, I'm glad at least those things have been accomplished, given the fact the holiday is only little more than six weeks away." Chloe gets up and begins to pace, kind of a difficult thing since this office is so small. "But doesn't Alberta realize what she's asking?"

"Maybe she doesn't think it's a big deal," I say. "After all, you did plan Topher and Lauren's wedding in like ten days."

"Yes, but weddings are my specialty. Also, I had help." She pauses, grips the back of the chair as if to steady herself. "Which is why I'm here. I know you're very busy with your new responsibilities, and you just moved into Marilee's house a few weeks ago and probably have loads of unpacking and organizing to do, but—"

"Chloe, of course I'll help you." Does she really think I wouldn't? Besides, even though I lived with Uncle Burt and Aunt Bea since Mama left me here in high school so she could travel the world and have her own adventures with my stepdad Kevin, I brought surprisingly little with me. And I haven't gathered much else in the years since. Clothes, a few mementos, pictures. There wasn't much to unpack.

What can I say? I'm a simple girl.

My friend slumps forward. "You have no idea how relieved I am to hear you say that. Once I tell others you're on board, they're sure to follow."

"I don't know about that." I wrinkle my nose, because I'm no leader. And I'm okay with that, actually. Being in charge makes it far harder to go with the flow, which is my natural state.

"Well, I do. I'm planning to hit up all the local business owners, as well as our friends." And by that, I assume she means Kelsey and Elisse Loveland, my cousin April Reynolds, and Marilee Moffitt, my best friend and new housemate. I moved into her family's three-bedroom house two weeks ago, after her former tenants left to get their own apartment together.

"Great idea. Just let me know what you need me to do."

"I'm thinking I'll put you on the food committee. Apparently there's a town-wide picnic every year on the beach?"

Chloe waves her hand. "I'll fill you in on the details. For now, just be at the first meeting on Sunday afternoon."

"You got it." I take in the natural glow of Chloe's skin but don't miss the circles under her eyes. They're only barely visible thanks to her expertly applied makeup, but I still see them. Perhaps she's just tired from all she's had going on, but I'd better check anyway. "You doing okay otherwise? Business all good? Freddy?"

She smiles, probably because I mentioned two of her favorite subjects. "I finally got all of the paperwork completed for Something Blue, so that's brilliant. And Freddy..." Chloe sighs, and I imagine her as a cartoon character with hearts in her eyes and doves circling her head. She moves around the chair and reaches for my hand, squeezing. "If only I could find such a wonderful man for each of my friends."

Oh, Chloe. She's a matchmaker at heart, but I'm afraid she'll be pretty disappointed in my prospects. Hallmark Beach is a tiny town, after all. "That's sweet, but I fully expect to settle for being the cool aunt who buys your kids all the annoying toys and goes home to her dogs. Or maybe I'll be the weird bird lady on the block."

The words roll off my tongue with ease. I won't let myself be bothered at the prospect of being alone forever. What good would that attitude do me?

Besides, being alone forever is better than having my heart broken like Mama's when Daddy died. Like my little teenage heart when Blake left for college and came home the next summer a different person—one who acted like we were never even friends. Like he barely knew me.

Nope. Alone is definitely better.

Chloe wags a finger at me. "Your time's coming, Miss Lucy Reynolds. I can feel it."

I smile and pretend it isn't forced. "You must know something I don't. Are you planning to conjure up my perfect man?"

Impossible. He's not here anymore.

Argh, stupid subconscious. *He's not anywhere, because he wasn't who you thought he was,* I argue back.

Sweet macaroni. That must be the tired talking.

But Chloe's looking at me thoughtfully, like she can hear my internal thoughts. I hope I'm not so exhausted that I'm saying any of this out loud. My new friend might have me committed to an insane asylum.

"What about Thomas?" she asks.

"Thomas Montrose? He's like a little brother to me." Two years behind me in school, the owner of the White Mocha coffee shop is one of the few, like me, who stuck around Hallmark Beach after high school.

"He's kind of cute in a puppy dog way. And he's clearly infatuated with you."

I roll my eyes. "You're obsessed with love. It's like you spend your days planning weddings or something."

Her laughter rolls off her tongue, a tinkling sound that lights up the whole room. No wonder Freddy loves her. No wonder the whole town does. "All right, I'll get out of your hair. Thanks again for your help. And I'll see you Sunday, yeah?"

"Wouldn't miss it."

We hug good-bye, and I spend the next hour attempting to clean the office, releasing my staff, and calling it a night at The Green Robin.

When I tell Tiny he can go home an hour early, he frowns. "Everything all right, Boss?"

"Don't call me that. And yeah, I'm sure things will pick up." I snap my fingers, remembering my earlier thought. "But if you can think of anything new to add to the menu, let me know. Maybe that will draw in some new guests."

He agrees to consider it, then clocks out. I sweep and wash down the counters, then flip off the lights, exit, and lock up. The streetlamps over Main Street illuminate the mostly deserted road, and almost all of the shop windows and restaurants are dark by now except The Black Hole, the club music of which I can hear thumping all the way from here. For a brief moment, I consider heading through the wide walkway between The Green Robin and Rainbow Ice and taking a moonlit stroll along the beach on the other side of the buildings, but my body begs for a shower and bed.

I curse my earlier self for not driving the five minutes to work, instead forcing one foot in front of the other as I trudge north on Main and then up Hillside Drive, which curves and overlooks our little downtown area. This is where most of the Hallmark Beach homes are located, and thankfully the Moffitt home—and now mine—is toward the beginning of the road at the edge of the bluff.

When I get to the sixteen-hundred-square-foot craftsman bungalow, I breathe a sigh of relief and enter as quietly as I can. Marilee has an early morning at the bakery, and I don't want to wake her.

The house is dark and buzzes with the white noise of the fridge's ice maker in the kitchen to my right. Something smells divine—is that banana bread?—and my stomach grumbles. Now that I think about it, I didn't eat dinner tonight, did I? "Yes, I'll feed you," I say, patting my belly. "But first, I have to wash away the restaurant smell."

So I do.

Once I'm showered and dressed for bed in my tank top and shorts, my long hair still damp from my shower, I tiptoe back to the kitchen and peek in the fridge, humming a Garth Brooks song to myself. I know it's not what the cool kids listen to these days, but I can't help it—it's the Texas girl in me.

But then, I hear a noise...and freeze.

My heart picks up speed, and I close the fridge door. Is that—?

The front doorknob wiggles, and I squeak, retreating until my back is against the granite countertop. Did I forget to lock the door? Surely not.

I'd call the police, but my phone is inside my backpack, which is in my room down the hall. Past the front door. I'm stuck here. My hand goes immediately to the wall, and I flip off the kitchen light so the intruder can't see me when he steps inside, the door creaking as he advances.

And it's definitely a *he*. I can only see the person's outline, but there are broad shoulders and strong arms. I'm no shrimp, but I'm definitely going to be outmatched against this guy.

Why is he here? Hallmark Beach isn't exactly a bastion of crime.

My hand trembling, I reach back onto the counter and feel for the closest weapon.

The guy turns away from me and starts heading for the hallway.

I start to breathe easier, because now I can escape. Except... Marilee. She's sleeping in one of those rooms. Innocent. Unaware that an intruder is headed her way.

So instead of doing the smart thing—which would be escaping out the front door, running for the neighbor's house, and asking for help—I decide to take on the giant.

By flinging the weapon I discovered on the counter.

It's not much, but it's all I have thanks to the darkness I created. The porch light is faint and coming through the front window—enough to show me where the guy's at.

But it's all I need. Something to aim at.

"Ahhh!" I yell as I lob the object with as much force as I can manage.

It hits him square in the back and falls to the ground.

He grunts. "What the—"

Then, before I know what's happening, he's turning—and coming straight for me.

I feel for another object, grab it, and toss it at him, this time smacking him in the jaw. Then I jerk away from his outstretched hand...

Which hits the same light switch I just turned off a few seconds ago.

Light floods the kitchen. I blink against the sudden glow, and my mouth falls open as I realize exactly how this "intruder" knew where to find the light. "Flake?"

"Nice to see you too, Lucy." But the way he says it—and the frown he's wearing—tells me it's really not.

Well, the feeling is soooo mutual, buddy.

Even if Marilee's older brother is more attractive now than he was at eighteen, back when I was maybe just a little bit in love with him. But looks don't make the man. Maybe if they did, the five o'clock shadow on his normally shaven jaw, his brown hair perfectly gelled just enough to actually look finger-combed, and those light blue eyes that used to make me weak in the knees would make Blake Moffitt the perfect guy.

But I know better.

He glances down at the ground. "Did you just throw *bananas* at me?"

I cross my arms over my chest. "I thought you were breaking in." And for all I know, he is. This may have been his family home once upon a time, but he lost all right to be here when he left six years ago—after his parents' funeral—and never set foot in Hallmark Beach again until recently. If Marilee hadn't asked him to provide the last-minute dinner for Chloe's brother's wedding out of his grilled cheese food truck at the beginning of April, who knows if he would have ever come back here.

So yeah, I threw bananas at him. But he deserved much worse.

As if he's tracking with my thoughts, he cocks an eyebrow. "I'm surprised you didn't go for the knives."

I lift my chin. "If I'd known it was you, I might have." Of course, that's not true. I'd never really hurt a living soul, much less my best friend's brother. I may have a major problem with him, but Marilee's forgiven him for his abandonment in her deepest time of need. She'd never forgive me if I maimed him in return.

Too bad the banana to the jaw didn't leave a mark on his annoyingly symmetrical face.

"What are you doing here, Flake?"

He flinches at the nickname he so deserves. "I—"

"You know what?" Shaking my head, I flounce out of the kitchen, then turn on my heel to face him again. He's standing there, looking impossibly handsome—and also like a statue carved out of stone. Just like his heart. "I actually don't care. You're just going to disappear again anyway."

three

BLAKE

Cooking is the thing I do when nothing else makes sense.

Just like two plus two equals four, runny egg yolks become solid when heat is applied. Baking soda reacts with acids, so dough rises. Water boils at two hundred and twelve degrees.

I don't have to think about how it feels. Whether I'm doing the right thing. Whether I'm doing *enough*.

As long as the chef is reliable and takes all variables into consideration, the cooking comes through.

Yawning, I glance at the clock over the stove in my family's kitchen. Just after four a.m. I barely slept last night, despite the fact I was tired from the four-hour drive north from Los Angeles. Probably had something to do with being back in this house for the first time in years.

Memories are everywhere. The little sign of my mother's sitting atop the microwave: *Be nice: I cook your food*. The large family photo over the fireplace mantel in the living room, where my parents and a teenage Blake and Marilee will live in memorial forever. That old floral couch my dad hated but Mom loved because it was the first thing they bought together when they were married at the age of twenty-four.

Blinking against the hot flashes at the back of my eyes, I start prepping for breakfast. A quick peek inside the fridge shows me what I have to work with. Thankfully, there's a decent amount, which makes sense. Though Marilee more enjoys the baking versus cooking side of things, our mother instilled a love of fresh food in us both.

Of course, cooking in and of itself was always too much of "an unlucrative hobby" for it to be *my* passion—at least in my father's eyes. That's why I also had to go to business school and get my MBA. That's why I've worked so hard, even after Dad's death, to turn my passion for food into a career. It's the first step toward the big, important life Dad always wanted for me.

It's also why I'm here, in Hallmark Beach.

At least, it's part of the reason.

The other part is sleeping down the hall.

I mean my sister, NOT Lucy Reynolds—that insanely attractive woman who is as much of a temptation today as she was my senior year of high school. When I saw her last night, standing in my family's kitchen, her long tan legs peeking out from tiny pajama shorts, the skin of her toned arms looking soft and silky, her hair hanging wet and wild—well, I nearly had a heart attack.

And it wasn't because she was pelting me with bananas, which was just...adorable.

Thankfully, she wants nothing to do with me. Because I don't need the distraction.

Grabbing a carton of eggs along with a block of cheese and some veggies, I close the fridge and select a cutting board from the collection beside the sink. Before I start on the food, I add some coffee grounds to the twelve-cup pot and hit the Brew button. Then I fall easily into the rhythm of chopping vegetables, and my whole body relaxes. When I'm done, I melt some butter in a small frying pan and toss in the onions and bell peppers, which combined with the brewing coffee soon create a delicious aroma.

I hear the squeak of a door down the hall, and Marilee emerges from her room into the living room. "Blake?" She blinks at me for a moment from behind her thick-rimmed glasses. Her brown hair's piled on top of her head, and she looks so much like Mom that my insides twist.

"Hey, Squirt."

She runs at me, throwing her arms around my waist in a show of exuberance. The top of her head only skims the height of my shoulders, and I wrap her up, squeezing her tight. Marilee's the most forgiving person I've ever met, and I know I don't deserve her kindness.

She pulls back and blinks up at me with her brown eyes. "What are you doing here?"

"Thought I'd cook you an omelet before work. That okay?"

"You came all the way to Hallmark Beach to make me breakfast?" She squints and scratches behind her ear, looking hilariously confused. Given the crazy early hours they have to keep, I've always been surprised Marilee chose a life as a baker. She was always the night owl among us, and it takes a load of caffeine to wake her up.

"No, Mare." I point my spatula at the coffee maker, which has finished brewing. "I'll explain after you've had some brain juice."

"An omelet *and* coffee? All right, what did you do?" she teases as she pads to the cabinet in her large fluffy Christmas socks. Doesn't matter to Mare that it's May and nearly summer. She'd do Christmas all year round if she could.

I know she's joking, but I hate the idea that it's not normal for me to do nice things for my sister. What kind of brother am I? If only I'd listened to Lucy six years ago and stayed after the funeral like she'd begged me to—for Marilee's sake, of course.

But I'd been on the verge of my cooking apprenticeship at Paprika, and Dale was taking a chance on a guy with no real kitchen experience except what he'd picked up on his own. It wasn't like that kind of opportunity was going to come along again.

And I'd had Dad's voice reverberating in my head: *"Do what I couldn't. Get out of this small town, and never look back."* With him gone, I was desperate to make him proud. And so afraid I wouldn't.

Still. I didn't have to reduce communication with Marilee to just a smattering of texts and calls each year and her annual visit to me in Los Angeles.

I crack a few eggs into a bowl and whisk them around, then throw them into an omelet pan. "I actually did do something. Just probably not what you think."

After snagging a pink mug from the cabinet, Marilee fills it with coffee. "I can't wait to hear all about it."

"What time do you have to leave for work?"

"Half an hour." She moves to the fridge and takes out some hazelnut creamer. "I've got time."

I grunt. "Good."

We are silent for the next several minutes while I make and plate her omelet, and she sits at the scratched oak table for four in the kitchen and sips on her brew, which is more creamer than coffee in my opinion. Guess bakers like their sugar in all forms.

Finally, I slide the plate in front of her. "Bon appétit."

"It looks amazing. Thanks, bro." Marilee forks a piece of the omelet and brings it to her lips. Groans. "Sweet macaroni, I've missed your cooking."

I raise a brow. "Sweet macaroni? You still hang out with Lucy a lot, I see."

"Oh. Yeah." She coughs. "Um, actually, you might want to know—"

"That you have a new roommate?"

She winces, and her glasses fall down her nose. "How'd you know?"

"Might have something to do with the fact I came in late last night and surprised her so bad she tossed bananas at my head."

That has my sister giggling. "She didn't."

"I have a bruise on my jaw to prove it." I point to a small spot that's been aching since last night. Who knew a banana could do so much damage? Then again, maybe it had more to do with the vehemence with which it was thrown.

Marilee laughs again, then sobers as she takes another drink. Her eyes study me over the top of the mug. She sets it down. "When I told you at the wedding that my other roommates were moving out and that I'd always have a room for you, that was the total truth. I'm not planning to get another roommate. The third bedroom is still open and available whenever you are here."

That both warms my heart and strokes my guilt. Because I know that weasel of an ex-husband Donny left her in some debt, though she won't tell me how much. If I had any money to spare, I'd give her enough to cover it in a heartbeat. "Squirt, don't forego another renter on my account." *In other words, don't forego the money.*

She shrugs and cuts another piece off her omelet. "You own half of this house fair and square. You should have access to a room as often as you'd like."

Technically, she's right. We used the life insurance money left to both of us from my parents' death to pay down the mortgage. Then I took the rest of my portion and invested it to buy an upgraded food truck, because the one that I'd started as a side gig in college was basically falling down around my ears.

I'm pretty sure Donny squandered Marilee's half.

"Yeah, well. After this visit, if you need to fill my room, please do."

She reaches for my hand across the table, squeezes. "I know that you and Lucy have a problem with each other, but I hope that won't scare you off from staying for a bit."

"*I* don't have a problem with *her*." Not that I really blame her for having one with me. "And no, it's fine. She's your friend, and I'll be on my best behavior. Scout's honor."

"Good." She smiles. "How long *are* you planning to stay?"

"That's what I wanted to talk to you about." Itching to do something with my hands, I stand and crack a few more eggs into the bowl. I'm not really hungry, but I could definitely use the steady calm that cooking brings. "If it's okay with you, I'd like to stay through the summer. Probably something like the end of July, beginning of August."

Marilee sets down her fork. "Seriously? Of course it's okay with me." She cocks her head. "But can you really be away from work for that long?"

"That's the thing. I finally sent Dale a business plan. Asked him to invest. And he went for it."

"Wait, what? You're going to get your own restaurant?"

"That's the plan."

"Oh my goodness! I'm so proud of you. You've been dreaming of this for...forever." Her hands go every direction in her excitement, and I halfway expect her to knock over her coffee.

Smiling, I flip my omelet. "Thanks. It's not a done deal yet. First, I have to come up with some new recipes. Dale doesn't think I have enough, so that's what I'll be doing while I'm here."

"Our kitchen is small, but it's all yours."

"You aren't using it to make cakes?" We didn't get much time to chat when I was catering the wedding, but she did mention that she'd made the wedding cake. I took a peek at it, and it was incredible—tall and glittering and perfect.

"I've done a few here and there, but..." She shrugs. "With my schedule at the bakery, there's not really time to do a lot on the side."

I feel like there's more she's not telling me, but maybe now isn't the time to broach the subject. Besides, we have all summer to get into the details. And that's good. Really good. Being here, it feels right.

Grating some cheese over my omelet, I then fold it over and plate it. "I actually won't need our kitchen. I brought the truck."

Marilee shifts in her seat, turns to face me fully. "Really? Are you going to open up shop here?"

I think of Dale's words back in L.A. over a month ago. "What better way to test recipes than with a live audience?"

"Great idea." Marilee drains the rest of her coffee and stands. "Won't it take a while for you to get permits and such, though?"

"Already done." I take a bite of my food. Hmm. A bit too salty, but still decent. "The second Dale told me to take the summer off, I got on the phone with the town council and started applications. In fact"—I peek at the clock over the stove for the second time this morning—"I've got a meeting at eight with Thomas Montrose to sign everything and get my truck set up in its new location."

My sister brings her dishes to the sink and sets them down. Turning to me, she gives me another hug where I'm standing beside the counter. "I couldn't be happier about this, Blake. I wish I could catch up more, but Marla's expecting me at The Blackberry Muffin."

I kiss the top of her head. "Go. I'll clean up."

"Oh, you don't have to do that. I'll do it when I get home." She scoots toward the hallway, then turns. "It's seriously so good to have you back, even if just for a few months."

"Thanks." I know not everyone will agree—Marilee's room-mate, for one—but if I can make a success of things here, then it'll be worth facing Lucy's wrath day in and day out.

The best thing I can do is play nice.

Just not *too* nice.

LUCY

I cannot let this stand.

After a restless night, I power walk down Main Street toward The Blackberry Muffin. Marilee and I need to have *words*.

Of course, as revved up as I am on the inside, those *words* will be sweet, gentle, and kind. It's not Marilee's fault she has a demon for a brother. The kind of guy who would walk into a house like he owned it (which, fine, he technically does, but only *technically*) and—without so much as an apology for scaring the living daylights out of a girl—have the actual gall to stay where he was so clearly unwelcome. (Which was on the other side of my bedroom wall!)

Thankfully, I was able to avoid the man when I left this morning, but not before I passed the bathroom and caught a whiff of his knee-weakening body wash that smelled like a flannel-clad lumberjack come to life. He must have just showered and left before I was up, because the steam still clung to the space.

Y'all. I can't even.

I breeze past The Purple Seashell, with its gabled windows

on the upper floor, its lavender walls, its brilliant ocean views. Not today, Seashell. I don't have time for your cheeriness. Or maybe I could use some of it to rub off on me. Either way, it won't affect my behavior. On the inside, I might be a roiling mass of *feelings*, but I know from observation that dwelling on them will do no good.

Directly across from the inn, I can tell The Blackberry Muffin is bustling even from the outside, where it sports a blue-and-white-striped awning and a wooden bench. I enter to find not a single table available—not surprising, since it's nine a.m. on a Saturday morning. The smell of sugar sprinkles the air, and the canary-yellow accent wall behind the register chirps a bright hello, as does the teenager working there.

And I can't help it. Just like that, the familiar sights, sounds, and smells bring a peace like nothing else can. Which is probably a good thing, because I don't want my irritation at Blake to make Marilee think I'm irritated at *her*.

Even though she could have told me her brother would be showing up. Give a girl a little warning and all that.

"Hey, Cynthia," I say to the owner, Marla's granddaughter, pushing all negative thoughts aside. "Is Marilee in back?"

"Yeah, she's finishing up another batch of muffins. You want me to get her?"

"Maybe just let her know I'm out here if you get a minute. For now, can I grab an apple fritter and a hot coffee with a splash of cream, please?"

"You got it." She flashes me a braced smile.

"Thanks, babe." I pay, then turn and scan the crowd for familiar faces—and let's be honest, most of them are. There's a few of the Loveland brothers, tossing back coffee and dressed like they're about to head out for a day of work in the fields or maybe even taking a break from a morning of already working, if the dirt on their jeans is any indication. Chloe's boyfriend

Frederick is with them, and he's joking and slapping Nathaniel Loveland on the back.

Then there's the older crowd—Earl Flanders and Ned Chamberlain, with their bald heads and raucous laughter—playing a rowdy game of checkers in the corner.

In the back, my friend Jordan Carmichael's hanging out with his son Ryder, who is coloring in a book and talking away, his adorable face smeared with chocolate. Jordan's got on his standard joggers and T-shirt, and he keeps looking over at the swinging door that leads back to the kitchen where Marilee works.

I've long suspected he's got a thing for my best friend, but the one time I mentioned it to her, she waved it off as impossible. In Marilee's mind, Jordan is simply a close friend (probably her next best friend after me). Besides, I think that after Donny, Mare's just closed herself off to love. It'll take something big and drastic to shake her out of the fear of being betrayed again.

Last, I see Greta Graber and her best friend—my aunt, Bea—chatting with their heads together by the to-go counter.

Sauntering over, I join them. "Morning, y'all. What's the latest gossip?"

"Look, Greta, it's our girl!" Aunt Bea grabs me into a hug, pulling me to her large chest. With her sturdy frame, the woman could have been a linebacker, but that doesn't mean she isn't the sweetest little thing this side of the Mississippi. "We sure do miss you."

Greta and I exchange a secret smile. "I've barely been gone a few weeks."

"But after having you around constantly for almost thirteen years, it's just not the same. Though I couldn't exactly call it quiet."

I laugh. "With April and Scarlett there? I don't imagine so." My cousin and her seven-year-old daughter moved back from

San Francisco at the end of March, and they're living with my aunt and uncle for the time being. It's one of the reasons I finally decided to get my own place. Not only because the three-bedroom house was feeling tight—and April and Scarlett definitely needed their own rooms—but because there was someone else there to help Aunt Bea around the house. Her arthritis has gotten worse over the years, and her quilt-making business tends to exacerbate it. But she refuses to give it up because she's stubborn like that. So I helped as much as I could.

Now, though, April's got it handled. Her sister Stephanie helps too when she's not busy running her clothing boutique, Just Peachy.

"Still, we miss seeing you whenever we want, sweetheart," Bea continues.

I nudge her. "In a town as small as Hallmark Beach, we see each other just as often as when I lived at home. Take this morning as a case in point."

"True, true."

Cynthia calls Aunt Bea's name and slides two drinks across the counter. After my aunt grabs them, she turns and holds them in the air. "I'd best get this hot chocolate to your uncle. You know how Burt likes his sugar hit in the morning."

I laugh, picturing my crazy, lovable uncle with his stained coveralls, slight hunchback, and wiry hair. In many ways, he's the opposite of my dad—a quiet man who died from cancer when I was eight—but the brothers were alike in all the ways that mattered, starting with their big hearts.

It's no wonder Mama completely fell apart when he died.

My aunt and her best friend leave, and I wait for my own coffee, watching for a peek of Marilee. She's probably flitting away in the kitchen, and you know what? I don't really need to disturb her. I can wait until tonight to talk with her about Blake.

But just as Cynthia finally delivers my drink and I turn to leave, Marilee breezes through the kitchen door, flour dancing across her cheeks and spilled down her apron. "Morning, Luce. Cynthia said you wanted to see me." She's about to hug me when she's nearly tackled by a tiny body. Apparently I wasn't the only one watching for her.

Squatting down, Mare pulls Ryder into a huge hug. "How's my favorite guy?"

"I had chocolate pancakes, Lee-Lee! They were delicious and I pretended my fork was a sword, but Daddy said I should probably stop, only when I said I didn't wanna, he pretended with me." He chatters on and on, and I might as well be dead to Mare in this moment, because the woman is only capable of focusing on one person at a time—whoever is right in front of her. I can't complain though, because it's what makes her an amazing friend.

Tapping my fingers along the edge of my cup, I take a sip— *ah*—and wait my turn with a smile on my face.

While Marilee and Ryder discuss the finer points of fork swordplay, Jordan joins us. "Let's let Lee-Lee get back to work, huh?"

Marilee glances up and grins. "Say that three times fast."

Ryder starts doing just that, and Marilee joins him until they're both in fits of laughter. Casually, I glance at Jordan to gauge his reaction. Pure adoration is shining from his face. Who knows? Maybe it has nothing to do with loving Marilee, and everything to do with seeing his boy laugh. The last several months have been tough since Ryder's mom, Georgia—who Jordan never really dated, but co-parented with well enough— passed away.

Jordan puts his hand on Ryder's shoulder. "Come on, little dude. We've got to get started on our hike before Grandpa and Grandma come pick you up tonight." He's really good about letting Ryder see Georgia's parents on the regular, despite the fact they live one town over.

Marilee straightens and swipes at her apron, which does nothing to dissipate the flour stuck there. "Wish I could join you. Have fun."

"Thanks. We still on for tomorrow night?" Jordan asks.

"Are you kidding? I wouldn't miss Sunday movie night for the world." She bends down and gives Ryder a kiss on the head, then squeezes Jordan's elbow before he leads the kid out the front door. Finally, she turns to me. "Sorry about that. How are you?"

"I don't know, Mare." I cock my head and offer a teasing smile that covers the sudden nerves zipping up my spine. I hate confrontation and any manner of unpleasantness. "How do you think I am?"

She blanches. "Right. Blake."

"Yeah. Blake." Wearing as big a smile as I can muster, I grab her hand and squeeze. "Couldn't you have at least warned a girl?"

"I swear I didn't know he was coming, Luce." Guess she can see through my facade. It's no secret that I've been holding a grudge against Blake on Marilee's behalf for the last six years.

Of course, that's not where my hurt concerning Blake Moffitt began. But it's definitely an easier offense to point to.

The bell over the door jangles, and in walks a tourist couple I don't recognize. We step aside, closer to the wall so we aren't in the way.

"It's fine. Really. I just wish I hadn't wasted the rest of our bananas."

"He told me about that." Marilee offers a wry grin. "Sounds like you had pretty good aim."

"What can I say? It's a gift." I shrug. "I'm the best darn banana slinger in the West."

After we both chuckle, Marilee sobers. "I know you aren't his biggest fan, but..." Her voice is tight, quiet. Soft. "Are you okay if he stays with us?"

"What? Of course. It's your house."

"It's yours now too. And I want you to feel comfortable."

"I don't feel *un*comfortable." Okay, maybe I do. Because somehow, the memories of high school Blake and what he meant still have the power to sear me when I really let myself sink into those feelings—which is almost never. But also... "I just don't want him to disappear and disappoint you again."

"You know I forgave him a long time ago."

Yeah, I know. That's the thing about my best friend. She's forgiving—a little *too* forgiving, if you ask me. It means people often walk all over her. Case in point: her terrible ex. And also, her brother, who put his own needs over hers.

But maybe I should be happy he's here, for her sake. I just need to let go of my protective instincts and allow her to enjoy her brother's visit without worrying about how I'm going to react.

I squeeze her hand again. "Forget I said anything, okay? I'm sure you guys will have a great time hanging out."

"You can hang with us too. Like old times."

Ha. No thanks. "Unfortunately, I've got a ton of work to do this weekend. I'll probably be working super late while he's here."

Her gaze meets mine, and her eyes squint. Uh oh. I know that look—the one where she doesn't want to tell me something that I'm not going to like.

"What?"

"It's just that...he's not leaving after the weekend."

Seriously? Well, it's not like he can afford too much time away from his fancy restaurant job that Marilee's told me he has. Maybe a week, tops? I can handle that. I paste on a bright smile. "That's okay. Have I mentioned my workload is suuuu-uper heavy lately? I can use a few extra hours of work time every day. When's he leaving?"

"Not soon."

"Define *not soon*."

The bell jangles again behind me.

"Maybe he should be the one to tell you. And he's not just here to visit. He's here...well, maybe he should tell you that too."

Ugh, seriously? "Mare—"

"Lucy! There you are."

I turn to find Tiny strong arming his way past the line of tourists waiting to be served. When did it get so crowded in here? The man finally reaches us, and he's huffing and puffing.

"Tiny, what's wrong?" I ask.

Hands on his knees, he sucks in air, holding up a finger. Finally, he straightens. "You've gotta come quick. I've tried calling you. Tried The White Mocha, then figured you might be here."

"Back it up. Where do I have to come, and why do I need to come quick?" I glance over at Marilee, who shrugs and looks just as confused as I feel.

"Because." He tosses a glare at Marilee. What the what? Then he points a meaty finger her way. "*Her* brother is moving in right next door."

"Right next door to what?"

"The Robin."

That doesn't make any sense. The Green Robin sits between Rainbow Ice and Just Peachy Boutique—both of which were in operation the last time I checked. "I don't understand."

"His food truck. He's parking it just behind the sidewalk

between us and the ice cream parlor. It's next to the walkway that leads straight to our front door."

Sweet macaroni. That little...

I swing my gaze back to Marilee. "Did you know about this?" I'm trying to keep my tone even, but in this situation, I feel the frustration edging my voice is a little bit warranted.

She holds her hands up. "He told me this morning that he was going to open his food truck for a little while this summer, but none of the details."

"Okay." I breathe in through my nose, out through my mouth. At least my best friend isn't turning against me. "I've gotta go."

"Lucy..."

"Sorry," I yell with a wave. Then I follow Tiny out the door, and I run with fire in my veins.

Because Blake the Flake may have weaseled his way into my house—my private sanctuary—for an indefinite amount of time. There's nothing I can do about that. But if he thinks he can also mess with my workspace? Especially when I'm in charge there?

He's got another thing coming.

BLAKE

After living in big cities for more than a decade, I almost forgot how anything out of the ordinary attracts a crowd in a small town.

"Just a little bit farther," Thomas calls as he waves me back, his arms flailing wildly about. "Alberta, Collette, come on, ladies. Please stay out of the way and let the man park his vehicle."

The two older women, who are standing extremely close to my food truck, sneer at him but do step back. A tad. Enough so that I won't hit them, anyway. They aren't there to help. Just observe. Of course, Alberta is the head of the town council, so she's got a vested interest in helping me settle in.

Collette, on the other hand—and the other random groups of people standing around, watching me at nine-something in the morning—is just there because there's nothing better to do. And because she's one of the local gossips and likes to have her nose in everyone's business. But I can't let their watching eyes upset me. They're hopefully going to be paying customers in the near future, and I can't afford to make them mad with what Dale calls my resting-grump-face.

So I offer a little wave of thanks to them for moving and use the truck's side mirror as a guide. I inch back so I don't hit anything. There's not a ton of space between The Green Robin and Rainbow Ice, but it's the only place on Main Street where the town council could accommodate my truck. Thankfully, it's actually the perfect spot, located right in the middle of the downtown hustle and bustle. The beach is just on the other side of the buildings, and across the street are more shops and eateries. The best part, though? Rainbow Ice already has tables, chairs, and umbrellas just outside, and the owner, Chad, has agreed to let my customers sit there if I pay him a monthly fee for the service. After all, our offerings don't conflict at all. If people want ice cream after they've eaten their grilled cheese lunch, they can just hop right inside the building and grab some. It's a win-win for all of us.

That's one thing I have always liked about my hometown—there's room for everyone here.

I finish parking, cut the ignition, and hop out of the truck, making my way toward Thomas with an outstretched hand. The guy's a few years my junior and doesn't look much like he belongs in a beach town with his fair skin, freckles, and poofed-up red hair, but he's nice enough from what I can tell. His coffee shop, The White Mocha, is just across the way. We met there this morning to go over paperwork, and he gave me a cup of Joe, on the house. It was quite tasty, and I can safely say I'll be back frequently.

He shakes my hand. "Alrighty, looks like you're in business. When do you plan to start firing up the grill?" He tosses some finger guns my way.

Dude's trying so hard to be casual, but it's difficult to take him seriously in his bright green Hawaiian shirt. Of course, next to him, I look extremely overdressed with my slacks and button-up shirt. I know it's probably too much, especially when I'm working the grill, but Dad always said to dress for the job I want. *"Respect is earned, not given,"* he'd say.

So even though I'd personally be more comfortable in shorts and a T-shirt, I am always sure to present myself as a businessman first, a cook second.

"As soon as I can," I say. "I need to buy some more supplies, finalize a few things, but if all goes according to plan, The Urban Melt will be open sometime next week."

"Over my dead body."

Whipping around, I find the last person I expect to see.

Lucy Reynolds is—thankfully—more fully clothed today than last night, wearing jeans that hug her curves, a blue shirt that says "Y'all Ain't Right," and a flannel long-sleeved shirt tied around her waist. Her blonde hair is pulled back in a bouncing ponytail just the way I remember it from when we were teens, back when I used to tug it playfully just to see her smile.

But unlike when we were younger (when she looked at me with something akin to hero worship), right now she's shooting laser beams with her eyes. And the goal appears to be slicing me in half. Or, at the very least, cutting me down to size.

I sigh and open my mouth to ask what in the world her problem is now, but Thomas steps around me. "Morning, Luce."

Luce? Is everyone that casual with her, or just him? Wait. Are they...together?

And why does the thought of that twist my stomach?

Lucy pulls her attention from me, and I watch in amazement as her lips press upward, her eyes un-narrow, and genuine affection fills her gaze. "Hi, Thomas. How are you?"

Wow. She either likes this guy a lot...or just really hates me.

Not sure which I prefer.

Thomas thumps me on the back like we're bros. "Just helping Blake here get his truck settled into its new home."

"What do you mean, its new home? That can't be right."

"I assure you it is." Thomas hooks a thumb toward Alberta. "The town council approved it and everything."

"Uncle Burt approved *this*?"

There's betrayal in her voice, but why? Does she expect the entire town to feel the same way about me that she does? She's acting like she's been personally victimized by the truck's location. "Why so glum, *Luce*? New business is always good for the economy. You know that."

She frowns. Tosses her hands onto her hips. "Maybe in most cases, but in this particular one, I am pretty sure your presence will be bad for business."

Unbelievable. My *presence* is the thing she begged me for six years ago. Now I'm finally here and, sure, it's later than it should be, but why has she done a complete one-eighty on me?

Perhaps I should apologize. Make peace with Lucy. Then again, maybe it's better to be on her bad side. Besides, this is my livelihood she's messing with.

I grind my molars. "I think we both know this has nothing to do with business."

Lucy's jaw drops.

A murmur goes up through the still-watching crowd. Can't the busybodies just mind their own business? But maybe this is good, for everyone to witness sweet home-town princess Lucy Reynolds losing her stuff. They'll know I did nothing to provoke her—nothing except dare to exist inside the same zip code as her again.

Thomas shifts. Looks at me. Back at Lucy. "Luce? Everything okay?"

She huffs, stomping that foot of hers in a way that's far more adorable than it should be. "No, everything isn't okay."

Lucy waves her hand at my truck. "His stupid truck is encroaching on The Green Robin's territory."

Thomas's nose scrunches as he looks at the grassy patch of land where my truck is parked. It *is* close to the sidewalk path that leads up to the restaurant next door, but it doesn't go over. "But he's not." Thomas scratches behind his ear. "He went through the process that all businesses have to comply with. I don't—"

"Fine, he's not technically encroaching," she says. Thomas is the one who's talking, but I'm the one and only recipient of her glare. "But the *spirit* of encroachment is clearly there." Then her attention shifts back to Thomas, and her face softens. It's like she's a different person with everyone but me. "Why wasn't I informed?"

Why in the world should she expect to be informed? I take a step closer to her. "I asked them to keep it on the down low."

Her cheeks turn red. "You asked them to lie for you?"

Does she really think that little of me? I may have unintentionally led her on when we were younger, but to call me a liar? That's low, even for her.

Thomas blanches. "He didn't ask us to lie for him."

"No, he didn't," I reply, taking another step closer to her. The toes of our shoes are nearly touching now. Lucy's taller than most women, and the distance between our glares isn't far. *The distance between our lips isn't too far, either.* I push the thought aside. "He merely didn't want his business broadcasted all over town before it was necessary."

Lucy rolls her eyes. "Stop talking about yourself in third person. You're not that important."

She's one to talk. "Why do you care, anyway?" If anyone would care, I'd think it would be Winona Lambert, the Robin's owner. It *is* unfortunate that the only place I could park my truck permanently happened to be next to one of the only other restaurants in town.

But such is life—and business.

"Maybe because I'm the restaurant's manager right now while Winona is gone for three months. *I'm* the one responsible for making sure the restaurant stays afloat and that no outside source *encroaches* on it."

Oh. Shoot. "I didn't know that."

"Sure you didn't." She tilts her chin sky high.

I open my mouth to protest, but close it again. She's got her mind made up. I won't waste my breath trying to convince her that all of my plans don't revolve around making her life miserable.

"So I don't know what game you're playing, Flake, but you can just turn that truck right back around and head home to L.A. where you belong."

"I will. Eventually."

Thomas lifts a finger. "I think—"

But Lucy doesn't seem to remember he's here—a fact that brings me waaaaay more satisfaction than it should—because she speaks over him. Right to me. "You can't park your truck here." Her eyes blaze.

Lucy might not be aware of it, but I'm conscious of the crowd that's still gathered. The one that seems to be straining to hear what we're discussing. I lean in and lower my voice. "I have paperwork in my truck that says I can. So you'd best get over it, Sunshine. Because it's here to stay. And so am I."

Her eyes narrow. "For now."

"For as long as I deem necessary." I've staked my reputation —and my business relationship with Dale—on this need to create more recipes, and in order to do that, I need an active audience. It's just how my process works.

And I'm not going to let some Siren with soulful eyes ruin it for me.

I wonder if she'd react differently to the whole thing if she understood that the other reason I'm here in Hallmark Beach is Marilee. But I don't need her understanding or her softening.

I just need her to stay out of my way.

"Sweet macaroni, you're so self-righteous." Her darts keep flying. "You just do whatever you want, the feelings of everyone else be darned, isn't that right, Flake?"

I don't need to stand here a moment longer and listen to her accusations—even if in the past, they might have been a little bit true. But I gotta play nice, or at least, appear to play nice no matter how Lucy Reynolds gets my ire up. So I pull a smile from my back pocket and force it onto my face. "It's not about being self-righteous. That's not why I'm here."

"Oh? And why are you here then?" The sarcasm is made even stronger by her Southern accent, which apparently gets more pronounced when she's upset. Before my parents died, I never heard a cross word from Lucy Reynolds, so I didn't know this side of her existed.

It's both the most infuriating thing—and darn it, the most attractive thing—I've ever heard.

"I just want a chance to return to my hometown," I say more loudly than necessary. Because if all the world's a stage, then right now I'm the main event at a Shakespeare festival. "And I think my hometown can benefit from having some gourmet food."

She scoffs. "That's very presumptuous of you."

"You're only saying that because you've never had my cooking. Well, not since we were kids." It sounds arrogant, but my food is maybe the *only* thing I'm truly confident about. For the rest, I just fake it till I make it.

"I have, actually. At the wedding." She looks toward the sky, where there's not a single cloud hanging out today. "But don't go getting a big head about it. There was nothing else to eat. I personally would have rather starved, but Marilee brought me a sandwich and it would have been rude not to accept."

Why does the thought of her eating something put together by my own two hands make it hard to breathe? "And what did you think?" I clear my throat against the unintentional huskiness. Her opinion shouldn't matter. It's not like food is her specialty despite working in a restaurant, though she always *was* good at assessing and critiquing my creations in high school.

I can't help but lean forward a bit, anxiously awaiting her reply.

"It was as terrible as its maker," she hisses.

But there's hesitation there, a glimmer of something unsteady in her eyes. She *does* think *I'm* terrible—but she liked my food. I know it.

Before I can say anything more about it, though, she continues. "I can safely say I'm never going to let anything *you* make ever pass these lips again." Then she turns on her heel and stomps away, her hips swinging in a way that shouldn't draw my eye.

Apparently there *are* some people here who don't believe there's room enough for everyone in this town. But it just makes me all the more determined to create recipes that these townsfolk will love. Not that I want to steal her business.

But it's not even *her* business. Winona will be back to managing the restaurant in a matter of months.

On the flip side, this opportunity is everything to me. And I'm not letting Lucy Reynolds—or the little tantrum she just threw—ruin my shot at getting what I want.

Granted, twelve-thirty on a Thursday afternoon isn't typically The Green Robin's busiest time of the week.

But looking around the empty dining room, I know something's off. It's never this dead—not unless there's an actual funeral or wedding going on in town. Even then, we usually have some tourists filtering in, especially since tomorrow kicks of Memorial Day weekend.

Winona would be in fits if she saw this. Am I just that incompetent of a manager, or is there more going on here?

I approach Sam, who's slumped at the hostess stand scrolling something on her phone. When the young woman sees me, she straightens and stuffs her device into the back pocket of her jeans. "Hi, Boss."

I rub my temple. "Has it been like this since we opened?" I've been holed up in Winona's office for hours, working on ideas for some summer promos and specials the Robin could run, as well as some initial ideas for the Fourth of July Festival. At Sunday's meeting, Chloe assigned me to the food committee with Thomas Montrose, and we are both supposed to bring our thoughts to the next one tonight.

Sam plays with one of her dangling earrings. "We had a few of the regulars around eleven-fifteen, but yeah. Pretty dead. I think it has something to do with that food truck opening yesterday."

Of course it does.

I blow out a steady stream of air, trying to not let my worries get the best of me like I did on Saturday. I still can't believe I got so worked up, and in public, no less. There's just something about Blake Moffitt that makes me forget that negative emotions do a person no good at all.

But it's not just about our personal history, whatever Blake accused me of last weekend. It's about how he parked his business nearly on my front lawn. Customers have to walk right past his truck to get to the Robin, and some are bound to be swayed by the delicious scent of frying cheese.

It has nothing to do with the actual *quality* of the sandwiches. None.

Although, fine, y'all, the sandwiches are amazing. If his offerings are anything like what he had available at the wedding, Blake's got gourmet recipes—everything from The Classic to one with pimiento cheese and apple-cherry chutney and another with ham, gouda, and caramelized onions. It's not surprising. He's always been talented. I remember how he used to make me and Marilee gourmet pizzas on their backyard grill when we were pre-teens. And how he and Mare would see a recipe of something new to try on TV and recreate it, asking me to be the judge.

Cooking always seemed to make him happy.

But right now, his cooking is making me decidedly *un*happy. And according to him, he doesn't think it's a big deal that he's opening his business right on my doorstep.

Well, my empty dining room says it's a very big deal.

And since nobody else is in charge around here, it's up to

me to set him straight. "I'll be back," I say as I head out the Robin's front door, Sam calling "Good luck!" behind me.

I halt and blink against the bright afternoon light. This can't be happening. There's Beach Boys music playing from somewhere—maybe the truck, maybe the speakers at Rainbow Ice next door—and a line stretches from the food truck straight down the sidewalk that leads between the two buildings and meets up with the beach boardwalk just west of us.

The truck itself ruins the aesthetic of Main Street, where all of the buildings are painted bright and fun colors. It's the kind of downtown where the very definitions of words like *adorable* and *quaint* were born. Each storefront and restaurant is unique, but they all tie together to create a wonderful kaleidoscope of color.

Blake's truck, though? It's white and black. Oh sure, with some red lettering—but it's all Los Angeles, big-city fancy, and doesn't belong here any more than its owner does. But I guess I'm the only one who thinks so, because sweet macaroni, there have to be at least thirty or forty people in this line! And just like inside The Blackberry Muffin on Saturday morning, I recognize a good majority of them. This is like a Saturday crowd, but on a Thursday in the middle of a working day.

My chest squeezes tight, and I back up against the front of the Robin, breathing in and out until air comes more easily.

Surely it's just the novelty of it, right? All of these folks want to try the hot new thing, but eventually that hot new thing will decide Hallmark Beach isn't where it wants to be—that Hallmark Beach isn't good enough for it—and it'll uproot and literally drive away.

It's happened before. No sense in thinking it won't happen again.

But what can I do about it? I already asked Uncle Burt to confirm the details of Blake's application for a permit, and it sounds like everything was on the up-and-up. Maybe I just need to have patience. To let the excitement die down and hope that the Robin's faithful service and longevity in this community will draw people back within our walls once again.

Nodding, I turn to head back inside and lick my wounds, but I catch sight of a group of women who work at the Golden Highlight beauty salon and come in every Thursday for our lunch special, the peanut butter bacon burger. They're walking up the path toward the Robin, but then one of them nudges another and points to the food truck. And I don't blame them— it's kind of hard to miss.

Glinda, a twenty-something with straight black-and-blue hair, heads toward the food truck and waits for Blake to slide an order through the window. He looks down at the woman and flashes her a smile—one that doesn't quite reach his eyes. Polite, but not effusive or flirtatious.

She asks a question, he gives an answer, and the woman turns and waves her friends over.

All three of them proceed to walk to join the back of the line.

Oh no. Uh uh. Bright and shiny is one thing. Outright thievery? Blake Moffitt will not steal from me.

I simply won't allow it.

I march toward the truck, my eyes darting this way and that. There's no way I can get a private audience with him at the window, so there's only one alternative. Before I can talk myself out of it, I rage-stomp around the front of the truck so as to avoid the line and sneak around to the back, where I fling open the truck door and climb inside.

The heat is the first thing to hit me. Even with a few fans going, it's warm inside this metal box. The galley is narrow, with a sink, prep station, and the sliding window on one side, and shelves, a fridge, and the grill on the other. The shelves are as organized as I imagined they'd be—not that I'd actually imagined ever setting foot inside this place—with loaves of bread and other ingredients perfectly stacked beside the boxes of extra napkins, cutlery, and disposable food trays.

I've never wanted to disorganize—maybe even vandalize—something more in my life, but I push the urge aside. I've got a food truck owner to deal with.

If only he didn't look so put together himself.

Despite the heat level inside, he's dressed in a blue button-up shirt that's rolled to his elbows, revealing nicely corded forearms—the kind that belong to guys who work out regularly but are too busy living life to be total gym rats. His khaki slacks are partially covered by a black waist apron, and his brown boots look more suited for a conference room than a food truck in Hallmark Beach.

And yet, he's still got that impossibly sexy business casual look going on. The kind that is only slightly mussed and partially unbuttoned—like it's the end of a long day of work, and he's coming home on a Friday night for pizza and wine and some movie watching and cuddling on the couch.

Gah. This look is not good for my heart. It's a reminder of those teenage years, when there were nights we hung out like that. Talking. Flirting—though ever since that almost-kiss on my seventeenth birthday, I've questioned whether I imagined it all.

This look hearkens back to those memories, almost making me forget that underneath that handsome facade beats the dead heart of someone who would never be satisfied with a small-town life. He's made that very clear. Which is why it honestly makes no sense that he's here running a business in Hallmark Beach anyway. There's got to be a catch. Maybe it's time I finally took Marilee's advice and asked Blake exactly why he's here.

Or maybe the *why* doesn't matter, so long as he leaves. Or at the very least, moves his dang truck far, far away.

Flipping a sandwich, he finally looks over at me. His expression doesn't change—like he has women pop into his truck every day. Like it's no big deal. "If you want a sandwich, you're going to have to wait in line like everybody else, Sunshine."

Sarcasm drips from his tongue. It doesn't suit him. He was always sweeter than that.

But people change.

"I'm not here for a sandwich." I walk right up to him and poke him in the chest. His much too muscular chest. The guy was always fit—he played football at his dad's insistence—but for goodness' sake. A guy who works around food all day should not have granite pecs. Or such a flat stomach. Or arms that...

Grr. *Focus, Lucy.* "I'm here to tell you to stop stealing my customers."

"*Your* customers?" Blake turns back to his grill, and my hand falls away. But I don't move an inch. Backing down would be admitting defeat. "They're in *my* line."

"Only because your truck is right there in front of my customers' faces!"

He butters a few slices of bread—quick as lightning—and tosses them onto the grill. "If they're so easily swayed by the mere presence of my truck, then maybe they aren't really loyal to you in the first place. Maybe they're just settling for what's here because they don't know any better."

How. Dare. He. "As if you would understand anything about loyalty."

Okay, it's kind of a low blow, I know. But I still stand by the sentiment.

Blake stiffens but doesn't respond for a few moments, so we just stand there, my face nearly touching his shoulder. It's irritating how good he manages to smell despite working with all this grease and dairy. If I worked in here, I'd be sweating through my shirt, my hair piled messy and high, my brow streaked with grime. But Blake somehow looks as put together as his shelves.

Finally, he lifts his spatula and points to the back door. "You've said your piece. Now it's time to go, Sunshine."

"Enough with the stupid nickname, Flake."

"You're one to talk."

"Yours is appropriate and well earned."

"And yours seems appropriate enough for an entitled brat who thinks she can waltz into my place of business and whine that *she* isn't doing enough to hold onto her own customers."

I rear back like he's slapped me. My hands curl at my sides. He did *not* just say that. Me, entitled? *I'm* the one who had to move to an entirely new town when I was sixteen years old after living in an apartment that was barely habitable, always wondering if Mama's job in the school cafeteria was going to be enough to cover food, rent, clothing, and our annual summer road trip ending in Hallmark Beach.

He's the one who grew up in the perfect town with the perfect family and never wanted for anything in his perfect life. Until his parents died, of course. But I lost people too. On that ground, we're even.

My lip curls, and I don't even feel like myself. All of this anger is going to give me early wrinkles. "If anyone's entitled, it's you, thinking you can come back here after what you did."

"It's not like I murdered someone, Lucy."

I find myself strangely disappointed that he called me by my real name. Sweet macaroni, I *hate* that he still has any sort of hold over my emotions. "No, but—"

"And I'm tired of you acting like I committed a crime at all."

"As far as I'm concerned, you did." Marilee needed him, and he left. He's guilty of being a terrible big brother, among other things. "But whatever. We're never going to see eye to eye on it. Just like, apparently, we're never going to see eye to eye on the fact that you're a thief."

He sighs, plating the sandwiches along with a pickle and some chips that look homemade, and slides them through the window, calling out "Jacobs!" before returning to the grill to toss on more sandwiches. "Yeah, I guess we won't. But answer me this. How can I be stealing from you when we don't even serve the same thing? Because that was the one condition the council put on my permit. If I ever try to serve the same thing as The Green Robin, I'll have seven days to pack up and leave." He flips another sandwich. "I won't be infringing on whatever your little restaurant serves. And if your customers are as loyal as you say, you won't have anything to worry about."

Wait a second. "What did you say?"

He pushes up his sleeves, distracting my eyes for just a moment, and lifts his eyebrows. "I said, I won't be infringing—"

"No, not that."

He said *if my customers are loyal...* That's it. "I've gotta go." I head for the back door.

"Finally, a little peace."

Stopping, I pivot and offer him a wicked grin. "Don't get too used to it. I'm taking back my customers. And we'll see who they're really loyal to after all."

seven

BLAKE

Lucy said she was going to take back my customers, and apparently, she's a woman of her word.

A week after our little chat, during which she invaded the peaceful sanctuary of my food truck, I pound out my frustration on the Hallmark Beach boardwalk. The sun's barely peeking over the horizon, and the temp is hanging out in the low sixties, but sweat clings to my skin as I run.

Normally, I like to run to a business podcast or even some music, but today it's just me and the sound of the surf. I like the constancy of it, the way it always moves in and out, the ebb and flow that's so much like life. Each individual moment or day may feel chaotic and unpredictable, but when you look at it as a whole, there's balance.

That's what I remind myself of as I pass a few cyclists going the opposite direction, away from downtown, where I'll finish up my four-mile run. My eyes can't help but take in the buildings, all still and mostly dark. In another hour or so, they'll be bustling with people—though I'm not sure if the same can be said for The Urban Melt.

Because while the first few days of my grand opening were

impressive and exactly as I'd hoped, as soon as Lucy left my truck last week, she started chatting up the people in line. Asking about their babies, their jobs, saying how much she missed seeing them at The Green Robin since she took over as manager.

She then joked—loudly, I'm sure so I could hear her—about how she could see the appeal of trying food from someone who will only be here temporarily. One woman looked over at my window, her face full of disdain, and asked, "Is that really true? I thought he was back for good."

And Lucy just shrugged her innocent little shoulders and said, "You know how quickly he left the last time."

It was a stab in the gut when she glanced at me, her eyes searing me before looking away like I wasn't worth her time. She didn't exactly guilt those customers into leaving my line, but several of them followed her to the Robin anyway. And though the tourists over Memorial Day weekend helped boost sales, ever since, I've struggled to get more than a handful of customers an hour, which has not exactly allowed the creative juices to flow. I'm at a stalemate on recipe creation, and it's all because of Lucy.

Essentially, she took her Hallmark Beach charm—charm I *should* have since this is *my* hometown—and used it against me.

I increase my speed, my lungs tight. My vision starts to blur a bit, so I slow to a walk, holding my hands behind my head. Why does she hate me so much? Yeah, maybe I was a jerk when I nearly kissed her on her seventeenth birthday and left the next day for college—but she knew I was leaving. Maybe I should have said goodbye, but after talking with my dad, I knew I couldn't promise her anything. That I shouldn't have spent the year flirting with her and getting to know her better. She was just so darn likable...

And when I came back the next few summers, she

smiled, laughed, and acted like she was fine. I mean, sure, we didn't interact as much as we had previously. I had to keep my distance, or I knew she'd pull me back in. But she didn't seem *mad*, and she never was the type to hold grudges. She was happy-go-lucky Lucy Reynolds without a care in the world.

At least, that's what I thought until I showed up here six years ago, and she begged me not to leave again for my sister's sake. And when I said I had to go, she gave me a look—not exactly angry, but disappointed, like I'd failed to be the man she thought I should be. I know she was just being a good friend to Marilee by arguing with me to stay, but my parents had just died. I was barely holding it together. The idea of staying? Of facing the loss day in and day out?

It felt impossible.

Clearly, the years of relative silence on my part since then have taken a higher toll than I thought. Because when I came back to cater that wedding in April, Lucy hated me.

Maybe she should.

"Hey, Blake! Wait up."

I turn to find Marilee's friend Jordan coming up behind me in joggers and a lightweight hoodie.

He pulls out an earbud. "Heard you were back in town." He reaches out a hand.

I shake it. "Yeah, for a few months."

"That's what Lee-Lee said."

I raise my eyebrows. "Lee-Lee?"

Jordan grins and shrugs. "It's what Ryder—my son—calls her."

"Oh, yeah. I heard you had a kid. She seems pretty taken with him." Mare caught me up life in Hallmark Beach—and all the gossip—during dinner together earlier this week. On the nights I haven't worked late, trying my hardest (and failing) to perfect new recipes, we've spent a few evenings together, which has been nice.

Of course, Lucy hasn't shown her face at all, probably waiting until she thinks I'm in bed to come home. The only way I know she's been there at all is the smell of her in the bathroom we share. Something citrusy and vanilla. Let's just say I'm in and outta there as quickly as I can be.

Why torture myself with things I can't have—and shouldn't want?

Jordan runs a hand through his hair, which doesn't seem sweaty at all, unlike mine. "Ryder's a great kid. I'm really lucky."

He seems like one of those good-natured guys who smiles a lot, and who's genuine about it. I'm glad Marilee has someone like him in her corner, though I've always wondered if there was something more between them. At least on his end. Maybe I don't have a right to play the part of the protective older brother since I've been gone for so long, and since I failed so epically to protect her from Donny.

Then again, I'm here now. Maybe there's a chance I can earn that right someday, even after I head back to Los Angeles in August.

"So remind me what you do for work around here." Marilee actually told me, but hey, I've gotta start the conversation somewhere, right? It would be way too obvious to just outright ask him what his intentions are with my sister.

We walk together, right past an older couple getting in their steps who wave and wish us a good morning.

"I own an adventure tours and beach equipment rentals company. Go Round Adventures. It's just south of downtown, past Red Sauce Pizza and the Golden Highlight."

"Awesome. You left for a while to attend business school, yeah?"

"I did."

"So what brought you back to Hallmark Beach?" From what Marilee told me, he moved home around the time our parents died. His son is only four, so he didn't come back to be near family for his sake. There must have been some other reason.

We stop walking for a minute, moving just off the boardwalk onto the sand. Jordan squints at the ocean, where there's a sailboat bobbing in the distance. "Guess you could say that everything I wanted was in this little town. It's home." Then he turns to me. "What about you? Why'd you come back?"

I clear my throat, unsure I want to share all of that with Jordan. So I stick with the easiest answer. "Had a break in my schedule and thought it was time to reconnect with Mare."

"I know she's missed you, so that's awesome."

It kind of rankles that this guy seems to know more about my sister than I do. "Just wish the rest of the town felt the same way."

He stretches his arm over his head. "How do you mean? Is business bad?"

"It wasn't, until Lucy showed up and sweet-talked all of my customers into leaving me."

"Ouch." Jordan shakes out his hand like something burned him. "I wouldn't want to go head-to-head with Lucy in a sweet-talking contest. Especially because that woman is genuinely sweet." He then lunges into a lower-body stretch. "Kind of makes me wonder what you did to earn her wrath."

"You and me both, man."

We both laugh, and I rub a hand along the back of my neck. "If you've got any tips on how to garner favor in this town, I'm all ears. I don't really want to be at war with Lucy, but she seems convinced that every resident is either her customer or mine—like we can't coexist somehow. And she's been busy convincing everyone else of the same thing."

Switching legs, Jordan nods. "What you need to do is remind people that you're from Hallmark Beach just as much—if not more than—Lucy."

"Yeah, but how?"

"That's for you to figure out, dude. If Lucy knew I was helping you, she'd have my head." He slices a finger across his throat and sticks his tongue out like he's dead. "But while she's my friend, I'm loyal to Lee too. And you mean a lot to her."

"Thanks, man. I appreciate it."

"No problem." He straightens and glances at his watch. "Aw, dang, gotta run. My elderly neighbor's keeping an eye on Ryder, and he should be waking up soon. Gotta get him off to my mom's and then shower before the festival meeting. You coming to that, by the way?"

"It's the first I've heard of it. What festival?"

"I'm surprised Chloe didn't hit you up for help."

"That's the princess, right?"

Jordan grins. "I see Lee has caught you up on all the local gossip. Yeah, she's a princess, but she's also the new owner of Something Blue and got drafted last minute to plan the town's Fourth of July Festival."

"Yikes." Now there's a job I don't envy.

"Right?" Jordan pauses, tilts his head. "You really haven't met her yet? She and Marilee are pretty tight, and you've been back, what? Two weeks?"

"Almost. But I've been pretty focused on getting the truck up and running." And starting—and scrapping—recipe after new recipe. "Haven't really interacted with many people except from behind the window."

"There's your problem, dude." Jordan snaps at me. "Hallmark Beach is all about loyalty, but you've got to remind them you belong here. That you actually care about the community and aren't just here to make a buck."

Okay, that makes sense. And it's something that I know about my hometown. Maybe I just forgot it. "I'm in. How do I do that, though?"

"I've got an idea. Are you free this morning at eight-thirty?"

"I'll make myself free." Whatever it takes to get my business plan back on track. To get customers so I can generate a test market.

And yeah, maybe to stick it to Lucy a little bit too.

"Perfect. See you then."

LUCY

I adore so much about this town.

The setting itself. You can't get much better than my current view on The Green Robin's beach-facing back patio, where Chloe's gathered us all for the third festival meeting.

The quirky characters. Like Earl Flanders and Alberta Jenkins, who are going at it right now like two toddlers fighting over an ice cream cone, and Uncle Burt, who's busy entertaining a few other old timers with tall tales of past customers and his heroics in rescuing stranded motorists passing through town.

But most especially, I love the way this community welcomed me into the fold summer after summer as a kid, even when I was just a guest among them. It's like they saw something in me that required comforting, and they became the safe haven I needed.

One thing I'm not a huge fan of, though? The way everyone knows your business. Don't get me wrong—it can be endearing, and usually it just means they care.

But right now, I'm surrounded by all of my best friends— save Chloe, who is flitting around in preparation for the meeting, and Marilee, who is at work on this Thursday morning—and they've started asking me about something they'd know nothing about if we didn't live in the tiniest of towns.

Because I certainly never would have brought it up.

"How are things going with your irritatingly good-looking new housemate?" Elisse's smile is wicked in nature as she pushes her brown bobbed hair behind an ear.

"No comment."

"I'm so jealous. Wanna switch?" My cousin April fans herself with an Abigail Fox novel that's got a cute illustrated couple on the front. Looks like this one's a hockey romcom. She's always carrying a romance book around—which makes sense, given she's both an aspiring author and works at The Bluestocking Bookshop in town. "My little housemate has been acting seven going on seventeen lately. When did kids get so moody, anyway?"

We all laugh. I reach over and squeeze her arm. "Believe me, I'd switch in a heartbeat, but something tells me Scarlett really does need her mama, even if she doesn't act like it." That something? It's called experience. Take it from the girl whose own mom can be difficult to get ahold of. I know she's having the time of her life gallivanting the globe with Kevin, and after all the sadness of losing my dad twenty years ago, I can't blame her for having a little fun.

But I'd be lying if I said I didn't miss her. Still, I don't need to dwell on it, and fortunately, my friends don't either.

Unfortunately, that doesn't mean they're ready to let talk of Blake die.

"So." Kelsey grabs my arm and tugs me closer, her gentle voice a soothing balm after her twin sister's teasing. "How is it going, really? I know how much you don't care for him."

"So she says," Elisse's voice singsongs. "What's that saying?

There's a fine line between love and hate? And we all know how much you haaaaaate Blake Moffitt."

"Shut up, Elisse." April hip bumps her out of the way and nudges close to my other side. "Let Lucy tell us all the good stuff herself."

"Good stuff?" I laugh. "This isn't a romance novel, cuz."

"I know." Huffing, April pushes her red hair out of her eyes. She recently got bangs and, upon coming home from the salon, declared that she regretted her life choices. "Real life is never as good as the books. But let a girl fantasize vicariously through you for a moment, okay?"

That makes me chuckle again. These ladies are good for my soul. "There's not much to tell—and definitely nothing to fantasize about. I've worked a lot of late nights, so we've pretty much missed each other at the house."

Elisse frowns at me. "And by that you mean Marilee texts you when he heads to bed so you don't accidentally run into him, right?"

"No, but that's a fabulous idea. Because I'm not wasting any more energy on him."

"Any *more?*" April latches onto the word with hope and a raised eyebrow.

"You guys are impossible." I roll my eyes. "I'm sure you've heard about the drama with the food truck."

"Of course. It's all over town, how Miss Sunshine herself got snarky with her best friend's brother," Elisse says in a low, saucy voice full of *knowing*.

I balk at her use of "Sunshine"—Blake's stupid new nickname for me—and narrow my eyes at her. Does she know more than she's letting on? Oy.

Either way, I hate how news of my lapse in emotional judgement spread so rapidly. At least I took my anger out on him in private the next time. Still, I wish he didn't affect me at all. *Lemons into lemonade, Lucy. You're good at that.* "He deserved it." I try to infuse as much conviction into my tone as possible.

"Sure he did." Elisse shoots me an exaggerated wink. "If I hadn't been busy at the vineyard helping Mom get set up for photos this week, I'd have been to town to see you two go at it myself. Would have brought my popcorn, parked myself outside, and enjoyed the show."

"Me too." April laughs, then presses her lips together when she looks back at me. "I mean…"

Kelsey just squeezes my arm again.

I dash a grateful look her way. "You'd have all been sorely disappointed, because after I set him straight last week and talked sense into the people waiting in his line, the Robin has been flooded with guests again, and I haven't said a word to him."

I can't tell you how extremely satisfying it's been to see his line dwindle after Memorial Day weekend. It was so good to know I've done something right, that—even though I may not have grand aspirations of opening my own business someday like Chloe and Marilee, and I'm not building a family legacy like Kelsey and Elisse or writing books like April—I've at least helped my community. I've provided some sort of service to Winona, who is depending on me.

And it doesn't hurt that I brought Blake a little kick in the pants too.

"In fact," I continue, "I don't think we'll be seeing much of Blake anymore. He's probably already contemplating whether to pull the plug and leave town." Do I really believe it? No. He doesn't strike me as someone who will give up easily. Then again, what's Hallmark Beach to him, really? If he finds himself facing too much opposition here, I *can* see him pulling up stakes and heading to the nearest place that will give him the opportunity for success.

That's all that matters to him anyway.

"I don't know, friend." Kelsey's turned her attention to the back doorway that leads out to the patio. "That doesn't look like someone ready to leave."

I follow her line of vision and hold back a sigh. Because there's Blake, channeling a used car salesman as he shakes hands with folks—those he's known all his life and a few newer faces to town, including Chloe's boyfriend, Frederick—and offers a smile.

Once again, there's something forced or uncomfortable in it, but he's schmoozing with the best of them. Apparently, he's figured out where he stands in Hallmark Beach and must be looking to change his reputation by volunteering and endearing himself to the community.

It's a brilliant move, and I hate him for it.

"Excuse me," I say to my friends as I push through the crowd, grab his arm, and tug him away from the group. "What are you doing here?"

"Do you mind?" Blake stares down at where my hand is touching his bare forearm.

Unwanted electricity shoots through me, and I pull my hand back to myself, flexing it. "Sorry." Dang it. I don't need to be apologizing to him. I straighten. "I mean..." Ugh, why is talking suddenly such a flustering activity? "I-I know what you're doing here."

"Funny." He pins me with a look while absently rubbing the spot on his arm where I touched him. "You just asked me, and now you suddenly know?" There's a tic in his jaw that draws my attention. And not because it makes his whole profile more intense. More chiseled. Nope.

I've been staring—gawking—too long. "I know, because I know you, Flake. You want to pretend like you care about this place, so you're at this meeting as some sort of goodwill gesture." I fold my arms over my chest. "But we don't want you here."

"You aren't the authority on all things Hallmark Beach, Sunshine." He pushes a hand through his hair, which doesn't budge an inch. The move is so nonchalant, like he doesn't have a care in the world. Like this conversation is just a pesky blip on the barometer of his day. "Need I remind you who was actually born in this town? So thanks for trying to speak for everyone else, but I belong here just as much as—if not more than—you do."

"Being born here isn't everything." I lean in, my voice sizzling. But I smile, because I know Elisse and company are watching—and her quip about the line between love and hate is reverberating around in my brain. If she knew our complete history, she'd never let me hear the end of it. Best to let all thoughts of me ever having loved Blake Moffitt die a painful death right here and now.

So, with a sickly-sweet tone, I manage to keep a straight face devoid of the grimace I really want to display. "It's the ones who stick around who are the true citizens of Hallmark Beach."

His face twists, and for a moment, I feel the tiniest inkling of guilt. But he deserves my ire. Doesn't he?

"Hey, Blake."

We both startle and turn to find Thomas standing there. Today he's wearing a bright orange polo that matches his hair. His attention shifts to me. "Hi, Luce." His cheeks pink up a bit. "I saved you a seat."

"Oh, thanks, Thomas. That was really thoughtful."

He nods once, twice.

Blake just glares at him. What in the world? What's he got against Thomas? Sure, the guy is a little...enthusiastic. But he's polite and sweet, which is more than I can say for Flake over here. Besides, Thomas is the one who actually stood up to me for Blake when he arrived. You'd think Blake would be his biggest fan.

Thankfully, Thomas doesn't seem to notice the daggers Blake is shooting his way. "When I saw you show up, Blake, I approached Chloe and told her we'd love to have you on our committee."

Hold the phone. "We what?" I practically screech.

Blake shakes his head. "Oh, that's really nice, bu—"

"Here's my brilliant Picnic Team!" Speaking of the princess, she appears out of thin air like some sort of good fairy. Except if it's true she assigned Blake to my group, she's dead to me. Well, not really, but she'd best have a good reason for her betrayal since she knows how I feel about him.

She claps twice and turns around. "All right, friends, it's about time to start the meeting. Please find your seats with your fellow committee members, and we'll begin shortly."

Then she faces us again and holds out her hand to Blake. "Chloe Huntington. You're Marilee's brother, yes? It's wonderful to meet you."

Blake, to his credit, doesn't seem to be affected by Chloe's royal blood. He merely shakes her hand and says, "Nice to meet you too."

"Brilliant. I'm guessing Thomas informed you already, but since you're one of our fellow foodies, I'd appreciate your help on the picnic committee."

"Yeah, of course." He glances at me briefly, then looks away. "Wherever I'm needed."

"Great," I say with extremely false enthusiasm.

Thomas leads Blake away, toward our table by the railing, and Chloe turns an eye to me. "Well, *that* was some of the hottest chemistry I've ever seen."

My nose scrunches. "What are you talking about?"

"The two of you. I was about to spontaneously combust watching you from over there. I can't imagine how *you* feel." She touches my arm then pulls back. "Ooo, yes, you're warm. Very warm." Then she laughs.

"All right, you've had your fun." I push her just a tad.

From out of nowhere, her bodyguard Tia appears at my elbow.

Chloe rolls her eyes. "Seriously, Tia, we've talked about this. She's my mate. Americans shove each other in love all the time. It's just the way they show affection."

"It's a blasted stupid way if you ask me," the woman mumbles. But she moves back against the railing nonetheless.

Frederick takes the opportunity to swoop in. "Princess, love." He places his hand on the small of her back, smiling, and whispers something in her ear.

She giggles and gives him a kiss on the cheek. "Later, yeah?"

"If you insist." With a wink, he turns to me. "Lucy."

"Freddy." I can't help but smile. The two of them are couple goals all the way.

If I *had* couple goals, anyway.

A love like they share is wonderful, I'm sure. But as I saw when my dad died, it can also break a person open when the one you love the most in the world leaves—willingly or not.

Frederick gives me a nod, squeezes Chloe's waist again, and heads back to the crowd, helping people find their seats and get situated. The way he supports his girlfriend is just the sweetest.

"I'm so happy for you, you know." And I really am. I may not have been there at the very beginning of their love story— which started when they were much younger—but I got a sideline view of them admitting their feelings for each other. It was, and continues to be, a beautiful thing. A scary thing. But a beautiful one to be sure.

"Thank you." Chloe spontaneously gives me a hug. How have we only known each other a few months? I seriously feel like she's a sister to me. One with way more fashion sense and poise than I'll ever have. But a sister all the same. "I want you to be just as happy as me." A pause. "You sure there's nothing between you and Mare's brother?"

Somehow, my eyes find Blake with ease.

I startle to see him looking back at me.

We stare at each other for a good few seconds before I pull my gaze back to Chloe. Clear my throat. "Nothing but supreme dislike." That, and a lot of baggage.

And words that can never be unsaid.

"And you're sure that dislike can never become...like?"

I press my fingernails into the palms of my hands. "I'm sure."

Because if I ever did let down my guard—if I ever *did* let Blake back in—I'm not sure the walls I've erected could hold back the tidal wave of emotions I've managed to keep at bay until now.

And the flood that ensued would be sure to decimate anything good I've managed to build in the wake of his leaving.

Hating him is far easier.

nine

BLAKE

A business plan is always just that—a plan.

Plans fail all the time. And when they do, you have to go back to the drawing board. Re-evaluate. It's part luck, part scientific process. You figure out what's working and what's not. Then you do more of the stuff that is effective and axe the things that aren't. You get creative—the part I hate, because I don't always have that gut instinct about what will work when it comes to marketing.

Now, if we're talking gut instincts about my food? I'm all over that.

But marketing? It's the shot in the dark I hate.

Which is why I was desperate enough to try Jordan's suggestion yesterday of showing up uninvited to the Fourth of July Festival planning meeting. Thankfully, Chloe Huntington was more than willing to have me aboard.

Lucy Reynolds, however? Not so much.

It's not as if she and Thomas have finalized any of their plans—far from it—but it was clear that she didn't want to hear my ideas for what food should be served during the festival. Whenever I'd suggest something, she'd shoot it down. At my suggestion that each of our respective businesses host booths with food for sale instead of serving one main meal like burgers, chips, and fruit—the same things that are always served—she said no way. Even though her restaurant could use the extra cash.

And sure, I understand the argument that this is not supposed to be about us profiting. It's supposed to be about the community, about us making the food as cheap as possible—while also making it delicious—so as many people as possible can enjoy a meal together.

But I also think that the woman's determined to be difficult.

Of course, that only extends to me. For Thomas, she's agreeable. For Thomas, she takes time to listen and really consider.

Look, Thomas is a nice guy. He really is. He even tried backing me up on the extra food sales, though, when she looked at him with hurt in her eyes, he instantly backpedaled.

But every time the guy called her *Luce*, I wanted to punch him and yell, "Mine" like some sort of caveman. Which is ridiculous, because Lucy Reynolds is the farthest thing from *mine* that there is.

"Earth to Blake." Marilee waves one of my fifty-percent-off fliers in my face.

I blink, and my sister's face comes into focus, as does the porch of The Purple Seashell, where we just dropped off a load of fliers with Lucy's aunt Janine, the owner.

After my chat with Jordan yesterday, I decided to try the classic coupon approach to entice new customers my way. I barely had time to run home, shower, and print off some fliers before the meeting, where I handed them out. It was a good opportunity to shake hands and give hugs to some of Hallmark Beach's oldest residents, many of whom told me that while "fancy grilled cheese" isn't really their thing, because it's me, they'll give it a try.

Here's hoping.

Now it's Friday morning around nine, and in the hours before I open the truck for the day, I've recruited my sister to help. Well, more like she saw my fliers in the kitchen this morning, and since she didn't have to work, volunteered to hand them out for me. It's a good excuse to spend time with her, so I let her tag along.

"Yeah, sorry. Just enjoying the view," I say, and it's not totally a lie as I peer past Marilee and take in the morning waves of the Pacific. It's June now, and the tourists have started to flood the beach in droves. Honestly, it's the ideal time to be running a food truck in Hallmark Beach, and Janine promised to distribute a flier to each of her customers when they check in.

"It does look like it's going to be a nice day." Her lips quirk up. "Maybe I'll take Ryder to the beach."

"You babysitting on your day off?"

She shrugs and tugs her hair up into a bun using a band at her wrist. "Jordan's mom had a flare-up of her multiple sclerosis, so I don't mind. Poor thing. It's been happening more and more lately, and Ryder has energy in spades."

We start down the steps of the Seashell and meet up with the boardwalk, heading south toward the rest of the downtown shops. Bits of sand crunch beneath my loafers. "I'm sure it's good for him to have a mom figure in his life." Ryder's own mom passed away earlier in the year after a brief battle with cancer. Poor little guy.

"Oh, I'm more like a fun aunt." Marilee's face stretches tight at the words as she forces a smile onto her face. I know it's forced because there's also a slight tremble in her voice. I must have said something that hit a nerve. Maybe Marilee will tell me eventually. Unlike Lucy—who only ever seems to be happy or angry (and only the latter with me)—my sister embraces her emotions. It just might take her awhile to process them. But eventually, she cries.

She reminds me a lot of Mom, and the thought has me looping my arm around her shoulders and squeezing.

Grabbing my hand briefly, she squeezes back. "I hope this coupon strategy works for you. How's the recipe creation coming?"

I hold back a sigh. "Not well."

"Sorry. You'll figure it out, though. You always do. And don't they say inspiration often comes from the most unlikely of places?"

"True. Here's hoping it decides to arrive more quickly than not."

"You can't rush genius. Then again, you're not a genius. Just my brother..."

I laugh at the goofy face she's shooting me, then pull her to a stop. "Come on, Squirt."

"Hey! You can't call me that anymore." But her giggle tells me she doesn't really mind.

It's good to hear her laugh after all the junk life has put her through. Good to see her happy. I wish she was pursuing her dreams and would find—or at least admit to herself she might have already found—a good man to settle down with. But for now, the laughter's enough.

And I'm glad I'm here to hear it.

"If the shoe fits. And you do have tiny shoes for your tiny feet." It's true. Mare's petite all over.

Unlike Lucy, whose tall willowy frame puts her much closer to my height. If she was the one standing beside me, I'd only have to tilt my chin down and see right into those big, beautiful blue eyes—

I nearly groan out loud at the path of my thoughts. *Get out, get out, get out of my head!*

"It's Mom's fault, not mine." Marilee's smile trembles. "Where are we going, anyway?"

"To find some inspiration. And finish handing out these fliers."

We wait for a couple of moms with jogging strollers and then duck up the sidewalk toward Olive Paradise, which sells olive-infused oils and other delicious-smelling knickknacks. Maybe here we can find something to use on my sandwiches.

My arm drops from Marilee's shoulders to open the door, and a bell jangles overhead. The proprietor, Ned Chamberlain, looks up from behind the reception desk and waves, then goes back to his computer.

Marilee starts toward Ned, but I snag her elbow. "Help me browse for inspiration first."

Her eyes light up, and she starts perusing. I do the same. Reaching for a bottle, she brings it close, her glasses slipping to the edge of her nose as she reads the label. Then she holds it up and smiles. "Okay, but seriously. Bacon olive oil."

"Hmm. That could work. But I already have a bacon-inspired sandwich."

"Oh, true. That's the one with the maple glaze, right?" At my nod, she purses her lips together and *mmm*s. Then she looks at the bottle again. "I wonder if this would jazz up my corn muffins? Ooo, or we could try it in Mom's mashed pota-toes. What do you think?"

We analyze the pros and cons of bacon olive oil for a few minutes before Marilee decides to give it a try. Sounds like Jordan—who she's cooking dinner for tonight since she's babysitting at his house—is going to be the lucky guinea pig of Marilee's genius. She definitely bakes more than she cooks, but Mom taught us both well.

And once again, I'm caught unaware by the equal parts grief and relief that fill my chest. Grief that I wasted so much time away from the one person who knew exactly what I was feeling the last six years. Relief that I'm finally here.

That I'm right where I should be.

"Mare." I turn back to studying the labels and absently pick up a bottle, reading the label but not really reading it. "I'm sorry."

I can feel the heat of her gaze on me. "Sorry for what?"

"That I wasn't here for you. After..."

Her hand touches my arm. "You were grieving too, Blake."

"Yeah, but Lucy told me I should stay. She told me about Donny. How bad he was to you." No, he didn't hit her, but he bruised her spirit all the same. I can see it now. That Lucy was right.

I shift my gaze again, forcing myself to look at the sister I more than failed.

Her bottom lip is tucked away between her teeth, and she's staring at the ground. Marilee shakes her head. "Donny was my stupid decision. No one forced me to marry him." Finally, she looks up at me, and her voice is quiet. "I don't want to talk about him."

"Fine, we won't. But I'm still sorry. You were dealing with a lot—probably more than I even realized—and then Mom and Dad died. I just..." I rub the back of my neck. This isn't easy to say, but it should have been said years ago. "I shouldn't have left like that. Can you forgive me?"

"I already have, Blake." Then my sister is hugging me around the waist. "I'm just so glad you're back, even if just for a little while. Though..." She shakes her head. "Never mind."

"No. What?" If my sister has a request of me, the least I can do it listen to it.

She pulls back and studies me, then plucks the bottle from

my hand and reads the label. "Mmm, cilantro and roasted onion. You should try that with some ricotta cheese."

My eyebrows lift at the sudden shift in topic—and also at the suggestion. "Good idea." I snag the bottle again and hold it over her head, where she'll never be able to reach it. "But tell me what you were going to say, Squirt."

She hesitates. "It's just that you mentioned Lucy. And the fight you had."

Great. My favorite topic. "Go on."

"Well, if you and I can move past it, then maybe the two of you can too? I hate you being at odds. You're two of my favorite people, and we all live together, at least for the summer. It would be nice if you could stop avoiding each other. If we could hang out like we used to."

Ugh. I hate it when she looks at me with those big brown eyes of hers, so like Mom's. When she pouts like she used to when she was three and I was five, and I'd give her the rest of my ice cream cone because she wanted it and I was the sucker who couldn't say no.

Back then, I sacrificed for her—and yeah, it was only ice cream, but ice cream is big in the land of five-year-olds. So maybe sacrificing is just what a good brother does. And to be honest, though Lucy's antics have gotten me riled up the last few weeks, I actually kind of hate that she dislikes me this much. Maybe being on Lucy's bad side isn't the best way to spend my time here in Hallmark Beach.

Of course, I'm not talking about rekindling any of those troublesome *feelings* I had for her in high school. Maybe not even friendship. Just...I don't know. A truce, maybe.

For Marilee's sake.

"Okay, baby sister. You can stop making puppy dog eyes at me. Now, give me that." I take the bottle of bacon olive oil from her quick as a flash and walk it and the cilantro one to the front, where Ned has apparently been watching our back and forth with his lazy eyes.

After I've paid for them both and plied Ned with coupons he promises to hand out, I turn back to Marilee, who is grinning at me.

"What?"

"Nothing." She slips her hand through the crook of my arm and tilts her head. "Do you think it's too early in the day for ice cream?"

I laugh and we head out the door. The sun is beaming at us almost as brightly as my sister's smile. Things are good here in Hallmark Beach.

Now I just have to figure out how to apologize to Lucy Reynolds. Or, at the very least, make her hate me a little less.

ten

LUCY

I'm not sure I'm cut out for management.

Not the people aspect—that's fine. Mama always said I could talk the ear off an elephant. Apparently that's some sort of special talent. And since I don't have many of those, I'll hold tight to what I can.

It's why waitressing came naturally to me when I was a teenager and why I've stuck with it ever since. I'm not a big reader. I can't really cook. And clearly numbers aren't my thing.

This has never been more obvious than right now as I stare at my laptop. I blink and stretch my neck, sinking back into the couch cushions in our living room, though only for a moment. It's nearly midnight on Saturday, my brain hurts, and my body is protesting still being awake. Marilee's been tucked in for a long while, and Blake is who knows where. Haven't really seen him since the meeting two days ago when he showed up to brownnose the town and interfere with *my* festival committee.

But as tired as I am, I can't let sleep claim me yet. I need to talk with Winona, and it's finally morning where she is over in

Europe. Hopefully she's as much of a morning person on this trip as she is in Hallmark Beach.

Because I've been working on a plan.

A plan inspired by Blake.

Well, not the man himself, but his idea. He spent a good chunk of time after the meeting on Thursday handing out coupons—something I never even thought to do. Winona has never done coupons, so I didn't think to do them either. But it seems fairly Business 101, right? Sometimes you have to give away free stuff to get new customers, or to give previous customers the push they need to return.

It certainly seems to be working for Blake. The Robin was busy enough today—thank you, weekend summer tourism season!—but the food truck was busier. What if he's figured out a way to come out on top? What if his schmoozing and business acumen are going to mean success for him?

And failure for me?

Despite what I said to his customers, I don't even know how long he'll be here. I haven't bothered yet to ask (because that would mean having a civil conversation). But even a few months of low sales could hurt the Robin.

I might be no match for Mr. MBA, but I've gotta try. For Winona's sake.

And speaking of Winona, I don't want to implement any new business strategies without her approval. Which means it's time to finally make that call. Sighing, I stand and set my open laptop on the kitchen counter. Then I take my phone and step outside on the back porch so I don't wake Marilee, leaving the door cracked behind me.

The evening is cool, and I zip up my hoodie as I lower myself onto the white, wooden porch swing and grab the blanket I left there a few nights ago. This is one of my favorite places to just think. The house may be old and small with locks that sometimes decide to jam (thus the cracked door!), but it's in a prime location, sitting at the top of Hillside Drive. That means the patch of grassy backyard faces downtown, and consequently, the ocean far below.

The phone rings a few times before Winona answers. "Lucy! How's my newest manager?" She sounds upbeat and happy, so different from the stress she exhibited the last few months of being here.

All the stress I've taken on lately has been worth it if it's given her the space she needs to find joy. Joy with her daughter. I have so many great memories of summer road trips with my mom—the ones that would always end here, visiting Uncle Burt and Aunt Bea in Hallmark Beach.

That was before she met Kevin, of course. Before she found a new travel companion.

But I'm happy for my mom. Seriously.

And I'm really hoping that Winona is having just as amazing of an experience as I did once upon a time.

"I'm good. How's the trip? Are you guys having a good time?"

I place my feet on the ground and push my toes back and forth to get a slow rock going while Winona exclaims and spends ten minutes telling me about all the sites they've seen and about their upcoming flight to London to start the UK leg of their trip. "Jessica is having a blast too. She's taking notes on where she might like to study abroad for a semester during college."

"That's amazing." There's nothing quite like the possibilities of traveling with someone you love. Mama and I might not have gone to Europe—mostly just national parks and other places her beat-up Civic could take us—but it was the spirit of adventure, the unknown discoveries before us, that were the best part.

That, and just being together.

I miss that. Miss *her*. Miss who I was back then.

My chest squeezes.

Winona laughs, a carefree lilt on the air. "So, how's the old girl holding up?"

She's talking about the Robin, I know. I run my finger along the chain holding up the swing. How will my boss feel about the state of affairs? I certainly don't want her to worry. "She's good. We're all good."

"You don't sound good." Winona pauses. "What's up?"

"No, no, everything's fine. We've just hit a little snag. Numbers are down a bit, but the summer rush hasn't started yet."

"It's June third, so no, it's not in full swing, but usually things pick up by mid-May." I can practically hear the frown in her voice. "Down by how much?"

"Um, about twenty-five percent?" Give or take. Mostly take. "But there's a new business in town. A food truck. It's stealing some of our business, but I have a plan to take it back."

"Wait, back up, please. What food truck? Who's operating it? And where is it located?"

I can practically hear Winona's mind whirling from here. "The Urban Melt. They sell gourmet grilled cheese. It's operated by Blake Moffitt." I avoid the topic of where it's located because Winona would probably come up out of her seat if she knew it's practically on her front lawn. I rush on. "But don't worry. I've got it handled."

"Twenty-five percent doesn't sound handled, Lucy." She's not mad, but she *is* firm.

I wince. "I know, but it's a new curveball. We've got to be flexible, right? So what I'm thinking is that we offer BOGO meals—you know, buy one, get one free."

"Yes, I know what BOGO means." Winona sighs, and I

hate that I've taken away her happy spirit. Maybe I shouldn't have said anything. "But I don't know. I've always firmly believed that the right customers would find us and stick with us. That we build loyalty one customer experience at a time."

A breeze picks up, rustling the branches of the only tree in the Moffitts' backyard—a stately Monterey pine.

"I think that's still true, but now there's the competition to consider." I chew on my thumbnail. "And I don't know if you remember Blake, but he's a really good businessman."

"Yes, but he doesn't know Hallmark Beach like we do. People like that forget what small towns are like. They run roughshod over everyone and don't develop any sort of loyalty."

"I think that was true at the beginning, but he's learning. Adapting." I can't keep the frown off my face. Thank goodness this isn't a video call. Taking a deep breath, I push away all of the doubt and fear creeping in. If I don't acknowledge them, they will go away. Better yet, they don't exist. Yes. "Winona, let me try this, okay? If it doesn't work, I'll stop."

"Make it temporary. Scarcity and a firm deadline are essential for creating a sense of urgency."

Good point. I make a mental note. "Yes. Of course. Oh, and I've also got Tiny creating a new dish every week. Something special and unique." He's been giving me samples, and I critique them. It's the only thing about cooking that I'm any good at—figuring out that a dish isn't quite right and giving suggestions for improvement. Not that I could fix it myself, unless I wanted something burnt to a crisp. I clear my throat. "That seems to be bringing some people back."

"That's good. But Lucy..." There's a long pause, and it's as pregnant as a woman in her ninth month carrying twins. "Do I need to come home early?"

"What? No!" Kicking the blanket to the ground, I push myself to my feet. My heart is pounding. I shut my eyes against the emotions coursing through my body. "Please. Just trust me, Winona. I can do this. I will make the Robin a success for you. You can count on me."

Winona sighs, and I can hear the tired in it. "All right. Keep me posted, though."

"Will do."

And with that, we hang up. I plop back onto the swing and put my head in my hands. My eyes burn with unshed tears, but I can't give into their pushiness.

Not even if I'm alone.

"Hey," a deep voice says from the doorway.

Blake.

My head bolts upright and I push my hands underneath my eyes, just in case a rogue tear has found its way out. Thankfully, my fingertips come away dry.

So much for being alone.

"What are you doing here?" And how much of that conversation did he hear? Knowing my luck, it was everything. Does my competition know my plan?

If so, this is war.

But he doesn't look ready to do battle. In fact, he's more casual than I ever remember seeing him in his flannel pajama pants and a white T-shirt. His hair is adorably rumpled, as if he's been running his hands through it. And there's something almost unsure in his eyes, in the way he sticks his hands into his pockets and slumps against the doorway.

"I live here."

I stand so we're on equal footing. "*Live* is a relative term." Because he's only here temporarily. Or so I assume. But after that conversation with Winona, I definitely do *not* feel like having a discussion with Blake about how long he's back in Hallmark Beach. Not sure I can handle the answer if it's going to be longer than, oh, say *another minute.*

I should just go to bed. Should just ignore his presence. Instead, I cross my arms over my chest and jut my chin. Because sure, he may be "living here" for the time being, but he has absolutely *no reason* to be out on the porch talking to me right now. Not unless he was spying on me. "I meant what are you doing out here?"

He studies me for a moment, then shrugs. "I got home a little while ago and came into the kitchen to make some popcorn."

From inside, the microwave beeps once, twice, three times. Right on cue.

He doesn't say anything more than that. Argh. Irritating man.

"Still doesn't explain why you're out here, eavesdropping on a private conversation," I say, fishing to see if he really did hear anything.

His silence is all the confirmation I need. Which means he heard everything. At least on my side.

"Fantastic."

"I just wanted to make sure you were okay."

Okay, those are not the words I expected from my greatest nemesis. They are also not words I can handle. Especially because in his eyes, I see something foreign. At least, foreign to this version of Blake Moffitt.

The Blake of my teen years had this kindness in spades.

Nope. Noooooope. Can't do it. *Can't think about that, Lucy.* "I'm fine." I practically spit the words. "And even if I wasn't, it's no concern of yours."

I've gotta get out of here, so I make a move to breeze past him.

But he stops me with a gentle snag at my elbow. "Hey."

I freeze. Look down at the place where the simple touch of his fingers is burning a hole through the fabric of my sleeve. Is it my imagination, or does his thumb move ever so slightly in what might be interpreted as a comforting stroke?

I glance back up at him, a question in my eyes. "What?" I say this with as much vehemence as I can muster, which isn't much.

For a moment, we just stare. And then—so quick that I'm not sure it actually happened—his gaze flits down to my lips. Back to my eyes.

Now it's his turn to clear his throat. Blake drops his hand. "Just...don't do that."

I move fully into the house. "Don't do what?"

"Pretend like everything's okay when it's not." He joins me inside and shuts the door firmly behind him.

Something deep inside me twists. "Everything *is* okay." And frankly, the fact he thinks he has the right to give me any sort of advice or directive is just so...typical.

"Lucy." He shakes his head at me. "You don't always have to pretend to be upbeat and happy."

The words trigger a memory, and my veins flood with heat. "I'm sorry if you find it *annoying*."

His forehead scrunches. Clearly he doesn't know what I'm referring to. Then again, I don't think he ever knew I overheard his little talk with his dad that summer night before he left for college.

My seventeenth birthday.

Marilee and I had spent the morning celebrating with my family and were ending the day with a going away cookout for Blake. A bunch of his high school buddies were out back, tossing footballs and hanging out, and Blake's parents and a few of their friends sat out by the firepit wiling away the hours, everyone chatting and laughing and eating an assortment of food cooked up by Mrs. Moffitt.

I'd gone inside for a refill on my lemonade...and found Blake standing at the counter alone, sipping from a red cup and staring at the living room. His brow was furrowed, and he looked a little lost.

To be honest, I felt a little lost too. We'd spent all summer together, though not much of it alone. I'd told him I'd miss him, and he promised to call me and Marilee when he could. To visit. But nothing more than that.

This might be my last chance to find out if he felt about me the way I did about him.

Squaring my shoulders, I sauntered toward him with a bright smile on my face. "Hey."

The clouds left his eyes and Blake straightened. His frown melted into a smile. "Hey, yourself, Birthday Girl."

"Hope I'm not interrupting your thoughts too much." The huge white jug of lemonade sat on the counter on the other side of him, so I squeezed past and pushed the dispenser button to fill my cup.

"Nothing worth interrupting."

"You sure?" I lifted the cup to my mouth and took a sip, soothing the dryness that was always there when I was in Blake's presence. "You looked sad. Or something."

"Good thing your sunshine is here to fix that."

I felt my cheeks warm under his praise. "What's wrong?" Maybe I shouldn't go there, maybe I didn't have a right to ask— but if I could offer him anything, it was a listening ear.

"I'm okay." He placed his cup on the counter behind him and sighed, running a hand through his hair. His T-shirt sleeve pulled against his bicep, and heat filtered through me at the sight.

But it wasn't just that he was the most attractive guy I knew.

He was easy to talk to. Kind. He listened when I talked. I couldn't help but want him.

But did he want me back?

Turning, I settled against the counter beside Blake, letting my shoulder press into his. "Doesn't seem like you're okay."

"It's just...I don't know. Tomorrow's a big day, you know?"

"Yeah." A terrible one too. But I didn't say that. "Aren't you excited?"

"Sure. But I also..." He paused, and I looked up at him. He was staring down at me, what looked like conflict roiling in his gaze.

My palms itched, and I realized just how close we were standing. Without thinking, I turned my body slightly toward his. Maroon 5's "Sugar" played in the backyard, but it was barely audible above the whoosh of blood pounding in my ears. "You also...what?" I managed.

His eyes bit into mine, like lasers with the ability to decimate. But there was something soft there, something I'd never seen when he looked at anyone else.

Was I imagining it? Was all of this just my high school delusions? A fantasy played out?

"I..." Blake swallowed, and he leaned toward me. Closer, closer, till his nose hovered above mine. "I'm going to miss this town."

Miss the town...or me? "This town is going to miss you too."

His lips quirked into a smile, and my whole body lit under it. I felt the barest whisper of his hand against my hip, the touch of his nose against mine, skimming down, down, and I closed my eyes, waiting for the best birthday present I could ever receive.

"What's going on here?" A voice interrupted my dream—making it a nightmare instead.

My eyes opened and landed on Mr. Moffitt standing in the doorway, an empty platter in his hand.

Clearing his throat, Blake stepped away from me quickly. "Lucy was just getting a refill, and we were about to head back out."

"Yep." I held my cup aloft. "Got it! So, um, guess we can go now." My voice sounded false and tinny, and I tried not to cringe at it.

"Hmm." Mr. Moffitt's gray eyebrows lifted. He looked as serious as ever in his khaki pants and red polo. "Son, help me reload this platter with more burgers from the fridge. Your mother wants to throw more on the grill."

"Okay." Something in Blake's voice shifted down. Being around his dad seemed to have that effect. "See you out there, Lucy."

Right. I was apparently dismissed. Or maybe saved. Whatever I was, I was sure my face was as red as the sliced tomatoes on the buffet line outside, and I needed to cool down before I faced the crowd. "I'll be right out. Gotta hit the restroom first."

I hauled booty down the dark hallway.

"I cannot believe you, Blake. What were you thinking, messing around with that girl?"

The way he said "that girl" made me halt in my tracks, turn, and flatten myself against the wall. Mr. Moffitt had never been overly warm toward me, but he'd never given me the impression he didn't like me.

"I wasn't messing around with her." The fridge snicked open, and I heard Blake rustling around inside.

"That's not what it looked like from here. Looked to me like you were about to kiss her."

Okay, maybe I shouldn't be listening in. But I couldn't help but want to hear what Blake would say...

"Why would I kiss her? I'm leaving for college tomorrow."

Ouch. Okay, okay, maybe he had a point. He'd be in Phoenix come tomorrow evening, and I'd be here for another two years at least. The whole thing was probably a bad idea.

But had I really imagined it—or was he just trying to throw his dad off the scent?

"Good." Mr. Moffitt paused. "The last thing you want to do is fall for a townie."

I couldn't help but huff. A townie? Seriously? Sure, I loved Hallmark Beach, but I was so much more than that.

Hopefully Blake saw me as more than that. He'd certainly seemed to...

I held my breath while I waited for his reply. Inched forward a bit so I could see his face. Thankfully, neither of them seemed to notice me.

"Don't worry, Dad." Blake's jaw ticked as he slid a platter of burgers across the counter toward Mr. Moffit. "I was just trying to be nice to Lucy. She's a sweet kid."

Kid? The word knifed my heart.

"That girl follows you around like an annoying little puppy, Blake. Don't tell me you haven't noticed."

What? Sweet macaroni.

Blake laughed, tight and low. "Yeah, but what else could I do? I didn't want to be mean to her."

No.

My chest tight, I couldn't breathe.

His dad looked him up and down with that exacting way he had. Finally, he nodded. "Good. Because a girl like that isn't a good fit for the kind of future you've got ahead of you."

"Don't I know it," Blake murmured—soft enough that his father didn't seem to hear, but loud enough to break my little teenage heart.

Because I'd been wrong. Blake hadn't been flirting with me all year. He hadn't almost kissed me. He thought I was an annoying child. A pest. Pathetic.

And not good enough for a guy like him.

I blink away the memory, and realize my fists are clenched.

It was more than a decade ago, and yet, here I stand, in the same kitchen where they once stood. Why am I letting those words affect me? They don't.

And clearly Blake doesn't remember them anyway.

"What?" he finally says.

Ugh, whatever. This isn't worth hashing out. "Nothing. I'm going to bed. Enjoy your popcorn." I pivot toward the counter where my computer sits, flip the lid closed, pick it up, and take a step toward the hallway.

"You could have some if you wanted. Popcorn, I mean."

I halt. Turn on my heel. Raise an eyebrow. "I told you. I'll never eat something you make ever again."

"Technically, the popcorn company made it." He runs a hand through his hair, and I can't help but follow the motion, as if my gaze and his fingers are magnets. The way his muscles still pop with the casual movement is completely unfair. "I just unwrapped the plastic and put the bag into the microwave." Then he offers me a small smile.

It's a jolt to my heart.

What's going on with him? Why is he being so...pleasant? "I'm good, thanks."

"Suit yourself." He pulls the bag from the microwave, dumps the contents into a large bowl, and shrugs. My treacherous nose can't help but notice how buttery the popcorn smells. And my growling stomach can't help but reveal the fact that I forgot to eat dinner.

Without a word, Blake pushes the bowl across the counter toward me, then opens a cabinet, pulls down another bag of popcorn, and unwraps it, the cellophane crinkling as he tosses it into the garbage. Sticking the bag into the microwave, he hits the Popcorn button.

Me, on the other hand? I stand here like a lunatic, just watching him in silence. I blame the tired. It's all the tired's fault. But sweet macaroni, he looks downright deliciously domestic.

And that smile earlier...it almost seemed like a white flag of sorts. Like he was choosing to lay aside the fact I've been doing my level best to tank his business. Like I haven't spent the last two weeks firing all sorts of potshots his way.

Analyzing his behavior is nearly as exhausting as being mad at him—especially since anger is an emotion I almost never give free reign.

I'm too tired to analyze anymore. I just want answers. "Why are you being nice to me?" I hug my laptop to my chest. My hand wants to reach for the popcorn he sent my way, but that feels like surrender. To what, I'm not sure.

"Well." He takes a step toward me, then another. They're slow steps, as if he's afraid of spooking me. "I've been meaning to talk to you. And this seems as good a time as any."

"Okay." I glance down at the popcorn. Can practically taste the salt on my tongue. Nope. My gaze pulls back to his face. Not sure that's better. "Talk."

"Marilee's upset we don't get along." Sighing, he runs a hand down his jaw. "So I was wondering if we could try for a truce. For her sake."

Oy. The last thing I want to do is hurt my friend. Still. A truce? Isn't that a bit...extreme? "I think ignoring each other and occupying the house at different times has worked just fine." Yep. Totally fine.

"Yeah, sure. That *definitely* sounds doable for the two more months I'm going to be here." He snorts.

"Two months?" I can't help the way my voice squeaks. It's finally confirmed—he *will* be here a long while. Not only will that be very bad for the Robin, but also for me. I'm honestly not sure I can do this for two more months. Eight weeks. Thirteen hundred and something hours. I'm drained just thinking about it. But I can't let him know that. "Oh, is that all?" Hopefully he's fooled by my nonchalance.

He doesn't react to my tone, just shrugs and says, "Yep. Have to be back in L.A. to work on a new restaurant opening at the beginning of August." The microwave beeps again, and he fishes the new bag of popcorn from inside. "And I think the next few months would go a lot smoother if we put aside our differences. Not just because it's exhausting." Blake eyes me, as if he can hear my thoughts. *Disturbing*. "But also because of Mare."

He shakes the popcorn into a new bowl. "She told me on Friday that her biggest wish is for us to be friends again."

I lift an eyebrow. "Don't think that's ever going to happen in this lifetime." Not only because I despise him, but because I don't think I could ever *just* be friends with Blake Moffitt.

"Didn't figure so. But how about housemates who at least tolerate each other?" He throws the popcorn bag away. "Do you think you could manage that much?" There's a sort of eagerness in his gaze, almost like he's asking me this for himself, not for his sister.

Sweet macaroni. How's a girl to stay upset—or hold onto her dignity—with a guy looking at her like that?

And not just any guy.

The guy she used to love.

Ugh. "Fine." I give him a solid glare though, just for good measure. "But this doesn't mean I forgive you for stealing my customers." Or for anything else, for that matter.

One corner of his lips turns up. It's only slight, but as Uncle Burt would say, *good golly*. Who knew only half a smile would make a man infinitely more handsome? What would I do if he ever went full watt on me? "Noted."

"Good."

"Great."

"Fabulous."

"We gonna do this all night?" Blake points at the first bowl of popcorn. "Or are you gonna eat something?"

"No and no." Then my stomach has the audacity to growl again.

"I don't think your stomach agrees." Blake waggles his eyebrows, taking a handful of popcorn and stuffing it into his mouth. He groans. "Soooo good."

And I actually have to bite my lip to keep from smiling.

What am I doing? One little truce and I'm practically flinging myself back into the Blake Danger Zone.

Nope. Not gonna happen. I take a step away. "My stomach doesn't know what it's talking about. So. I guess I'll go to bed then."

Because my room is literally the only place I can go to escape these pesky feelings that are just dying to reawaken. All because of one little word: *truce*.

And *that's* a good reminder too—that he's only saying this, being nice, because his sister asked him to. He probably doesn't find the idea any more palatable than I do.

He cocks his head. Seems to consider something. "We could flip on *The Great British Bake Off* if you want."

I suck in a breath. Does he remember that we used to watch that together? Him, me, and Marilee? Sometimes their mom would join us too.

I have so many fun memories of that. And Blake's asking me to go back there.

My mouth opens. Closes. Because I want to say yes. But instead, I force the next words out of my mouth. They shouldn't be this hard, but it feels like walking through a patch of drying concrete. "I don't think that's a good idea."

"Right."

Before he can say more, I turn to go, but stop. Because while I don't want to go back to where we once were—my heart can't take that—I don't want him to think the truce means nothing. That I won't try.

So I take the dang bowl of popcorn and hightail it outta there.

"Night, Sunshine." His words filter down the hallway after me. This time, I hear his smile in the nickname, and the warmth of it melts my insides.

If I knew I'd only have to handle the heat for another week or so, I'd be fine. But two more months of this torture?

Sweet macaroni. I'm in trouble.

BLAKE

There's just something about closing up the truck for the night —something I never felt at the restaurant.

It's just me and the grill as I scrub it clean. I can whistle and not disturb anyone. Massage the ache in my lower back from standing and bending all day long. And there's this soul-deep satisfaction in having done an honest day's work that didn't involve crunching numbers and dealing with diva chefs and stressing over whether that was a food critic frowning over his mushroom risotto in the corner.

Mom used to say that food nourishes more than the stomach, and—even though it's just an ordinary Monday and my food isn't anything Michelin-star-worthy—I hope I've done that for somebody today.

I finish up with the grill and check my watch. Darn. Not quite enough time to run home and shower before my meeting in The Green Robin kitchen with Lucy and Thomas. I've been double and triple checking my watch all day. Once again, I haven't been able to stop thinking about Lucy.

It's become a terrible habit.

But ever since our interaction at home two nights ago, I

keep picturing the way she looked, all lit up by the glow of the stars. She was dressed casual like always—a sweatshirt, jeans, and sneakers, her hair pulled back with a tie—but her expression was different. It wasn't filled with rage or disdain.

No. This expression was guarded. And yet, almost wistful at times.

I can't even put my finger on it, but it made me sad. Made me wonder if things would have been different between us if I'd never left. What would have happened if I'd stayed after my parents' funeral. If I'd listened to her.

If I hadn't listened to my dad years before that.

What would happen if I chose to stay now.

But I can't even contemplate that. Dale is counting on me to come home in August to work on opening the second restaurant. *My* restaurant. And if Dad was here, he'd be counting on me to leave too. To not get stuck in a small life. A normal life.

He always wanted big things for me, and big things are finally happening.

Of course, I need to get my creative mojo back first. Because despite many attempts, I'm still no closer to a new recipe. So far, nothing I try has turned out right. It's like my brain has forgotten how to be creative, if it ever was. Maybe tonight's meeting will help with that. We're planning to discuss and try out a few recipes for the festival, and being around other food people can sometimes motivate and inspire.

I'm just hoping my truce with Lucy holds up. Since our little chat on Saturday night, I've only caught glimpses of her coming and going into the restaurant from my food truck window, so haven't had a chance to test out our tenuous agreement.

There's a knock on my back door and I frown. My window's locked and the sign is flipped to Closed, so it should be clear the truck is shut down for the night. I trudge toward the door and swing it open. Jordan's standing there, a pizza box in his hand. "Hey." He holds it up. "Have you eaten?"

Wow, that was nice of him. Or was it? I smirk. "Did my sister send you?" She said something the other day about me not having any friends in town. I told her I was busy working, and that she was the only friend I needed.

"Guilty." Jordan has the good sense to look chagrined. "To be fair, I had to work late, and Ryder's hanging out overnight with his grandparents, so I didn't have anything else going on."

I hop down from the truck and land in the grass. "Thanks for the offer, man, but I'll need to take a rain check. I've got a festival subcommittee meeting in a few."

"Ah. No problem. I'll just see if Marilee wants to hang out." His eyes light up at the mention of my sister. Dude is so far gone. I wonder if my sister knows. He nods toward the truck. "How are things going since our last chat?"

Guess that was only four days ago. Feels like a lifetime. "Better, I think. Your suggestion to help out on the committee is much appreciated. Seems to have gotten people warmed back up to me, so that's good. The last few days of business have picked up. And I've had a lot of customers use the fifty percent-off coupons I handed out. All in all, it's on an upward trajectory."

Which is more than I can say for The Green Robin. I really didn't mean to overhear Lucy's conversation on Saturday night, and I hate that my presence has cut her profits by such a drastic amount. But I know it won't last forever. My truck will only be here for a few months, and then any customers I've "stolen" will go right back to the Robin.

"That's great, man. Super stoked for you. Told you things would work out."

"Yeah, it's been good." I check my watch again. Time to go. "For real, I want that rain check."

"You got it, man." We fist bump before Jordan tugs on the brim of his baseball cap and walks away with his pizza.

Meanwhile, I lock up and head over to the Robin, which is dark inside. Lucy said she'd prop open the side door to the kitchen, so I walk around the side and into the white space where she and Thomas are standing side by side at the large white island, their heads bent over something.

They look entirely too cozy.

I have no right, but something in me just protests.

I clear my throat. Thomas jumps and turns, but Lucy just straightens without facing me. Wonder if she's as annoyed at Thomas's attention as I am. Or if she's just taking her time in greeting me because Marilee's call for a truce is hard for her.

Thomas holds up his hand for a high five. His hair looks shorter than it did the last time I saw him, and he's got it gelled within an inch of its life. "Welcome to Team Foodie."

I slap his palm—probably harder than necessary—and smile just a little when he shakes out his hand like it hurts. "I like the sound of that." Then I saunter to the counter and stand beside Lucy, lowering my voice for her ears only. "Evening, Sunshine."

She peeks at me, then glances down at a notebook with our food ideas scrawled in it. "Flake."

Her tone is monotone, devoid of any emotion. What's going on with her tonight? Another bad few days at the restaurant? But I thought her BOGO coupon idea had merit. Maybe she hasn't started handing them out yet.

Does it matter what's going on with her? I chide myself.

No, it doesn't. We aren't here to be friends. We are here to figure out an awesome dessert to serve the whole town at the festival picnic.

Lucy straightens and turns, leaning back against the counter beside me. Not too close, but the fact she isn't insisting on being fully across the room from me is progress. "Now that we're all here, we can continue the discussion we began on Thursday." She taps the notebook with the end of her pen. "After our last meeting, I asked Chloe if the food budget could be revised at all to give us more flexibility and scale up the amount of offerings we serve, but it seems the funds were a bit on the paltry side this year. So, our only choices are to either do a potluck-style barbecue for the whole town—something Chloe isn't super keen on because we usually get a lot of tourists in, and they won't be contributing—or we serve up something like burgers we can easily mass produce."

One of the fluorescent lights flickers over the large granite island.

Thomas scratches his neck, just above the collar of his lime-green Hawaiian shirt. "I'm all for the latter option."

"Same." I cock my head before trying once again for the easiest option of them all. "But are we sure that we can't cater the food ourselves with our various businesses? Seems it would be a good opportunity to help out the Hallmark Beach economy. And we could still provide the dessert for free."

"I've already told you," Lucy says. "Tiny is going to be out of town that week, and the Robin's backup cook wouldn't be able to handle it." Then she purses her lips in my direction. "And don't bother suggesting again that your truck bear all the load either. We will all be needed to pitch in on the burgers."

"Wasn't going to say a thing." Mostly because of the truce. But also because, while I do think the festival would be an amazing chance to gain some valuable feedback—events with large and varied crowds like that always are—I don't want to emphasize the "feud" between my food truck and the Robin now that I know how much she's struggling there.

She squints at me. "You weren't?"

I want to laugh at how suspicious she looks, as if I've told a joke and she's waiting for the punchline. Or maybe wondering if there *is* a punchline in the first place. I nudge her sneaker-clad foot with the tip of my loafer. "No, Sunshine, I wasn't."

Lucy stiffens and licks her lips like she's nervous. But why would she be? Maybe all of her energy is being funneled into not biting my head off, and I'm poking the bear. I pull my foot back to myself and determine to behave.

But I have to admit—I like touching her, even if it's fabric on fabric. What would it be like to *really* touch her? Would that skin be as silky as it looks? Would her hair, which is back in its usual ponytail, be thick as spun gold, or would it fall easily between my fingers as I—

Yikes. These thoughts are dangerous. And can't lead anywhere.

"Blake? What do you think?" Thomas spears me with a look and rubs his hands together.

Shoot. "About what?"

"A bake-off." Thomas laughs and walks over, slapping me on the shoulder. Kind of hard. Maybe he's fighting back. Though if he wants Lucy, he can have her. Seriously. They're two peas in a pod, at least as far as their love of Hallmark Beach goes. Dude's on the town council and he owns a business...one that's not going to pick up and drive away.

So even if I did want Lucy for real—which I don't—then Thomas would still be the better guy for her.

Focus, man. "A bake-off? For what?"

Lucy's squinting at me again. "To figure out what dessert we want to serve." She pauses, eyebrows lifted. "Haven't you been listening?"

She's speaking, and I'm mesmerized—not by the words coming out of her mouth, but by her mouth itself.

That saucy little mouth that's tipped up at the corner, the one no doubt trying hard not to launch into a diatribe about how annoying she finds my lack of attention. That mouth that, she promised, will never again taste *my* food.

Which gives me a really wicked idea. And I know I shouldn't test the boundaries of our truce like this, but something inside prods me along. "A bake-off sounds like a great idea."

"It does?" She's surprised. Maybe she thought I'd say no.

"Yep. Thomas and I will both bake a dessert, and you will be the judge. Winner gets their dessert featured at the festival." I flash her a grin.

Her returning smile is weak, and her eyes flick to Thomas, who is nodding along with my suggestion. "Oh, but I thought I'd try to come up with something too." Her voice is weak.

"But then how will we decide which one is best? No, we need a judge, and you're the perfect candidate."

Lucy's eyes narrow at me, but I blink back innocently at her. She turns her body slightly toward mine and leans in, lowering her voice. "I know what you're doing."

"And what's that, Sunshine?"

"Stop calling me that." She grits her teeth.

"Why would I do that, when it makes you smile so pretty?" I close the gap between us and take a sharp inhale of her orange-vanilla scent. Her nearness is so heady that my vision blurs around the edges, and I have the sudden urge to pull her into my arms.

Yikes.

I should step away. I really should. But then she might become aware of how she affects me.

How she's always affected me.

"I think Lucy as judge makes total sense." Thomas is either oblivious to...whatever *this* is, or is pretending to be as he joins us at the counter and leans in. "What are we whispering about?"

Lucy blinks and jumps away from both of us, dropping her notebook in the process. "Nothing." She squats to retrieve the notebook, then rises again. "Fine. I'll be the judge." Her eyes speak resignation, and my fist wants to double pump the air.

But I haven't won yet. Now I need to really wow her.

Make something she can't help but declare the winner.

Do I care about having my dessert featured at the festival? No. It won't contribute to my overall goal for being here in town, though it might make more people aware of my business if my name is splashed everywhere. "Winner gets their name and business on a big banner at the table where the dessert is offered."

"I'm all about that," Thomas says. He stands at the large industrial refrigerator, his eyes skimming the contents inside. Most likely he's taking stock of what's available to him, brainstorming ideas.

As for me, I've got...nothing.

Which isn't all that unusual, at least lately. I have literally no idea what to make Lucy. Searching my memories for our high school conversations, I try to recall whether there's any sort of dessert that she loves more than others, something that will secure me a win. I remember she likes baklava, but that's time consuming. And besides, it's not a *wow* dish.

And I need a wow dish.

"All right, I'm starting the clock now." She punches something on her phone, and Thomas gets to work pulling things from the fridge and pantry, working with a frenzy I wish I had.

Instead, I stand there and stare at the counter.

"Giving up already?"

I glance up, surprised at the tease in her tone, at the taunting smile in her eyes. Opening my mouth to reply, I stop as her phone vibrates on the island beside her.

"That's not the timer already, is it?" I say, knowing full well it isn't.

"Of course not." She rolls her eyes as she picks up her phone—and her jaw drops. "Sweet macaroni."

I can't help but smile. She's so dang adorable. Adorable and sexy too, leaning one hip against the counter, her hair hanging forward over one shoulder, her long lashes splayed downward as she reads something on her phone.

Then she frowns.

"Everything okay?" I know it's not my business, but if someone's hurt her...

"What?" She glances up, something vulnerable in her eyes. "Oh, yeah. It's just my mom." Lucy blinks. "I haven't talked to her in over a month. Tried calling her on Mother's Day but didn't hear back. I assumed she was traveling again, and she'd call me when she could."

I've always felt bad for Lucy, how her mom and stepdad just dumped her here her sophomore year of high school because they wanted to go sailing around the world and didn't want a teenager tagging along. Oh sure, they said it was because it wouldn't be good for her schooling, but they could have done things differently.

Sounds like not much has changed.

I also catch no hint of anger in Lucy's voice. Just a mixture of surprise, pleasure, and maybe a hint of sadness too. Does she truly not feel any animosity, or is she just really good at bottling it up?

Thomas is knocking things together and cracking eggs behind me. Shoot. I need to get my head into this competition, though I still have no sense of what I want to bake.

Lucy's attention is back on her phone, and now she's biting her lip, her thumb hovering above the screen as if she can't decide whether to respond. Or maybe what to say. "Sweet macaroni," she breathes out again.

And suddenly, I have it. I know what to make.

The next hour is a whirlwind as I fling ingredients together. My movements are quick but not frenzied. I know exactly what I'm doing. Somehow, I fall into a trance, ignoring everything else but this certainty building inside my chest. This rightness in what I'm making.

Honestly, I haven't felt this way in...years.

I boil the pasta. Combine flour and butter in a small dish and create a roux. Add the whole milk, the vanilla bean, the salt. Then comes the mixing of the cream cheese, the sugar, the eggs. A batter is formed and added to the pasta, along with blueberries. I top the custard with sugared panko breadcrumbs and set the creation in the oven.

And when I pull it from inside—slightly puffed and golden brown—I know that my mojo is back. And sure, it's not a grilled cheese recipe, but it's something new. Creative.

Exciting.

I turn triumphantly to Lucy and Thomas, who are chatting next to the cooling tin of Thomas's espresso brownies, and set my dessert on a trivet beside them.

Lucy eyes my contribution. "What is it?"

And I don't back down from her gaze when I say, "Dessert pasta." I pause. "Or, as some would call it, sweet macaroni."

She blanches and blinks, rearing back.

Thomas leans closer to examine my creation. "Impressive."

I step back, crossing my arms over my chest. "Thanks, man. Yours too." His brownies *do* look and smell good, and I'm not surprised he made them coffee-flavored, seeing as how he owns the coffee shop. But I know I've got this in the bag. Just like when I hit on a winning grilled cheese recipe, I'm confident in this.

I redirect my confidence toward Lucy, who is still staring at my dessert as if it's diseased. My confidence slips a bit. Maybe this was a dumb move.

Her lips twist, and her eyes finally find mine. They're appraising, and there's a question in them. She's confused, and I get it. Up until a few days ago, we were at each other's throats, and here I go making a dessert inspired by her token phrase that's as cute as she is.

But like Marilee said...sometimes inspiration comes in the most unlikely of places.

It's not like I *asked* to be inspired by Lucy. Not like I wanted to be. I just...was. It doesn't have to be a big deal.

"All right." Thomas rubs his hands together and then starts to slice into his brownies with a knife. "Moment of truth." He slips a piece out onto a thick napkin, crumbles of chocolate falling onto the counter. Then he lifts it toward Lucy's mouth.

Is he going to try to *feed* it to her?

I literally have to hold back a growl.

Thankfully, he switches directions and hands it to her, so I don't have to go Hulk Hogan on him—not because I'm feeling anything in particular for Lucy. No. I'm just...grateful to her and the inspiration she provided. And she's my sister's best friend, which means she falls under my protection.

Yeah, keep telling yourself that, Blake.

She takes an enthusiastic Lucy-sized bite of the brownie— tearing into it like she tears into life—and *mmm*s. "That's so good, Thomas!"

You'd swear the guy had just been told he'd found the cure to cancer. His smile is bright enough to light the Vegas Strip for days. "I'm glad you like it, Luce."

Oh, come on.

I swipe a hand across my mouth to keep from saying something not so nice.

When Lucy is done chewing, she turns her eyes to me and flashes me a grin that looks super forced. "Your turn." The words ring falsely bright in the air, vibrating like a bell.

And I don't know what possesses me to do it. I honestly don't.

But I step around Thomas so I'm standing right in front of Lucy, grab a fork from the counter, sink it into the soft, puffed mass of noodles and custard, and hold the bite up to her mouth, which rounds into an O. Steam wafts from the dessert, twining upward between us.

I blow on the food to cool it down.

Her eyes widen.

One of my hands is just below the fork in case a bite drops, and the other guides the food to her waiting lips. And I can't even begin to describe the primal satisfaction that wends through me when she takes the bite of something *I made* between those lips, closes her eyes, and groans. Not a polite *mmm*. This is a sound of pure pleasure, a sound that holds nothing back. A sound I could sink into. One that leaves heat swirling in my stomach.

"Well?" I both hate and love how low and husky my voice has gone and how my body involuntarily hovers closer to Lucy. She's got just a tiny bit of custard on the corner of her mouth, and it's all I can do not to lean in and remove it with my own. "What do you think?"

As if I need to be told she loved it. Her response said it all.

Her eyes flutter open, and she jolts like she's just stuck her finger in the electrical outlet. Her gaze flicks upward, then past me to where Thomas stands. "Um."

I take a step back to give her space because *what am I even doing?* I shouldn't be flirting with Lucy like this. First of all, the woman hates me. She might like my food, and she might be tolerating my existence for Marilee's sake, but if the way she's acted recently is any indication, she can't stand me.

But even if she could, I can't promise her anything. I'm leaving again in two months. Just like when I left twelve years ago, there is no future here.

So before she can say anything, or declare my food the winner, I grab a pinch of Thomas's brownies and shove it into my mouth. Hmm. Not bad. Could use a bit more sugar, but pretty decent for a first attempt.

Then I take the same fork I used for Lucy—hopefully she doesn't notice—and take my own bite of the dessert macaroni. It's perfection, just like I thought it'd be.

And yet.

"Wow, dude." I turn and offer my fist for Thomas to bump. He's eyeing me curiously, his head cocked. "You are definitely the winner. Awesome job. Let's get these on the menu." Then I glance at my watch. "Oh, dang, look at the time. I need to get to bed. Early day tomorrow."

And I hustle out of there before I do something even more stupid than flirting with a woman who despises me.

Something like...kissing her.

LUCY

Who does Blake Moffitt think he is?

I slash toothpaste across my brush and re-cap the tube before whipping the brush into my mouth, determined to get every bit of his "sweet macaroni" out of my mouth.

If only Blake himself was as easy to scrub from my mind.

What was with him tonight? He was being so...sexy.

Ugh, not that he isn't always sexy. But this was more than a sexy existence. This was raw male power—perhaps even flirtation—and it was allllll directed *my* way.

It was all I could do not to tip my head upward and pull his face toward mine.

But then—then!—he backed off. Shook off whatever was between us. Declared Thomas the winner (he wasn't). And ran away.

Just like he did nearly twelve years ago.

Of course, back then I told myself I must have been mistaken. In all my teenage adoration of him, it was easy to put the blame squarely on my shoulders.

But now I'm an adult.

And adult Lucy saw what teenage Lucy couldn't—that man is into me.

Or at least, he felt *something*.

Doesn't mean adult Lucy knows what to do about it, though.

I wince as the bristles of the toothbrush swipe my gums with ferocity. Ouch. If I'm not careful, I'm going to bleed my mouth dry. Spitting into the sink, I wash my mouth out with water and clean the paste from the brush. Then I give myself a quick once-over in the mirror—since Blake moved in, I've started wearing pajama pants and baggy T-shirts to bed—and open the bathroom door into the hallway.

Where a shirtless Blake is standing.

His hand is extended like he's reaching for the doorknob. *Because of course he is.* "Sorry. Didn't know anyone was in there."

I should speak. I know I should. But my eyes are busy drinking him in.

Gaaaaah. He's so beautiful, with his golden skin on display, his muscles well-defined and just the right size. His clavicle sweeps down from one shoulder, across him, to the other. And the rest of him—his pectorals, his flat stomach, his gym shorts hanging low on his tapered waist—beckons my hands, which I fist at my sides to keep from reaching where they shouldn't.

"You okay there, Sunshine?"

"What?" My guilty eyes dart back up to his face, where his gaze is lit with a faint hint of amusement. Sweet macaroni, I've been staring like a lovesick fool. But I'm not. Lovesick, that is. I'm just a woman, appreciating the form of a man. I don't have to think more of it than that. He has no reason to be amused.

Maybe he's laughing at me. Maybe earlier, at the Robin, he just wanted to see how far he could take things before I broke.

Well, Lucy Reynolds doesn't break for anyone. Most especially him. And since I can't show him ire anymore—darn truce!—I'll just have to be overly nice.

I paste on a smile and dip into an exaggerated bow, directing my hands toward the bathroom. "All yours, roomie."

Then, with his chuckle low in my ears, I run toward my bedroom, a move that I'm realizing is becoming all too common where Blake Moffitt is concerned.

"Hey."

I squeal and throw a hand to my chest at the feminine voice that greets me as I enter my room. "You scared me!"

Marilee's sitting on my bed, her arms wrapped around the knees pulled into her chest. She's got on black sleep shorts and a tank top with Grinch faces all over it, despite the fact it's summertime. "Sorry. I came to deliver that"—she points to something on my side table—"but stayed because we haven't seen much of each other, and I don't have to work tomorrow, so I thought we could catch up a bit."

"Of course we can." I plop down beside her on the bed and give her a hug, then grab a postcard off the side table. A photo of some European countryside beckons.

My heart thumps. A text and a postcard from Mama all in one day? Not that the text said much. Just that she missed me— but was having the best time in Italy.

I set the postcard down again, determined to savor the message on the back later when I'm alone. Then I flick on my second fake smile in a matter of moments, this one directed at my bestie. "I've missed you. How are you? How's work? And cake making?"

Last I heard, she was taking on a few cake commissions here and there as part of her job at The Blackberry Muffin. Even though I can tell that's where her passion lies, she's hesitant to start her own business. I can't exactly blame her—she's still fighting every month to get out from under the debt Donny left her with four years ago.

Her face lights up as she tells me all about a Barbie cake she made for one of the young Painter girls' birthdays and a fiftieth anniversary cake for our town librarian Anita Draper (who is Alberta Jenkins's twin sister and quite her opposite in terms of kindness and tact go) and her retired doctor husband Donald.

While she talks, I pull a few bottles of nail polish from my side table drawer and toss her one that's Christmas-y red. I unscrew the bottle of a lime green color and begin to spread the polish onto my bare toenails. I'm not really a girly girl, but even us casual women like to have cute summer toes.

The strong smell of the polish permeates the air as Marilee finishes updating me on her life—including her last few "hang-outs" with Jordan and Ryder, whom she oh so clearly adores. Then she makes a face, sticking out her tongue. "I just monopolized that conversation, didn't I? I'm sorry. How have you been? How's the restaurant? Did you hand out the BOGO coupons yet?"

"Yep, delivered them around town yesterday. Now, we wait to see if it works." My insides twist.

"I'm sure it will. Blake's fliers worked well." She picks up the unopened red nail polish. "Speaking of Blake..."

Smooth, Mare. Smooth. My eyebrows lift her way. "Go ahead. Ask what you really want to."

"Hmm? I don't know what you're talking about." A droplet of red falls from her brush onto my comforter, and she sucks in a breath as she wipes the excess from the fabric with her pinky. A small red smear is left behind on the lavender. "Oh no. I'm sorry!"

"Don't be." I casually screw the lid back onto my polish and set the bottle aside, admiring my toes even though they're far from perfect. "A little mess adds character. Besides, that's the benefit of buying things secondhand for cheap."

"I guess." She frowns, and her glasses slip down her nose a bit as she resumes painting her nails. Then my best friend sighs, and she glances up at me again. "Fine. There *is* something I wanted to ask." A pause. "How are things between you and Blake?"

I glance through the open door toward the hallway, but the bathroom door remains shut. "You mean since our Marilee-inspired truce?"

She bites her bottom lip. Nods.

"Things are..."

Suddenly, the ceiling—with its old popcorn texture, its slight cracks in the paint, the old battered ceiling fan—is the most fascinating thing in the world. Because I can't be fully honest with Marilee. That would require giving voice to all the doubts and questions swirling in my heart and brain.

"I see." And there's such sadness in her voice. Her hand shakes a bit as she applies the polish.

"No, Mare. You don't." How can she, though? I've never told her how I felt about Blake. Never wanted her to think I was friends with her because I liked him. But maybe that's done a disservice to our relationship. I inhale a steep breath, gently take the polish brush from her fingers, and move on the bed so we're facing each other as I start to paint her toenails. I can't look at her when I say this. "You know I was crazy about him in high school, right? I never told you as much, but Elisse likes to mock me for it, so I assume it was fairly obvious."

"I always thought you might be. But then things changed when he left for college. You changed."

Me? It was him that changed. "What do you mean?"

"I don't know. You just seemed even more distant. And happier—but like, a fake happy."

The brush hovers over her nails. My best friend is even more perceptive than I've given her credit for. "Yeah. Maybe."

"What happened? I know about your fight after the funeral. Last week, Blake apologized for how he left, how he wasn't here. He admitted that you were right."

Did he now? "That's great." I lift my chin, wink at her. All bluster and tease. Because I don't want to show how much that news elates me. How warmth is flooding my heart. To know not just that he thinks I was right—I don't care about being right for being right's sake—but also that his relationship with his sister is important enough for him to make amends. That he recognizes what his leaving did to her.

"It *is* great." Marilee reaches toward my hand, snatching the polish brush back. "So you guys can be friends again. Not just tolerate each other for my sake. Right?"

I choke out a cough. "Yeah. Right."

"You sound so convincing." Marilee sighs and recaps the nail polish, her toes only half painted. Then she spears me with a look. "Time to come clean, Luce. What happened between the two of you in high school?"

"Nothing." I sputter. And sigh. "And that's the problem."

Now it's her turn for an eyebrow lift. "Care to explain?"

"Um, not really." But maybe it would be good to get it off my chest. To just...I don't know. Release it into the ether. Bottling up the emotions for so long hasn't really done much for me, has it? I've tried making lemonade out of those lemons, but clearly (based on my reaction to Blake tonight) my old crush is rearing its ugly head.

I just need to spit out what happened in the past so that someone else can reassure me that he never had feelings for me. Because that would be easier, honestly. If it all was truly in my head, then nothing is Blake's fault. Then it's not like he chose big-city life over me. If it all was truly in my head, then I wasn't part of the equation at all.

And that's better.

So I tell her everything. About what I considered flirtation—all of those little moments, interactions—sophomore year while I lived in Hallmark Beach. What I thought might have been an almost kiss on my seventeenth birthday, just before junior year. The conversation I overheard between Blake and his dad later that night.

And how I felt that whole year after he left for college, when I didn't hear a word from him.

How I wrestled with feeling abandoned. Feeling stupid. First, for falling for him. Second, for thinking he cared about me as more than his sister's friend.

When I'm finished, I get the courage to look at Marilee again, praying her next words are reassurance that I misunderstood everything. That I was just a foolish teen girl with her head in the clouds, seeing things that weren't there.

But that's not what I see in her eyes.

Instead, there's pity there. She tilts her head, and her messy bun lilts to the side. "I'm sorry, friend." She squeezes my knee. "I kind of want to murder my brother for how he played around with your heart. For what it's worth, I think he did care about you. But I also know how persuasive our dad could be when he had strong opinions about something."

My stupid heart sparks hope in my chest. Sweet macaroni. Nope. Nooooo. Cannot let that little ember turn into a flame.

I shrug. "It doesn't matter. I got over him a long time ago."

She shoots me a skeptical look.

I wave my hand in dismissal. "And now that I know the two of you are truly good, he and I will be good. Promise."

And because I'm not a liar, I'm going to have to make it so.

I'm going to have to do more than "make nice" with Blake.

I'm going to have to be friends with him again—and somehow, this time, not fall for my best friend's brother.

thirteen

BLAKE

I am officially an idiot.

And, once again, an eavesdropper. Curse the thin walls of my parents' home!

"Ugh," I say as I fling several boxes of graham crackers into my tiny cart at Al's Grocery.

"Blake? You with me?" Dale's voice barrels into me from the phone cradled between my cheek and shoulder as I navigate the small grocer at eight-thirty in the morning. For a moment, I forgot I was talking to him.

"Yeah, I'm here." Physically, at least. Mentally, my brain is still back at the house, in the hallway outside Marilee's room where I stood last night when I overheard Lucy telling my sister about the conversation she heard between me and Dad so many years ago.

I didn't mean to stop. I was on my way back to my room—after a purposefully cold shower, during which I tried to forget the previous events of the evening—when I heard Lucy say my name. Then, it was as if my whole body shut down. I slumped against the wall and listened while Lucy's gut-wrenchingly sad voice talked about how much teenage Blake had hurt her.

And just when I was about to storm inside, confess my sins, and apologize, she ended with, *"I got over him a long time ago."* Because of course she did. Yet here I was, being that jerk trying to stoke back to life the feelings she'd once had. And for what?

I won't do that to her. Not again. And I *will* find a time to apologize.

But not right now. Because right now, I'm busy plotting with Dale about our restaurant.

That, and buying the ingredients for a new grilled cheese recipe I want to try. Inspired, of course, by last night's escapades.

By Lucy.

I snag a few bags of mini marshmallows while Dale drones on about details I should find interesting. The location he's secured for our restaurant is at once upscale but not stuffy. It's modern but has some architectural elements that will lend a mid-century vibe to it as well. He's already signed the lease to begin July 15, once the current tenants move out, and he's put out feelers for sous chefs. "Unless you want to be fully in charge of selecting your staff?"

Above me, a fluorescent light flickers. I'm one of the only shoppers here this early, though I've seen a handful of older folks come through buying cans of soup and loaves of bread. I blink at the two bags of chocolate chips I'm holding, one with mini chips and one with regular-sized. Everything in me wants to hang up this phone and get to my truck. My fingers are itching to experiment. But I can't put off Dale like that. "Uh, to be honest, I'm not sure."

"Really?" He pauses, and I can picture that vein that pops in his forehead when he gets worried or upset. "Is everything okay there, Blake? Are you still committed to this?"

"What?" I laugh, and it comes out stilted. "Of course I am."

"You sure? Because for a guy on the brink of all his dreams

coming true, it doesn't sound like you've been thinking much about that dream at all lately."

I toss both bags of chocolate into the cart and push harder than necessary. The wheels squeak and grind, and I grunt with the effort to maneuver around the corner, nodding at old Earl Flanders as he hobbles past me in his cowboy hat. The bell at the front of the store jangles. It's getting later, and I'm running out of time to experiment before I have to open the food truck for lunch.

"Look, Dale." I draw up my shoulders and continue my trek to the spice aisle. "I haven't been as focused on the business side of things because I know you've got it covered. Besides, my main focus right now is getting these recipes ready, right? I'm doing everything in my power to get feedback on my offerings so I know what's going to sell like hotcakes when we open the restaurant." Here's hoping he doesn't see through my bluster, though, of course, there is some element of truth to what I'm saying.

To be honest, I'm not quite sure *why* I haven't been obsessing about all the details of the restaurant. But maybe it's better to just concentrate on one thing at a time. Maybe it's a blessing in disguise that Hallmark Beach has a way of sucking you in and making you forget the outside world.

Hallmark Beach...and certain residents.

"I suppose that makes sense." Dale's voice hums with consideration. "So, you're making headway on the new recipes then?"

Sure, if you call serving the same limited offerings for the last three weeks progress. Although after last night, I've got a spark back that I haven't felt in a good long while. So I'm hopeful. Which is why I assure Dale that of course things are moving forward—so he doesn't worry—and fly through the aisles grabbing the last ingredients for what I need after hanging up with him.

I reach the only occupied register with a decently loaded down cart, and Alberta Jenkins herself is acting as cashier. The seventy-something has bottle-red hair with gray roots nobody would dare point out to her. She purses her lips like she's swallowed a vat of vinegar and inspects my cart as if its contents hold all my secrets. "That it?"

Uhhh, what else was she expecting me to buy? I'll never know, because right when I open my mouth to say, "Yep," Alberta's eyes pop behind me, and her jowls wobble as she yells, "Earl Flanders, you put down that glass vase before you break it," and waddles away, finger waving in the air.

Okay, then.

My eyes sweep the counter while I wait for her return, and they land on a stack of fliers with The Green Robin's simple logo and information about their BOGO special going on this week. Lucy must have dropped them at all the local businesses like I did when handing out my own coupons. I glance back at Alberta, who is now following Earl around with her wagging finger as he clutches a vase to his flannel shirt, his nose tipped in the air as if he's ignoring her. Then, before I can stop myself, I grab half of the fliers and stuff them into the back pocket of my slacks.

Finally, Alberta returns, muttering under her breath about insufferable men, and rings up my items without another word. I help bag everything to make the process quicker, and her eyes seem to soften around the edges. But of course, she doesn't say thank you. The president of the town council is known for her forthrightness...and sometimes, her rudeness. Still, after I pay and she hands me the receipt, she tips her head toward me and says in a quiet voice, "I hope this town is being good to you while you're back."

"It is."

"Good." She blinks at me. "Your parents were fine people, and we sure do miss them around here. Glad you're back, if only for a while."

Whoa, what alternate universe have I stepped into where Alberta Jenkins—the woman who used to literally yell at all the school kids to GET OFF HER LAWN—is being nice to me? I clear my throat, nod. "Thank you."

Then I'm outta there, making sure Main Street is clear of cars before I cross and walk down past the bookstore and Rainbow Ice to where my truck is parked. I set the groceries on the ground and dig my keys out of my pocket, waving at Chad Painter as he cleans one of the tables between the food truck and Rainbow Ice, which he owns with his wife Amber. In his early forties, he seems like a nice guy, but I haven't had much time to chat with him. Between the business and his wife and their three young kids, he's a busy dude. Plus, he closes up right at five and lets a few college students take the last shift.

I wonder what that's like—to have a family to go home to, and to make that a priority. My last significant relationship lasted only three months and ended because Chelsea couldn't handle my long hours. Not that I blamed her. Whenever I did see her, I was so tired I could barely keep my eyes open, and my mind was always back at the restaurant even when I wasn't physically present there.

Is it bad that I kind of dread going back to that fast-paced lifestyle?

Shaking myself from the not-so-pleasant memories and the terrifying contemplations, I unlock the food truck and drag my grocery haul inside. Another spark of excitement zings inside my chest as I pull out what I purchased. Flipping on the grill, I refrigerate what I'll need for later, and—before setting to work —tug Lucy's fliers out of my back pocket. They're a bit wrinkled, so I do my best to smooth them out, then set them on the sill of my window so I remember to put them beside the condiments station where patrons will be sure to see them...and hopefully take one to use later.

It's not much, but I want to support her. Because she's right. I'm only here for the summer, and I don't want my success to mean her failure. And the sooner I get my new recipes figured out, the sooner I can stop "stealing her business."

So, I pop on some jazz music...and start buttering some bread.

LUCY

I have never been more in need of a bubble bath than I am right now.

Dragging myself from my ancient Corolla, I close the door and breathe in the crisp ocean air wafting from the Pacific up along the edge of the hill where Marilee's house is situated. Somewhere, an owl hoots, and the light of the full moon flickers in and out as clouds chase it in the sky.

I rub my lower back, which aches from sitting at Winona's desk—staring at the books, wondering why-oh-why my BOGO coupons haven't increased our numbers this week, despite how many people I saw come back through the door. My legs hurt too, from the hours I spent pitching in on the floor because Jason called in sick for the dinner shift, and we needed an extra server during the rush.

It's Saturday, which means it was busy (thankfully). There were a lot of requests for Tiny's latest special—a jalapeño burger with Worcestershire sauce, crispy onions, and pepper Jack cheese—and yet, in between serving them, I heard nothing but rave reviews over Blake's new dessert grilled cheese that he introduced several days ago.

All of that to say, I think a bubble bath is calling my name tonight.

I push through the front door and freeze at what I see. Marilee's sitting at the kitchen table—despite her early morning shift—and she's chatting with Blake, who is at the stove. There's one of Mare's pink tea towels draped casually over his shoulder, and he's shucked off his button-up shirt, leaving just a white tee on with his beige slacks and black socks. He's holding a spatula, and there's a relaxed curve to his whole body, like he's settled in and plans to stay a while.

The smell of cooked butter rends the air, and my stomach growls its approval. Not surprisingly, it looks like he's making some variation of grilled cheese. The counter is strewn with ingredients of all sorts. It looks like it does after Marilee bakes— and yet, neat-and-orderly Blake is the one in the kitchen. Huh.

At my entrance, they both turn and stop talking.

Blake stares at me and presses his lips together. I can't get a read on him at all. Finally, he nods—polite, but not effusive— and turns back to the stove.

But there's no such reticence in Mare, who smiles and waves. "Hey, stranger."

She's not wrong. I've been so busy at work that we've been like ships passing in the night since our late-night dish session on Monday.

I hang my purse on one of the hooks to the left of the entrance and shut the door. "Hey, guys." My instinct tells me to let them have their privacy, to run straight for the bathroom and dunk myself in the tub. To get far away from this domestic picture of Blake.

But I promised Mare that he and I could be friends again. And so far this week, I haven't had a chance to prove it. Looks like my bubble bath will have to wait.

"Something smells divine." I toe off my shoes and let my

feet sink into the carpet. Mmm, that feels nice. I pad over to the table and pull out a heavy chair next to Marilee. She's already changed into comfy lounge pants and an oversized, purple T-shirt. "And I'm starving."

Blake turns toward me with surprise in his eyes that quickly turns to teasing. "Oh, you think this is for you?"

"Well, me and Mare." I pretend to be confused as I look at my bestie. "Aren't we re-enacting our high school days when Blake used to cook for us?"

"That's an excellent idea." Marilee raises her hand. "I second the motion."

Blake snorts and grabs a plate from the cabinet. He sets it beside another plate, which must be for Mare. "Actually, this is good. I need you guys to taste test some samples for me."

Now that I'm not "mad" at Blake anymore, I don't have to pretend to not want his food. (Just his food, y'all. That's all I want. JUST HIS FOOD.) "I guess I could be up for that."

Mare giggles, Blake spears me with a look like he knows what I'm about, and I rub my hands together with a rumbling *mua-ha-ha*. While Blake cooks up a few more sandwiches—and I do a masterful job at ignoring how his back muscles bunch and gather under his shirt as he reaches for various ingredients and artfully adds them to the pan—Marilee and I catch up from the week. Sounds like hers went much better than mine.

Meanwhile, waiting here is a whole experience. The smell of melted cheese, the sound of sizzling butter, the taste of antic-ipation on my tongue, the gnawing of my empty stomach. And when Blake finally turns to us with two plates in hand—each one arranged with four sandwich halves—I'm like one of Pavlov's dogs, practically salivating with the need for these sandwiches.

"Ooo, what did you make us?" Mare asks as she examines the contents of her plate.

I take mine as well and can't help but notice the way Blake studies me. His gaze is intent, his light blue eyes slightly darkened around the edges. His cheeks are flushed, and I can't help but think he's the most handsome man in the world here, in his element.

Friends, Lucy. Just friends, my subconscious murmurs in my head.

"Thank you," I blurt out, loudly and awkwardly enough that Blake rears back a bit.

He rubs the back of his neck, shakes his head, and moves his gaze to Marilee's plate. Points. "Um, yeah, so I've been experimenting—"

"Ooo, like the s'mores grilled cheese you made earlier this week?" Marilee lifts her shoulders and squeezes her eyes shut for a moment. "Mmm. So good. Lucy, did you try it?"

Two sets of eyes swing my way.

"No. Haven't had a chance yet."

"You'll have to fix that."

My forehead wrinkles at Blake's simple statement, said so casually. And yet—with his arms folded across his chest like that, his eyes blazing with something dangerous—in this case, simplicity can be deceiving. "Guess I will."

"Good." He holds my eyes for just a second longer, then points to our plates again. "All right, so I cooked up four different recipes. Just experimentations. I want your honest thoughts."

The vulnerability in his tone brings a dip to my stomach. There's something there. Some reason he cares. "Why the sudden burst of creativity? Don't you already have a full menu?"

"He needs new recipes," Mare says as she bites into the first sample. Chews. *Mmms*. Pats her lips with a napkin. "For his restaurant."

He mentioned a new restaurant the other night—but not that it would be *his*.

Something like pride wiggles through my chest, and I'm surprised at myself. That I could go so long "hating" this guy, and yet still feel pride for that high school boy who told me all about his dream of someday owning a restaurant featuring his recipes. "It's happening? That's awesome, Blake. Congrats."

And I find that I mean it.

Well, if that's not the scariest thing in the world, I don't know what is.

I peek up at him and he's staring at me, leaning one hand against the counter as if bracing for support. He swallows hard, and I see his throat bob. "Thanks, Lucy."

The way he says my name—all warm and gooey and filled with meaning—is not good for my peace of mind. Because the whole reason he's here, serving me food in the first place, is because he's leaving again.

Remember that. Remember.

But given my knack for critiquing recipes, that's what I need to focus on right now. While Marilee *oohs* and *aahs* over the next sandwich—something with chutney, maybe?—I pick up a different kind and peel back the sourdough bread a bit to find apples and fontina cheese.

Then I bite into it. Chew. Close my eyes. Assess. Flavors pop in my mouth but end quickly. Hmm.

"Well?"

When I reopen my eyes, Blake swims in my vision and he's...pacing? Like, he's actually nervous. Does he really care what I think? He definitely didn't seem this nervous with Mare. Of course, Mare is over there licking her fingers as she devours her last sandwich, and all she's managed to say is "delicious!", "amazing!", and "that's the best sandwich I've ever had in my life"—and two seconds later, "never mind, that one is!"

Maybe he just knows I don't give out compliments easily. At least, to him. Even in high school when I'd critique his cooking, I didn't tell him what he wanted to hear. I was honest, although always upbeat (and slightly afraid he'd hate me for my truth telling). The goal was always to help make his food better. To help make him a better cook.

And, if he's truly my friend (and only my friend, okay, y'all?), then I will still want that for him. I will want him to knock the socks off the folks in L.A. when he opens his restaurant—his dream—and offers killer sandwiches that will cause rave reviews.

"It's good. Really good." I pause.

"But?"

I sigh. I always hate this part. "But something's missing. I can't quite put my finger on what it is."

"Really?" Mare lets her bun loose, her long brown hair falling in waves around her shoulders. She combs her fingers through it. "I thought they were all amazing."

"Yes, but you're only ever critical of your own work." Blake swoops in and rumples her hair like only a big brother would.

She smacks him in playful protest. "That's not true."

He looks at me, a wry grin on his face. "Back me up, Sunshine."

I can't help but laugh. "It's not *un*true."

Standing, Mare puts her hands on her hips in a very poor attempt at a haughty pose. "Well, excuse me for thinking my brother is the best chef in the world."

"Aw, Squirt." Then he grabs her in a half hug and kisses the side of her head before swooping in, grabbing her empty plate, and heading for the sink. "You have way more faith in me than I have in myself."

My heart squeezes at the sight in front of me. I'm so glad for the smile on my best friend's face, the light of adoration in her eyes. She's always looked up to Blake, and I know how crushed she was when he left. But now I'm starting to see that it wasn't easy for Blake either. He lost his parents too. And just because my way of dealing with hard times is to hold tighter to the people I love—to never want to leave them—that's not the same for everyone.

Some people need to deal with grief by escaping. Not saying that's the healthiest way, but now I can see that Blake wasn't escaping forever. He's come back to himself. Back to Marilee.

Back to me.

Ugh, there I go again. I cannot be thinking like that. He's not here for me. He's not. And that's okay. Even if I'm only ever Marilee's annoying friend, I'm glad he's here.

For her sake.

I reach for another sandwich, bite into it. There are hints of cilantro and roasted onions and tomatoes. As Uncle Burt would say—Oh. My. Golly. Gee. "Blake."

I wait for him to turn from where his hands are plunged in soapy water at the sink. "Yeah?"

"You *should* have more faith in yourself." I wave the newest grilled cheese in the air. "Because what we have here is a winner."

BLAKE

"Here you go. Enjoy." I serve up the last five sandwiches for the day, handing them through my truck window to a guy about my age with a young family.

"Sure will, man. Thanks." He's clearly on vacation—if the board shorts and rash guard aren't an indication, then the sunburn he's sporting on his forehead and cheeks surely is—and he does an impressive job of balancing the disposable baskets with their sandwiches, homemade chips, and pickles. One of his kids rushes him, and he nearly drops it all but manages to bribe the little pig-tailed princess with a traditional grilled cheese, which she takes in hand before skipping back to the tables outside Rainbow Ice.

Chuckling, I double check to be sure nobody else is waiting or approaching before I roll down the window screen. Whew. My hand finds the back of my neck and massages there, working the muscles that are tired but satisfied from a long Sunday that started with a busy lunch and ended with never-ending dinner lines. Thank goodness for the air conditioner blowing coolness onto my skin or I'd be a sweaty mess in addition to a weary one. But despite my exhaustion, there's energy too. It's buzzing underneath my skin, moving like a swarm of bees.

Because last night's cilantro grilled cheese creation was a hit. All day, excited return customers ordered it with enthusiasm, and lots of newbies still chose it over my classic offerings.

It's definitely going on the restaurant menu.

Now if only I can figure out what Lucy thinks is missing from the apple and fontina sandwich. She's right, though. After she gave her critique, I tried making it again and couldn't help but see things from her perspective.

Of course, she could have been saying it to mess with me, but I don't believe that. Not really. Lucy Reynolds is many things (many things that I will not say out loud because admitting them would be admitting *other* things), but vindictive is not one of them.

In fact, last night, things almost felt normal between us. Comfortable. She was the old Lucy—the one she is with everyone else. The one she used to be with me.

I didn't realize before then how much I'd missed her.

Of course, I knew that she'd inspired me—I've been a creating machine since the bake-off nearly a week ago—but this was about more than inspiration.

It was just about...her.

I groan because I really need to stop being so sentimental.

Then, as if the woman materialized out of my mind, there's a knock at the back door and Lucy's voice. "Blake? You in there?"

"Yeah." I hurry to the door and fling it open.

Lucy's standing on the bottom step, looking so casually gorgeous in a bright pink tank top and white shorts. Her hair is in two braids today, and she looks sporty and strong with her tan shoulders and arms on display. "Hi." She's got something held behind her back, and there's a somewhat shy smile that she's also trying to hide. "Sorry to interrupt."

"You're not interrupting. I was just closing up."

She bounces on her tiptoes. "Okay, well, I know you're probably tired, but I couldn't stop thinking about last night."

Her words are a gut punch. She can't? "Me either." I find myself saying the words, wondering what revealing them means. Wondering why I'm openly admitting that I can't get her off my brain.

She squints at me. "Really?" Her head tilts as she studies me. A breeze blows the grass just below her. "So have you already come up with a solution?"

"A solution?" To what? How we could possibly be together?

"For the sandwich?"

Okay, slow your roll, Blake. What an idiot. I want to curse. Of course she's talking about the sandwich. I clear my throat. "Yeah, of course."

"Hmm." She looks past me, as if she can see something by studying the contents of the truck. "Guess you won't be needing this then." With a flourish, she takes the last two steps so she's standing even with me, then draws a small container from behind her back.

Whole-grain mustard.

My mind goes berserk.

"Lucy freaking Reynolds. You're a genius."

"Of course I am." Then she reaches into the back pocket of her pants and pulls out a small bag of something else. "Aaaaaand try a few of these to go with it."

I grab for the bag, but get her hand instead, tugging her closer to me so her hand is pressed between us. Her skin is soft, and my rebellious thumb reaches for a silky stroke before I can stop it. The apples of her cheeks turn pink.

I could stay in this moment forever.

"Sliced chives!" she blurts out, just like she did last night, all loud and awkward. I think she must do that when she's uncomfortable.

Immediately, I drop her hand and take a step away, because I refuse to be the guy who makes her uncomfortable. Then my brain processes what she said. Mulls it over. I blink. "That could really work."

"Of course it could. It will." She flips a braid over her shoulder with a confidence that's as sexy as the curves she shows off as she pushes past me and hops up onto the counter by the window. "Wanna see if I'm right?"

She's just teasing me like a friend would—really taking that truce to heart—and can't know how much I both want to be trapped in these close quarters with her and dread it too. Thankfully, my hands will stay busy with the sandwich making. "Let's do it."

I grab a loaf of sourdough off my well-organized shelf. Flipping the grill back on, I let it heat up while I pillage my refrigerator for an apple and some fontina. "So." What? I never claimed to be a riveting conversationalist. "Where did you get the mustard?"

Oy. That made it worse, didn't it? But I just can't think right now, not with Lucy's bare legs dangling close to my backside. With her orange-vanilla scent quickly overtaking the small truck. Thank goodness for rote actions that my hands immediately know what to do.

Slice apple. Check. Apply mayo to bread. Check. Slide on the mustard. Check. Arrange the apples and chives. Check.

While I do all of this, Lucy talks. "I got it from the Robin. I was busy waiting tables all day because one of my servers was out sick again. But that gave me time to figure out what the sandwich was missing. I was running in and out of the kitchen and spied this on the counter because Tiny was using it for one of his burgers, and BAM. It hit me. And of course, chives are good on everything."

"Everything?" I tease, peeking back at her.

"Within reason." She smiles at me and I'm a goner. Yep. Total goner. Especially when she lifts her head a bit like she can see over my shoulder. "How's it coming?"

"Patience, woman."

Her laugh fills up the whole truck. My heart too. And I'm the biggest sap that's ever walked the planet as I toss that sandwich onto the griddle and hear the satisfying sizzle. I take my spatula in hand and turn, leaning back against the opposite counter to face her. My truck is decent-sized, but there's still only inches between us in the cramped galley.

Her eyes flit away from my face and onto the sandwich. Then back to me. "You know, I really shouldn't be helping the competition." A little bit of the light fades from her gaze. "But if I can't help the Robin do better, at least maybe I can take some credit for your success." Her smile's back, but there's something strained in it. Like she's pretending again.

"Ha ha." I turn back to the sandwich, peek under the slice. Ready to flip, so I do. Then, "Are things really that bad for you?"

She shrugs a delicate shoulder, and guilt pummels me. "I'm sorry, Lucy. If I hadn't moved in here, then—"

"No, Blake. It's not your fault. We were failing before you ever arrived. You opening your truck just made things..."

"Harder?"

"More interesting."

"Ah." I frown. "I know it's not any of my business, but why is all of this falling on your shoulders?"

"I'm the one in charge."

"Well, yeah, but it's Winona's company. Her ultimate responsibility."

She sighs. "True, but I want her to be able to enjoy her trip without worrying about it, you know? I don't know what I'm doing, though. I sit and stare at the numbers and try thinking up ways to change them, but...I guess I don't really have a head for business."

I pull the sandwich off the griddle and set it quickly on my wooden cutting board. "What about a business plan? Have you tried creating one? You start with the vision, identify problem areas, and then that can help you figure out some solutions for those areas. It kind of lays things out in a more helpful and purposeful way." Setting down my spatula, I slice the sandwich in half—the melty cheese pulling deliciously from slice to slice —and scoot one half onto a paper towel. The heat bleeds through, as does a bit of the grease.

"I wouldn't even know where to begin."

"I can send you the one I put together for the restaurant. It might help you get started. And I can look yours over when you're done. If you want." Turning, I offer the sandwich to her.

But she just blinks at me, frozen. "Really?"

"Really, Sunshine." I press the sandwich into her hands.

"Thanks." She takes it and blows on it, not taking her eyes off of me. I like her here, all casual in my domain, like she belongs.

More importantly, I like the pretty picture she makes when she finally closes her eyes—her nose scrunching ever so slightly —and takes a happy bite of the sandwich. She gasps, and her eyes fly open. "This is it!" Lucy waves the sandwich in the air like a victory flag. "Try it. We are geniuses."

So I do—and she's right. It's even more perfect than the cilantro sandwich that flew out my window today.

"Sunshine, I could kiss you right now."

And whhhhhy did I have to go and say a thing like that?

Her arm drops onto her lap, and she swallows quickly.

My brain isn't computing. It's short circuiting. One thought—must recover. Must recover. I laugh. "I just mean, it's really good. I couldn't have done it without you."

Her shoulders relax and she laughs along, though again, it's stilted. Hopefully my inane comment didn't make her uncomfortable again. I'm really going to have to rein things in with her. Because it's clear that I've still got a mad crush on Lucy Reynolds.

Not on the girl she was then, but the woman she is now.

And that is a very big problem.

Because I can't be the guy I was then. And I can't let myself give in to what that guy wanted, either. What my dad said is still true—I don't want any regrets. I don't want a small life. And even if I did, I have to press on, to make him proud. If I fail at that, well...there's really no other option for me, especially since he's not here anymore.

Lucy bites her lip and slides off the counter sideways to avoid running into me. "I guess I'd better go. See you at h—" Her jaw drops, and before she can say the word "home," she's reaching across the counter toward the window.

Where there are still some of her BOGO fliers.

I ran out of the ones I stole from Alberta, so I finagled these from Burt's auto shop. Burt promised not to tell Lucy. But now, it seems I've told on myself.

She lifts the flier. "What's this?"

I scratch the back of my head. "A coupon."

"Thanks, Einstein. I recognize it. Quite well, in fact. But why is there a stack of *my* coupons in *your* truck?"

Now it's my turn to shrug. "I know you say we can't

possibly share customers, but I don't think that's true. Consider this my way of making up the theft you accuse me of."

Will this upset her? Make her mad? I've known people who would be mortally offended by something like this, wanting to be able to prove they succeeded all on their own.

But not Lucy. Instead, she tackles me with a hug, pressing her face into my chest and wrapping her arms around my middle. "You didn't have to do that."

I take this opportunity to hug her back, setting my chin on the top of her head so I don't do what I'm dying to—which is bury my nose in her hair and take a big whiff like some sort of stalker. "I wanted to."

She looks up at me, and her eyes are watery. "You aren't so bad, Flake."

I chuckle softly. "Neither are you, Sunshine."

Lucy pulls back far too soon, wiping at her eyes and heading toward the door. At the last minute, she turns, her hand on the doorknob. "I'm sorry for how mad I let myself get at you six years ago. About how I've been treating you."

Aw, Sunshine. I stick my hands into my pockets. "I'm sorry for leaving. You were right. I should have listened to you. Should have been here for Mare."

"You're here for her now. That's what counts." She opens her mouth as if to say more, then must decide against it. "I'm happy for you. That your dreams are coming true. Those L.A. foodies aren't going to know what hit them." Then she softly slips out the door and it latches behind her.

And I slump back against the counter, my heart beating double time. Because I'm no L.A. foodie. And unlike them, I know exactly what's hit me.

And yet. I can't pursue it. Can't chase this feeling. It wouldn't be fair to Lucy. To me. To Dad and his dream for me.

I have to do better at maintaining my distance. If I keep letting Lucy in like this—literally and figuratively—then I'm bound to break down.

I'm only human, after all.

sixteen

LUCY

At twenty-eight, I wouldn't exactly call myself *old*.

But when you've just spent thirty minutes giving romping, alternating piggy-back rides to a three-year-old, a five-year-old, and a six-year-old, you start to understand the phrase, "Oh, my aching back."

"Okay, guys." I slide Felicia, the youngest, off my back onto the bottom stair, then lean against the railing to catch my breath. "Aunt Lucy is getting tired."

They protest for a moment, and five-year-old Leonardo narrows his striking blue eyes that stand out even more against the darker skin tone he inherited from his Hispanic mama. "You promised me next!"

"Please, auntie? One more?" Isabella bats her little lashes at me and twirls.

I'm not really their aunt—I can't be anyone's aunt, since I don't have siblings—but my littlest cousins don't know the difference. Their dad, Jeff, my oldest cousin who is in town visiting for a few days with his wife and four kids from Dallas, is eight years older than me, so he was already away at college when I moved here sophomore year. Still, he's come back a few times every year to visit, so as far as his kiddos know, I'm just like another one of his sisters.

Speaking of his sisters, Stephanie is on her way to this little impromptu Monday night gathering—working late—and April is huddled on my uncle's beat-up recliner in the corner of the tiny living room with her computer. I don't know how she writes with all the chaos ensuing.

Five children (including her own seven-year-old, Scarlett) ranging in age from three to twelve have spent the last hour shouting, running up and down the stairs and out to the backyard, tossing balls and snatching bits of food from Aunt Bea, Aunt Janine (my dad and Uncle Burt's sister), and Jeff's wife in the kitchen, where my stomach rumbles at the smells of the Mexican food Maria is an expert at making.

My uncle Burt and Jeff are sitting at the kitchen table, loudly discussing the Cowboys' chances this year at going to the Super Bowl. (Which, yes, is eight months away, but these Texas men love their football.)

But despite the cacophony surrounding her, April is still zeroed in on whatever she's writing. That woman loves a good romance novel, and I'm convinced that someday she's going to be published. Whenever I ask her how it's going though, she just shrugs me off. I've heard authors are never satisfied with their own work, but I remember when April let me read some of her stuff before she left to study at the University of Washington's creative writing program. I'm not a big reader, but even I could tell that it was good.

"Give me fifteen minutes, all right? Shoo now. Git." I lunge like I'm going to pat my cousins' tushies, and they run up the stairs screaming like little banshees.

It's glorious, and I'm right at home in the chaos.

After a few moments of rest, I haul myself up and sit down on the end of the couch closest to April. She's got on a pair of slouchy socks and bright red lounge pants that match her shoulder-length red hair, which is back in a clip and—from the looks of it—several days unwashed. There are some dark circles under her eyes, and she's got a stain on her black T-shirt. I haven't seen her looked this harried since Scarlett was a newborn. She had to move home from college, pregnant and a dropout at age nineteen, severely depressed but also determined to somehow carve out a life for her daughter.

And that's exactly what she did. By the time Scarlett turned two, April had built up a little nest egg from her job at Aunt Janine's inn, The Purple Seashell, and moved them both to San Francisco, where a friend from college offered her a job as an administrative assistant at a publishing house.

April is fiercely independent, and I know that moving home again recently wasn't something she really wanted. She did it for Scarlett, to grow up with family around, and also for her parents, since they're starting to get up there in years. But maybe the move has been harder on her than I realized.

"Hey, cuz." I nudge her with my big toe.

She jolts at the contact and slams her laptop shut as if on instinct. What in the world is she working on that *that's* her reaction? I don't think she writes steamy scenes in her books, but then again, what do I know? I have no clue what's popular these days.

When she notes that it's me, her shoulders relax. "Sorry. I had a moment of inspiration and had to get it down." She laughs softly and slides the computer onto the coffee table. "How are you?"

"I'm fine. But I'm more worried about you. You look tired." I pull one of Aunt Bea's bulky quilts from the floor between the chair and couch and tuck it around my legs—not really because it's cold, but because it's comfortable. That's how this whole house feels, because that's how my aunt and uncle make everyone feel when they come inside. It's nothing fancy, just random knickknacks and no real decorating theme. But the way the living room leads right into the kitchen in a great room style, the comfy sitting area, the big-screen TV, the quilts—it all somehow comes together to say, *"Stay a while."* (Or in my case, nearly thirteen years!)

April pushes back the side-swooping bangs hanging in her eyes. Shakes her head. "I'm just on a deadline." She blanches and hurries to continue. "I mean, I've given myself a deadline and don't want to miss it."

Hmm. I mean, my cousin is kind of hard on herself, but this seems like more than that. Maybe she's worried about Scarlett. "How's Scar doing? Adjusting to life in Hallmark Beach?"

"She's thriving. Loving it. Honestly, she slipped right into first grade like she'd known all those kids her whole life—not just as a toddler before we left." She rolls her eyes, and there's the sassy cousin I know and love, finally coming out of her writing coma. "When school ended last week, she was queen of the playground. Apparently everyone wanted to be Scarlett's friend. Hopefully it doesn't go to her head."

"Takes after her mama, that one." I wink. "So what's she doing now that school's out? Hanging with Aunt Bea while you work?"

"Some of the time, but I enrolled her at the summer day camp that Go Round Adventures is running."

Oh, right. Marilee had mentioned that Jordan's company was expanding this summer to try out a program for kids. "That's the one Sarah and Mandy Hubbard are running, yeah?" The sisters actually are the reason I snagged a room at Marilee's house. They moved here last year to work for Jordan, lived with Marilee in the rooms Blake and I now occupy, but decided to get their own apartment together, which made room for me at the beginning of May.

"Yep. She loves it. Especially all the sports. Football is her favorite."

And that makes me snort. "Who knew *your* daughter would be sporty?" The only time I've seen April run (other than forced gym class in high school) was when she once won an all-you-can-grab-in-two-minutes book sweepstakes at The Bluestocking Bookshop where she now works.

"Yeah. Funny." Her gaze slips away toward the women in the kitchen, almost as if she's contemplating escaping our conversation to help cook—which is even more laughable, because she's like me when it comes to her kitchen craftiness. Why is she...

Ah. Of course. She must be thinking of Scarlett's dad. None of us know his identity—she's always refused to say, and I've just always assumed it was some jerk she met in college who left her high and dry when she told him she was pregnant —but maybe *he* was sporty.

I reach over and squeeze her arm. "I'm glad she's doing so well. And I have no doubt you're going to crush that book deadline, even if it's self-imposed."

She flashes me a genuine smile. "Thanks, Lucy." Then her mouth tilts even more to the side, and I recognize the look in her eyes. The prying one. The teasing glint that says she's about to ask me something personal. "Sooo. How are you, really? I've heard rumors about you and a certain food truck owner and have been meaning to ask you if they're true."

I cough. "Depends on what you've heard. We haven't murdered each other yet."

"Yes, I can see that." She leans forward, grinning. Whatever was on her mind just a few moments ago has clearly fled. "Elisse texted me that she saw you sneaking out of the truck last night, and even though it was dark, she could tell your cheeks looked flushed."

Darn that Elisse, always looking to stir up trouble for me. Hmm. Maybe the ladies in the kitchen do need help…

I do my best to maintain a neutral expression. "For your information—and you can tell Elisse this too—I was helping Blake with a recipe and standing near the stove. Naturally, I'd get warm." I mean, yeah, it's the truth. But there was also the heat from Blake's body so near mine, from his gaze as he pinned me to the spot while I tried his—our—creation…

The warmth exploding inside me when I realized that he'd been handing out my coupons.

It started as embarrassment that I'd needed the help but quickly morphed into something more. Something that very nearly made me rise up on my tiptoes and fuse my mouth with his.

Instead, I sank into his arms. Because clearly, he's working at a truce too. The fliers were his white flag. Doesn't mean I need to go making a fool of myself. He's leaving, after all.

But I still can't get it out of my head the way he looked at me. The almost near certainty that he's feeling what I am. That the spark is there.

I just don't know what to do with that. Probably nothing.

From the way her eyebrows are rising and waggling, April's not buying my story. "Helping with a recipe, huh? Is that what the kids are calling it these days?"

Sweet macaroni. Her implication makes me blush here and now. I feel my cheeks heating hotter than a Fourth of July firework. Taking one of the couch pillows beside me, I toss it at her head.

She dodges it and laughs. "Kidding, kidding. I know how much you loathe the man."

"Yeah. Totally." But my voice lacks conviction.

Her eyes narrow, and she studies me like a lion assessing its prey. "Oh, no. Lucy."

Oh, no, Lucy, is right. "What?" I fold my arms over my chest.

April frowns. "You know I love to tease you, but you haven't honestly fallen for the guy again, have you?"

"No." Again, I'm as convictionless as a felon intent on a crime.

My cousin hauls herself out of the chair and comes to plop beside me on the couch. She turns her body so she's facing me, and I do the same, one leg pulled up underneath me. "Lucy, I know I'm two years younger than you, so we didn't exactly hang out a lot in high school, but even I saw how you felt about him. And you never talked about it, but I saw how it tore you up when he left for college."

I open my mouth to protest—because that's what I've always done—but my recent conversation with Marilee comes to mind. Maybe I need to start being honest with not just the people I love, but myself too. "It did." My words are soft. "But... I don't know." I run my finger along the couch's blue weathered fabric.

And finally, I get the courage to voice the question that I've been trying to bury the last week, since Blake and I made our truce. Since I've started seeing I was wrong about him. That maybe the old Blake is still in there somewhere. That work *isn't* all he cares about. And that maybe he really does have feelings for me too. "Maybe things could be different this time around."

"Aw, cuz. You know I'm the queen of happily ever afters. Reading about them, not living them out, clearly." She gives a wry smile. "And you know I'd be sooooo happy for you if you found the man of your dreams. You deserve happiness more than anyone I know."

My eyes sting, and I push my finger harder along the rim of the couch.

"But just...be careful, okay? Those first loves have a way of holding onto you and never letting go."

And now I wonder if April's talking about me or her—and Scarlett's dad, whoever he is. But either way, she's got a point. Maybe what's happening between me and Blake is inevitable. Maybe my feelings for him are so wrapped up in the past that what's happening now is just a continuation of that.

Maybe there's nothing real there now. Maybe it's all a result of the years of longing.

Ugh, I don't even know if I'm making sense. Thankfully, my brain is given a break when Aunt Bea declares it's time for dinner and says everyone better get in the kitchen and grab all the fixins for tacos and enchiladas. Then it's chaos again, and that drowns out the doubts and questions in my brain for the time being. I'm not thinking about Blake or the failing restaurant or anything except the joy of being with my family.

Even if I've always felt a little on the outside of it all—an honorary aunt and daughter only—I'd still do anything for these people, and I love being with them. But being with them always brings out a longing deep inside me. One I don't often let myself dwell on.

I want this. I've always wanted this—to build something like Burt and Bea have built. Something I didn't have growing up with my parents because I didn't have siblings and Daddy died so young. Mama did her best, I know, but part of her best was bringing me here, letting Bea and Burt have a hand in raising me. I'm grateful. But I'm also sad that it wasn't different in my own home.

Still. Maybe someday, I could have this with someone.

If I can find the courage to risk my heart—to risk the heartache that Mama felt when Daddy died—then a version of this could be mine.

I'm quiet as dinner goes on, as plates are filled and then

emptied, as stories are swapped and laughter rings out. I'm just soaking it all in.

As I'm leaving, there are hugs all around. Uncle Burt gathers me up and pulls me off my feet with a "boy, howdy, we sure miss you around here." Aunt Bea pulls me to her large chest and kisses my head, then slips a postcard into my bag. "From your mama. Not sure why she sent it here." She pats my cheek, as if she knows how that probably hurts to hear.

Mama—that's another subject I have pushed to the periphery of my mind, because thinking about the unanswered text I sent her in reply to *her* text a week ago makes my chest ache.

"Oh, Bea, don't forget to ask her about Sunday." Burt winks at me, stuffs his hands in the pockets of his overalls, and walks away whistling.

"What's next Sunday?" I ask.

Bea studies me, pensive. "Father's Day. He wanted me to make sure you were coming over for dinner. Said it wouldn't be a good day without all three of his girls here." Her eyes go all misty, and I'm hit in the chest with my aunt and uncle's love for me all over again.

It's strange—losing a parent at a young age. You grow up with this sense that you're missing something, but because you only had that something for a handful of years, the memory of the actual thing kind of fades, and you're left with a hollow that can never be filled...because you're not exactly sure what actually fits there. Only what you think maybe should.

All of this—Mama, Daddy, Blake, my failings, April's warnings, the postcard—hits me at once.

And it's all I can do to hold it together as I kiss Aunt Bea, assure her that of course I'll be at dinner next Sunday, and race out to my car without completely losing it.

Tomorrow. I'll deal with the emotions tomorrow.

Because right now, I'm going straight home and getting that bubble bath I promised myself two nights ago.

I did *not* go straight home for the bubble bath.

Instead, like an idiot, I pulled the postcard Aunt Bea gave me from my purse and, leaning against my car, read it with starlight streaming down around me as I stood in my aunt and uncle's driveway.

The postcard was bright blue, and the picture showcased rows and rows of white buildings on a hillside. The words scrolled in a flourish across the top: *Greetings from Santorini.* I flipped it over and saw Mama's chicken scratch: *"Had some baklava today and thought of you."*

A memory teased and shot forward in my mind. The two of us had been out taking a walk in our old neighborhood in Texas. I was nine, maybe ten. We walked past a Greek restaurant, one of those fancy kinds where they put the menu in the window. I assumed because there were no prices on the menu, it was all free. Mama had laughed and said, "Not quite, Baby Girl."

My eyes immediately roamed to the desserts section (um, hi, whose wouldn't?) and I'd tried to pronounce baklava. Pretty sure it came out back-lava. "What's that, Mama? Can we try some?"

That might have been the first moment I really realized we were poor. Daddy's life insurance (I later learned) ran out quick, because there wasn't much to it in the first place, and Mama had gotten a job as a lunch lady at my school. I'd always worn second-hand clothes she'd bought at Goodwill, but I was never much into fashion, so I didn't mind.

But what I saw on Mama's face that night...well, she was

sad she couldn't take me into that restaurant and let me have baklava.

Still, when Mama puts her mind to something, she makes it spectacular. And her solution was much better anyway. We hightailed it to the nearest grocery store, bought all the necessary ingredients, and made our own baklava in the tiny kitchen of our apartment. We threw on *My Big Fat Greek Wedding* in the background, and then we baked up a storm. (And when I say "we," I really mean she. But she let me help smash nuts with a kitchen mallet and do a few other things.)

And when we were done and tasted our creation, I didn't even care that it wasn't the best thing I'd ever eaten. (It was fine—but come on. Nothing compares to chocolate cake!) All I cared about was the memory we made.

Which is how I find myself here, in my kitchen at nine p.m. on a Monday night, an hour after wishing my family a good night and just twenty minutes after arriving home with a trunkful of groceries.

The good thing is, Al's is open until nine, and they had all of the ingredients I needed.

The bad thing is...oh, yeah. I CAN'T COOK OR BAKE TO SAVE MY LIFE.

The recipe I found online looked so simple. Pound out some nuts, add some dashes of sugar and cinnamon, and then create a dough.

This is where I run astray. After blinking at the instructions for a few minutes and making sure I have the ingredients lined up on the counter in front of me, I realize I don't have the faintest idea what a flour sifter looks like. Or where one would be. I could ask Mare, but she's asleep, and Blake isn't home from work yet.

I blow out a breath and shake my head. No backing out now. I may not have Mama here with me, but I can try to channel her cooking expertise. To pretend I got even an ounce of her genetic cooking abilities. Something—anything—to feel like she's given me more than just a lousy postcard or two and a handful of short visits since she left me here.

The backs of my eyes burn. No, no, no. I will not cry.

Instead, I will bake. And I will be glorious.

Two minutes later, I am anything but glorious.

I've added salt to a mountain of flour in one of Marilee's purple, plastic bowls. Then I create a well in the flour. Actually, it's more like a crater, but how is someone supposed to know how deep a "well" is when it comes to recipe lingo?

Next, I crack five eggs into the well. My nose wrinkles at the instructions when they say I'm supposed to mix it with my hands, but I plunge them in anyway. That's when I realize my hair, which I normally keep pulled up and out of my face, is hanging loose and long today, and there's a piece that's shorter in front that careens into my eyelashes. I try to blink it away, but it doesn't budge. Closing that eye, I try to read the instructions, but it's harder to do than you might think with only one working eye. Not only that, but apparently I'm supposed to add warm water and olive oil to the mix.

I know for a fact that the water sitting in a measuring cup on the counter is no longer warm. It's taken me way too long to get this far and it has to be cold by now. How much will that affect the result?

Why am I so stupid and bad at this? Why didn't Mama take the time to teach me more before she left? It's not like Aunt Bea didn't try, but there are certain things that mothers should do, right?

And there's a lot that Mama and I didn't get a chance to do before she left.

Without warning—with my hands plunged into a flour-y, eggy mess—long-suppressed tears start to stream down my cheeks. I want to wipe at them, but that would leave a terrible mess on my face instead. So I let myself cry into the flour.

And then there's a noise behind me—the creak of the front door, the clink of keys sliding into the small metal tray in the entryway.

Great. Just great. Of course I'd have a witness to this moment of uncontrolled emotion.

Stiffening, I quickly sniffle in an attempt to clear away evidence of my utter meltdown, but my nose honks and my throat emits one loud hiccup like it's going out of style.

"Lucy?" Then I feel the heat of Blake next to me. "Are you okay?"

I turn to face him, shrug. Attempt a smile. "Sure, why do you ask?"

"I..." He lifts his hands like he wants to take my arms, to feel that I'm solid, that I'll be okay. But he doesn't touch me. He glances back, toward the hallway, and I can only imagine he's dreaming of his escape from the crazed lady in the kitchen with dirty hands, streaming tears, and flour all over her tank top because she forgot to put on an apron.

But—for better or worse—Blake is too good of a guy to abandon a crying woman. "Did someone hurt you?" The words come out a bit of a growl—which is strangely comforting. "Tell me what's wrong, Sunshine."

There he goes with that nickname again. I think about April's warning a few hours ago, but at this moment, I feel broken open, raw, and it's almost a relief to show him that I'm *not* always fine. "No one hurt me," I manage, my voice wobbly. With my hands still plunged into the wet bowl—the so-called "dough" beginning to harden and cake on my skin—I nod to the postcard resting on the counter. "I just got that and...it made me kind of weepy."

He picks up the postcard, turns it over. Frowns. "Does she send you these a lot?"

"Off and on."

"When was the last time you talked with her?"

"She texted me last week, remember?"

"So you talked to her after that?"

My silence is my answer.

I sniffle and look up at the ceiling so my tears will be forced back into my eyes. Gravity and all that. I don't want him feeling sorry for me. Ugh, this is a new low. "She calls and visits when she can. My stepdad doesn't really like to stay in one place for long. He's the kind that just likes to up and go when he feels like it, you know?"

And Mama is more than happy to go with him. Because she loves him. I think she also loves the lavish lifestyle he's given her—much more than my daddy ever could give her, though I know she was happy with him too. I huff at the thoughts that are a betrayal to my mother and her generous heart. "She's just...busy."

It sounds so lame, but I know it's partially true. Mama was my anchor, and I was hers for so long, so I know she loves me. I may not understand her distance, but I will never doubt her love.

I can't.

Because what would that mean—that everyone I love eventually leaves me? It's probably why I've never given Marilee, my aunt and uncle, and all of my friends here a choice. It's probably why I stay.

Though I do love this little town and can't imagine where I'd go anyway.

He's frowning. "It's okay to admit that you're upset with her, you know."

"I'm not!" My voice is overly bright as I pull my hands from the sludge. "She's finally happy in a way she hasn't been since Daddy died. How can I begrudge her that?"

"Because she left you. And even if you understand why, doesn't that hurt even a little?"

"Nope." I can't afford to let it hurt a little—because if I give an inch to my thoughts and feelings, they'll take a whole freaking thousand miles. "All that to say, the postcard put me in a mind to…" I wave my hands around the kitchen, as if what I'm doing is obvious.

And apparently, to Blake, it is. "You're making baklava?"

"Correction." I laugh caustically. "I'm trying—and failing—to make baklava."

"Okay." Then Blake sets down the postcard and swivels toward the pantry, where he ducks inside to pull out an apron. Scratch that. Make it two aprons. He pulls the first—a black one that says "Kiss the Chef"—over his head and ties it at his waist.

I narrow my eyes at him. "What are you doing?"

"I thought we were making baklava."

"No. I said *I* was making baklava."

"Then I'm making it with you."

"You're kind of bossy, you know."

He has the audacity to wink at me. (And my heart has the audacity to like it.) "I think you can handle it." Then he steps toward me with the other apron—a pink one—and chuckles. "Here. Put this on. You look like Mare."

He's not wrong. My best friend is a wonder in the kitchen, but she's also messy. There's always a streak of flour on her cheek or forehead after a baking session. I don't have a mirror, but I can see my black spaghetti strap tank is already speckled on the front. It probably doesn't matter whether it gets even dirtier, but I should embrace the cooking experience fully and get aproned up, right?

Only one problem. I hold up my messy hands. "I can't exactly put that on right now." Because, sure, I could wash these hands, but I'm just going to get them dirty again, and this stuff is seriously caked on. It'll take days to get it off. Maybe I used concrete instead of flour.

Rather than letting my excuses deter him, Blake swiftly loops the apron over my head without asking.

"Hey!" I protest.

"What? We can't let you get even messier. Now turn around and let me tie it."

Oh my goodness, I like bossy Blake much more than I should. Mouth numb, I do as he asks. I feel the tug of the apron ties at my waist—but now his movements are achingly slow as he steps closer. I feel the warmth of his presence at my back, the swoosh of his fingertips against my shirt, and it's almost as if he's touching my bare skin.

I shiver and peek over my shoulder at him.

He's staring at the back of my neck, where the top loop of the apron is flattening my hair in place. If I had put it on myself, it would be nothing to sweep my hair out from under the apron loop. Maybe Blake isn't quite sure what to do. I'm guessing he doesn't want to be presumptuous.

But I *want* him to be presumptuous, April's warning be darned.

"It's okay," I whisper, and his eyes flick briefly to mine. "I don't mind."

He swallows, nods, and I turn back around, bracing myself against the counter. (Because who cares if *it* gets dirty? Not this girl.) His fingers find the nape of my neck, brushing slowly along the sensitive skin there. I imagine what it would feel like for him to press his lips to that very spot, and I have to bite my bottom lip to keep myself from begging him to do just that.

Then he gently pulls my long hair out from under the

apron strap. When my hair thumps down against my back, I nearly groan with disappointment because it wasn't enough. And even though I know he's leaving in another month or so, I can't deny that I want more of his touch.

More of him.

I think he feels the same way. And heaven help me, I want to see how far I can push him before he breaks. To see if there is something here worth exploring. I'm suddenly not just a crazed crying woman, but a crazed woman on a mission.

So, I turn around and offer him my wrist.

He looks down at it, eyebrows knit together.

I smile and wiggle my finger at the rubber band that I keep there whenever I leave my hair down. I'm never without a way to tie back my mane—and now I'm congratulating myself on that feat of genius. "My hair keeps getting in my eyes. Would you mind pulling it back for me?"

A muscle tics in his jaw, and the rings around his irises darken. He clears his throat. "Sure. I mean, no." Swallows. "I don't mind." His words burst out short, staccato, and he looks pointedly at me until a giggle burbles up in my chest, and I turn away from him again.

This time, instead of dropping my hair like it's hot lava the moment he touches it fully, his hands gather it slowly like someone might collect flowers in a field on a languid summer day. I might imagine the deep rumble in his chest, but I definitely am not dreaming up the way his fingers comb gently through my hair to get any tangles out. Or the way he releases it, gathers it again, the way his fingertips brush up and down the sides of my neck and he takes his dear sweet time tying my locks back.

How can something as simple as having this man touch my hair be more sensuous than anything I've ever known with anyone else? Granted, my dating experience is pretty limited, but Blake's touch is so innocent—yet it's burning a trail across my skin, wreaking havoc on my entire nervous system, my respiratory system. My circulatory system too.

And when he's done and sets the ponytail gently against my back, I'm in luck, because a few wisps still hang in my eyes. "Hey," I say, my voice as delicate as spun glass. I'm afraid of breaking this spell.

"Hmm?" He leans closer, his breath warm on my bare shoulder.

I turn around fully to face him and point to the eyelashes on my right eye, where another piece of hair has gotten stuck. "Can you get that hair out of my eye, please?"

"Okay." With great care, he leans closer, squinting as he looks for the blonde hair in the boxed light of the kitchen. Finally, he finds it and swoops it out of the way, his thumb trailing over my cheekbone as he tucks the hair behind my ear. "There." His voice is husky, and it's all I can do not to clutch his clean blue shirt with my doughy hands.

We hang out here for what seems like hours, the most delightful game of chicken I've ever played, staring, blinking, breathing. After stroking my cheek, his hand drops to my shoulder, then skims down my upper arm, falling to my waist as he takes one step nearer, closing the gap between us. My hip is scalded by the heat of his hand through the thin fabric of my shirt, my mouth as dry as this flour caked onto my hands.

Heart pounding in my throat, I tilt my chin up and wordlessly dare Blake Moffitt to kiss me.

And he wants to. I know he does. His breath is stuttered, his eyes blinking rapidly. A vein in his neck jumps.

But with pursed lips, he finally steps away. Clears his throat. "Ready to start?"

What. Was. That.

Of course, I can't show him how much he's affected me.

How much I wanted that kiss. It's probably good that one of us is keeping our heads. We're right back where we were more than a decade ago, except this time, there's no father influencing his decisions. This time, it's Blake making the call.

It makes sense. He doesn't want anything but Marilee tying him to Hallmark Beach. To anywhere that isn't L.A., where his dream job awaits.

So, I shake off the rejection and wiggle my mucked-up fingers at him. "Ready."

"All right. Show me that recipe."

I point to my phone, and he opens it and laughs. "Aw, Sunshine. You went straight for the hardest version of baklava, didn't you?"

"What do you mean?"

"I mean, sometimes, homemade is best." He waltzes to the fridge, rummages for a moment, and emerges with a white box. "But other times, just go with the premade stuff."

Oh, thank goodness. I breathe out a sigh of relief as I head to the sink to wash my hands and he unboxes the phyllo dough and quickly cuts it to fit a small rimmed pan he pulled from underneath the oven. We work in relative silence for a while, him patiently showing me what to do and then watching while I do it. His critiques are never harsh, and his gentle undertones are relaxed and calm.

"You remind me of her, you know," I find myself saying.

"Who?"

"Your mom." The air is heavy with the admission, and I rush on. "She loved baking with you guys. And the way you're teaching me now...it's the way she taught you."

"Thank you, Lucy. That means more than you know." He's quiet for a long while, and I look up to see him run a hand along his jaw. "When we'd cook together in the kitchen, it was like the whole world disappeared. All the pressure, all the fuss to make good grades and play football and do something big and important with my life."

He means the pressure his dad put on him. Maybe he and Marilee didn't talk about that, but I was in their home enough to see it.

"I miss her." The words rush out, and then he's focusing on the recipe again.

I can't help but touch him, and this time, it's not for my own selfish reasons, but for him. With a squeeze of his elbow, I lean my head against his arm. "I miss her too. Both of your parents. They were like my second pair. Well, my third, I guess, after Burt and Bea."

He chuckles and lifts a knife to cut the baklava diagonally. "I think they liked you more than they liked me half the time."

"Well, *that's* certainly not true." When he hands me the knife, I try to mimic his slicing but the knife sinks in too deep. With a grunt, I try again and this time, victory!

I finish up and stick the pan into the preheated oven, setting the timer for an hour as per the recipe.

While I'm doing that, Blake quickly creates a mixture of water and sugar in a saucepan and sets it to boil. "What did you mean by that?"

"By what?"

"That it wasn't true. About my parents liking you better."

"Oh." Is it hot in here? "Nothing."

"No, you were thinking of something specific." He leans back against the counter, arms crossed. "You're thinking of what you overheard that night, right?"

Immediately, I know the night—the overheard conversation —he's referring to. "So you do remember."

"I actually didn't. Not until I overheard you and Marilee talking the other night in your room." Now he has the decency to look chagrined.

"Blake Moffitt! You're nothing but a…" Words escape me. Because I don't quite remember what I said that night, but I do know it was not meant for his ears. Only Mare's.

"Believe me, I know." The mixture on the stovetop is boiling, and he flips the burner to simmer, then turns back to me. "The truth is, Lucy, I remember the conversation with my dad, but I don't remember calling you annoying. If I really did that, then I was an idiot."

Oh. "To be fair, it was your dad who called me annoying. You just sort of…didn't contradict him."

"Still. It wasn't accurate."

"So, you didn't find me annoying?"

"Never."

Hmm. I kind of like this groveling side of Blake. "What about now? Do you find me annoying now?"

"Maybe in a really cute sort of way."

Laughing, I smack his arm. "Ha. Guess I wouldn't blame you if you did find me annoying. I might too if I came home and found a crazy person crying in my kitchen." Then I smile. "Thanks for the pity baklava, by the way."

"It wasn't pity baklava. If anything, it was apology baklava." Then he takes my hand in his and stares at it, turning it over so my palm faces upward. "I'm sorry, Lucy."

My throat feels like there's a heartbeat inside of it, thrum, thrum, thrumming higher and higher. "Sorry for what?" Then, for levity's sake, I add, "Finally admitting to stealing my customers?"

But he doesn't even chuckle. Oh my. He really is sorry about something. He blinks at me. "For the past. For…flirting with you my whole senior year. For nearly kissing you, and then leaving without a word. I should have been man enough to tell you the truth. To tell you that even though I cared about you, I couldn't be with you."

Sweet macaroni. Did he just say that? Did he finally confirm that I wasn't nuts back then? That I wasn't just a girl with an unrequited crush, haplessly falling for her best friend's older brother? That he felt it too? "I thought I'd imagined it."

"You didn't. But..." His stunted reply is clear this time.

"Nothing's changed," I say. He might still care about me, but he can't be with me.

"I'm sorry." Blake's choking it out, so I know it's not easy for him.

And though I wish I could change his mind, it's probably better this way. "Don't be." Lifting up on my tiptoes, I skim my lips against his cheek in a soft kiss. "We're good. I promise."

He holds me there, right against him, and I feel his breath feather over my cheek. Blake sighs. "I wish..." Then he groans. "Sunshine, if things were different, I just want you to know that I..."

I draw back and frame his face with my hands. His stubble is rough under my palms. "You'd what?" I dare him to answer. To admit that what he's feeling right now matches what I am.

"I shouldn't say."

"Say it anyway."

His hand finds my waist, flexes against my hip. "I'd say to heck with all the *why nots* and kiss you right now."

Sweet macaroni. Am I brave enough to ask him to do just that? Even if there's no future here? The seventeen-year-old girl inside of me waves her white flag of surrender. "And what if I said that was okay?"

His eyebrows go up. "You're not making it easy on me, are you?" Fingers slide tighter around me, resting on my lower back. "I won't be that guy. I can't lead you on again."

"You've made your intentions clear." I shrug as if this kind of conversation happens for me all the time. "And what's a small peck between friends?"

"Is that what we are, Lucy Reynolds?" A wry grin finds its way across those lips I've been dying to kiss for years. My own mouth tingles with the want, the longing. And I know one kiss with Blake Moffitt will never be enough. But right now, I just don't care. "Friends?"

I draw his head down until our foreheads sink together. "I hope we're at least that."

He grunts. Then he pulls back a little, studies me. "You're sure? Just once? I can't promise you any more than that. I'm leaving again and I—"

"I know."

With a nod, Blake tips up my chin with his index finger and angles his mouth down to meet mine. It's soft and sweet and gentle, chaste and lingering as we breathe the same air and finally, absolutely finally, give in.

It says more than a simple peck should.

It says, "I wish," and "I want," and "I'd like very much to," and "why can't we," and "because."

And when Blake steps away from me after far too short a time, my head is spinning and my heart is banging and my lips are tingling.

We stare at each other, and I feel the pull back toward his arms. The air stirring between us is a force that's almost too strong to be denied. It's a tornado, and I'm the lone barn in a dry field that's trying to hold onto its roof but about to lose more than that. I'm about to be completely uprooted.

And all over a "peck."

But before the winds can take me away, Blake squeezes my elbow and smiles in the sweetest way. "We still good?"

And I know our moment is over.

"We're good." And we are, because he's making this easier on me in the long run. He's stopping things before they even start—and if he doesn't see a future of any sort with me, that's the kindest thing he can do.

At least we'll have this night of apology baklava and memories made.

The problem? I finally know what I've been missing all these years, and somehow, I have to live with that knowledge while Blake is literally right next door for another month and a half.

What have I done? I should have said no.

But as I head down the hallway, leaving Blake behind to pull the baklava from the oven, I can't find it in me to regret that kiss.

seventeen

BLAKE

I tried to keep my distance from Lucy. Tried...and obviously failed as royally as a toddler trying to make creme brûlée.

If I had any doubts about her feelings, I don't anymore. Not after Monday night. The way she looked at me. The way she bravely put herself out there.

Tying that apron without leaning in to kiss her bare shoulder tested the limits of my self-control. But when I finally let my fingers run through the thick, luscious strands of her hair, I nearly came undone. It was all I could do not to wrap my arms around her, to spin her around, pick her up, put her on the counter, and kiss her senseless.

And then, that kiss. I didn't want to stop there. I wanted to devour her. To let her have as much of me as she wanted. I wanted everything with Lucy.

But I refuse to be a cad. I will not hurt her again.

Which is why, instead of joining the Friday night beach volleyball game she's currently engaged in with various friends —Kelsey, Elisse, Landon, Chloe, Frederick, several of the Loveland brothers, Marilee, and Jordan, who arranged the whole thing as a practice run for the Fourth of July tournament he's in charge of organizing—I'm sitting here alone by the bonfire, contemplating life.

Okay, I'm man enough to admit it. I'm avoiding Lucy.

The gang invited me to join in after closing up shop early tonight, but I know that if I was over there right now, I'd be tempted to tease Lucy about her competitive streak. To laugh at the goofy victory dance she does whenever her team scores a point. To flirt with the woman I have no business being crazy about, because I'm leaving.

And maybe sooner than I thought.

I mean, nothing's for sure, but I chatted with Dale earlier today. He asked how things were going, and I couldn't lie. They're smashing. My creativity has been on fire. I've already come up with six new sandwich recipes, and four of them have sold well this week, especially the apple and fontina cheese one that I've dubbed The Lucy.

People have been so intrigued by the name—and yes, the busybodies have definitely read into it, despite the fact I also called my cilantro-inspired sandwich The Marilee—that I ran the idea by Dale of naming the recipes after people on the restaurant menu too.

He loved it.

He also loved that things are going so well on my end. Even alluded to some "exciting things" being in the works on his. He'll let me know more when he can, but for now, he wants his "superstar" to keep moving forward with market testing.

And then his next comment kicked me in the gut. *"Sounds like you might only need a few more weeks of that, and then you can come home earlier than planned."*

Home. Why did that word feel so...wrong?

Lucy's laugh floats through the air again, and I stand, suddenly too warm near this fire. I need to walk.

Kicking off my loafers and peeling off my socks, I leave

them behind and walk toward the surf. The sun's a burning ball sitting on the horizon, and the breeze off the ocean cools me down in an instant. It's the middle of June but I've yet to experience a truly warm day, which is kind of how Hallmark Beach is. Never hot, never super cold.

Perfect, really.

Rolling up my pant legs to my knees, I wade into the water. When it hits my ankles, a delicious shiver rolls against my skin, a reminder of a thousand different memories of growing up here, away from the hustle of the city. Don't get me wrong—there are some things I love about L.A. But to experience *this* on a Friday night there, I'd have to first take off work (not easy), and then fight terrible traffic that would leave me flustered and grumpy before I even hit the sand.

A seagull squawks as it flies overhead, and the ocean's roar today is more like a mew. Someone calls my name, and I turn to find Mare coming toward me, a spare volleyball tucked under her arm. She waves at me with the other. "What are you doing way out here?" she shouts.

I'm not that far from the group, but I guess it probably does look like I'm off in my own world. I step closer to her, so I don't have to yell. "Just enjoying the peace and quiet." I look at her pointedly to emphasize the fact she is neither of those things.

Wading into the water too—apparently unconcerned about the jeans she's wearing—she laughs and tosses the ball at my head.

I easily catch it and bring it down to my chest. "Did you steal the game ball?" But when I peek back at the group, I see them still going strong.

Even from way over here, my eyes find Lucy. Take in her strong muscular legs in those cutoff shorts. The long hair flowing down her back—the same hair I had my hands in four nights ago.

When my eyes finally drift back to my sister, Marilee looks pensive. Like she sees more than I want her to and knows exactly what I was just looking at. What I was just thinking.

But then she shrugs. "I know you like volleyball. Thought we could toss it around a bit."

Ah, she wants to get me busy so I'll open up and talk. Using Mom's old tricks. I'm fully convinced that's one reason Mom starting cooking with me.

But, sure, I'll humor her.

"Come on, Squirt." I head back up the beach to where we can hear each other better and the water isn't soaking her pant legs.

She joins me and I hit her the ball. She does her best to volley it back, but a great sportswoman, she is not. Those hands were created for baking brilliant artwork, not spiking a ball. It's probably why Jordan had to prod her to stop playing with Ryder and one of his buddies and join the "big kids" game earlier tonight. But then again, the man never seems to see her flaws.

We pretend to be playing our own version of volleyball for a while, and I catch her up on my conversation with Dale.

"Wow. I wonder what things he has in the works?"

I have my suspicions, but don't feel like going into it now. "Guess I'll find out when he's ready to tell me." I overhand serve the ball her way.

She jumps up to slap it but misses. Laughs at herself when she falls to the ground.

I rush over to make sure she's okay, but she's smiling and sits upright. When I reach down to help her up, she stands and brushes off the seat of her jeans. Sand clings to the wet part of her pants, but she doesn't seem to care. "I think I might be done with volleyball for the night. Wanna take a walk?"

"Sure."

We start off walking south at a slow pace along the water's edge. We could head up to the boardwalk for more even footing but know from experience how clogged with tourists it gets around the late dinner hour.

As we pass by the volleyball game, Mare tosses the spare ball back toward the group, where it rolls and eventually stops. Ryder and his friend—who are building a sandcastle—shout and run for it. Mare waves at them before turning back to me. "So you might leave sooner than expected?" She's not judging me or guilt-tripping me with the question. She's just invested in the answer. Invested in me.

I kind of lucked out in the sister department. And I hate that it's taken me thirty years to really figure that out. On the one hand, leaving early means I won't have as much time with her. On the other, we're good now. We've made peace. Regarding Marilee, I've done what I came here to do. No matter when I leave, I know I'll be back. We're going to stay close.

It's not *her* I'm worried about.

"Maybe." My hands find the pockets of my pants. "Nothing's for sure."

"And how do you feel about that?"

I huff out a laugh. "There's no reason I shouldn't feel fine about it. I've got the recipes I came for. You and I are good." And yet. Nights like this are so rare back in Los Angeles. Nights when friends' laughter is on the air and I'm enjoying the outdoors instead of stuck inside in an office at the back of a crowded, noisy restaurant. Maybe it'll be different when I'm in the kitchen instead.

But even then, I'll be cooking for strangers. I won't have old ladies coming up to me in the kitchen and bugging me about eating my vegetables or finding a wife. Won't have young kids saying, *"Mr. Blake, can you pleeeeeease add extra cheese to my sandwich?"* with their gap-toothed grins. Won't have buddies stop by and invite me to hang out after work—because work won't end until midnight or later, and by that time, I'll be wrung out and exhausted.

But I'll be living my dream. The one I've had since I was a kid.

Beside me, Marilee just *hmms*, communicating without words like she's so good at doing. "And what about Lucy?"

That makes me stop and turn to face her. The sky's darkened, but I can still somehow see the meaning in her eyes, hear it in her tone. I grunt. "It'll be better for Lucy if I leave sooner than later."

She tilts her head. "You really believe that?"

I think about the desire in Lucy's eyes on Monday night. The trust I've finally earned. "If my truck isn't here stealing her business, she'll be better off."

"The Robin was already struggling before you got here." She holds up her hands. "I know it makes me sound like a bad friend to say that, but it's the truth." Then Marilee pauses, sighs. "I've seen the way you look at her, Blake. The way she looks at you."

She lets the words hang there between us before resuming our trek down the beach.

I follow in silence, my mind working overtime. My sister and I have never broached this subject in quite this way before, but I shouldn't be surprised she's doing it now. She's Lucy's best friend. She wants to protect her heart.

"I won't hurt her again, Mare."

"Oh, Blake." She crosses her arms, stopping again to stare up at the moon. "Why'd you do it the first time? I wasn't blind back then, just like I'm not blind now. I know you liked her. Maybe even loved her. So why'd you leave like that?"

How can I tell her without sullying her memory of Dad? "I had my reasons."

Then she surprises me. "She wasn't good enough for Dad, right?"

"What? No." But then I remember, Lucy's told her about the conversation she overheard. "It wasn't Lucy. It was any small-town girl."

"But Mom was a small-town girl."

See? This is why I didn't want to go here. "We don't have to talk about this if it's going to upset you, Mare."

It takes her a while to respond, but finally, she inhales sharply. "No." Her voice is soft. "I need to know. Was Dad... was he not happy with his life with Mom?"

"I don't think it was Mom. You know he loved her. But I think he regretted what marrying her meant. What he gave up, you know?"

"No, I don't know. Sure, he always talked about how his college roommate got that fancy job in New York after Dad turned it down to stay in Hallmark Beach, but..." She turns to me. "So he really warned you off of Lucy because he didn't want you to end up like him?"

What can I say? "He just wanted me to be the best I could be. To not get distracted, stay stuck in a small town because of a girl. To live a big life that means something. To be the best I could be."

"Wow." That word is full of fire—and fire isn't something I'm used to in Mare's voice. "That's so...short-sighted."

Definitely not the reaction I expected from her. "What do you mean?"

"I mean, have you ever thought that maybe Dad *was* the best he could be *because* of Mom? If he'd gone on to New York and gotten that job instead of working here as an insurance broker, we would not even exist. Did he think of that?" Now she's moving back and forth, and I'm a little scared she's going to set the sand on fire with the ferocity of her pacing.

Suddenly, she stops and spears me with a look. "Blake, Dad might have talked about regret and not wanting you to have the kind of life he did. But do you think that if he'd known he was going to die in that accident, he would have wished for one more job promotion—a 'bigger life'—or one more day with his family?"

The question rends the beachy air, hanging there, twisting and bending. Forcing me to look at it. Refusing to let me ignore it.

She continues, her voice softer. "I'm willing to bet, for all his bluster, that in the end, he saw what mattered most. And his biggest regret wasn't that he didn't live a big enough life. It's that he didn't appreciate how big the life he already had was."

Then my baby sister drops her proverbial mic and crushes me in a hug.

And leaves me with a lot to think about.

LUCY

If my life was a song, it'd be that old Alanis Morissette number about irony.

Because a month ago, I was avoiding home (and Blake) because I couldn't stand him.

But now, I'm avoiding it because five nights ago, I let him kiss me—and haven't been the same since. It's seriously all I can do not to think about it.

To not think about doing it again.

So here I sit on a Saturday morning in Winona's office, working on a business plan. Yes, I—Lucy Reynolds, with no college degree and no expertise of any sort except knowing how to keep a customer smiling—have spent the week working on a Green Robin business plan like Blake suggested, using the one he sent over as an example.

And I'm not saying it's good, but it's a start. A way to maybe make some sort of progress. The BOGO coupons have helped a bit, but it's still not enough.

Basically, until Blake's truck leaves, we're in trouble. And Winona has been texting me daily for updates. I'm afraid she's going to pull the plug on her trip—and I can't have that.

My phone vibrates on the desk, and I glance up. How long have I been here, staring at my computer? A few hours, at least. I grab my phone and see that Chloe's texted me.

Chloe: *I feel like I haven't seen you in forever! But we're still on for Wednesday, yeah?*

Crud. What's Wednesday? Tomorrow's Father's Day, so I know I've got time with the family all afternoon after the lunch shift. But what's later in the week? I flip to the calendar app on my phone and groan. Right. A spa day for the twins' birthday in Morro Bay, which is about thirty minutes from Hallmark Beach. I really shouldn't take the time off, but I could use a girls' day. Chloe isn't the only one I haven't spent quality time with. Sure, I was on the beach for the impromptu volleyball game last night, but left after an hour or so to—you guessed it— work on this stupid business plan some more.

Besides, I said I'd go. And my friends are everything to me. I have to be there for them.

Lucy: *I know, I miss you! Yep, I'll be there Wednesday. Can't wait!*

Setting my phone down again, I rub my temples and try staring at the business plan some more. What am I doing? I'm seriously no expert. Maybe I should just let Winona come home. This is her restaurant, after all.

But then a memory flashes—the last day of third grade. I came home from school, expecting Mama to be on the couch asleep or listlessly watching a soap opera like she had for the past year after Daddy had died. Instead, when I climbed from the bus steps and got to my house, she was waiting on the stoop.

She jumped up, and the first thing I noticed was her hair. She'd gone to the salon, had it cut and colored a bright red to match the pants she was wearing, along with a polka-dot blouse that made her look so pretty. She pulled me into a hug and asked if I was ready to go on an adventure.

My mouth fell open. "Really?"

"Yes, baby girl. I'm tired of being sad. And maybe that sadness is always going to be there. Maybe it's just a part of us now. But you know what? We're gonna ignore it from now on. We're gonna make lemonade out of the lemons life's given us." She took my backpack from my shoulders and slipped her arms around me and pulled me close so I could smell the vanilla and cinnamon on her skin. Then she walked me into the house, where there were two ratty suitcases, all packed and ready to go. "We're gonna outrun that sadness and start living our lives again."

And we did our best.

That summer, and every summer after, until I was fifteen, we drove her beat-up Civic all over the United States, always ending in Hallmark Beach.

They were the happiest memories of my life.

And I know that Winona and Jessica are making their own happy memories. I can't let them come home early. I can't fail her.

Pushing away from the desk with renewed vigor, I march down the hall past an empty restaurant—we don't open for another thirty minutes—and into the kitchen, where Tiny has already started working on a few dishes for the day.

He grunts at me. "You're here early again, Boss."

"I've told you." I saunter over to the first large stockpot and peek inside. Mmm. Chili. "Don't call me that." I grab a spoon and stick it inside and then laugh when he growls his displeasure.

"Don't go critiquing my food like you do that boy's."

Great. How did he hear about me helping Blake? I take a bite and smile. "No need. It's perfect."

"I know." The man rolls up his sleeves, revealing his beefy

forearms with an anchor tattooed on one bicep like a real-life Popeye the Sailor Man. "What do you want?"

"Aw, don't act like you don't love me in here."

"You in my kitchen spells trouble. Leave me in peace and quiet."

"You'd like that, wouldn't you?" I snatch his chef's hat and laugh when he simply grabs another off the fridge. He's no fun. "Seriously, though, I was wondering if you've got any more good ideas for specials this week. That seems to be helping move the needle a bit."

He stirs the chili and glowers at me. "I do, but you're not gonna like it."

"Oh? Why not? You know I'm open to anything."

"Why so desperate?" He blinks at me. "We in trouble, Boss?"

I try not to sigh. "Of course not."

"You think I'm dumb?"

"No."

He harrumphs. "Then talk to me straight. I know a stressed-out Lucy when I see one."

Aw, Tiny. I tap him on the chest with my spoon. "So you do have a heart in there."

He grabs the spoon and flings it over his shoulder into the sink. It clangs, shattering the quiet. "I'm serious. I have an idea for a special that would knock that boy's food outta the park."

That boy, as in Blake. My blood heats at the thought of him. Ugh. I clear my throat. "I'm all ears."

"You do still want to beat him, don't you?"

"Yeah..."

"Because last I saw—"

"Spit it out, Tiny." I know what people in this town think, especially after Blake went and named a freaking sandwich after me. "My loyalty is first to the Robin."

Though maybe I don't want Blake to fail like I did a month ago. So sue me.

Tiny continues stirring, considering me. Then he nods and strides to the counter, where he's got a stack of notecards—presumably recipes. He filters through the stack, pulls one card loose, and walks it over to me.

I stare at it. My gaze narrows. "Tiny, this is a grilled cheese recipe."

"And it belonged to my sister, may she rest in peace."

I never met his sister, but from his stories, he was close to her, and he remains close to his nephew, who is some hotshot hockey player that Tiny visits in New York at least once a year. In fact, that's why he won't be here for the Fourth of July.

"It looks delicious." Four different types of cheese. A few spices, hints of garlic. Yum. "But we can't serve grilled cheese. That's Blake's department, and he got his permit on the condition that he didn't serve the same thing we did."

Tiny shrugs. "We don't have anything in *our* permit that says we can't serve grilled cheese."

I hand him back the notecard. There's no way I'm doing that to Blake, even if he's my competition. Because he's also my friend. And besides, he's only here for another six weeks or so. We have to find a way to survive—and thrive—with or without him here.

And definitely without sabotaging him in the process. "Tiny, we can't do it."

His scowl clouds the whole kitchen, and he waves his dirty spoon at me. "That boy's gotten to you."

"No." My face heats, and it's not the chili's fault. "I just..."

"Lucy." My teen waitress, Jenny, comes racing into the kitchen. "I need your help now. One of the toilets is overflowing in the men's room. Help!"

Saved by a crisis! I press the notecard back into Tiny's

hands. "I love the initiative you're taking. Keep up the good work in here. We'll talk about this later, okay?" And we will. Mostly about how I can't undermine Blake, even if it makes me look weak.

But no time to think about that now, because here I go again, rushing off to try to solve yet another disaster that I feel unqualified for—because what am I? A plumber?

Then again, maybe I'd make a better plumber than a businesswoman. Because a good businesswoman probably would have jumped at any chance to squash her opponent. She'd see a weakness, a chink in the armor, and dive right on into the fray, not caring one bit what happened to the guy who'd stolen all of her customers.

But then I think about those BOGO coupons sitting on Blake's counter. About the way he helped me make baklava. About how it felt last night at the bonfire when he ignored me, trying to keep his distance despite the looks he kept sending my way.

And I know that my heart has already decided what my head can't comprehend. That Tiny's absolutely right.

And it's possible my inability to *not* fall in love with Blake Moffitt will be the downfall of The Green Robin.

BLAKE

My relationship with my dad was complicated. But Father's Day still hits hard every year since he's been gone.

"Thanks for closing up early today." Marilee sighs from the passenger seat of my dad's red sports car, which I've taken to driving around when I don't want to walk. "It was nice to go visit them together."

"Yeah, it was." I put the car into Park beside Lucy's Corolla, pull the keys from the ignition. The house's front window is dark, which probably means Lucy is in her bedroom. Possibly sleeping, given the late hour. Reaching over, I squeeze Mare's elbow. "I'm glad I was here this year."

And even though my sister and I are good, the same old guilt pricks me—because for the last five Father's Days, Mare has had to visit the cemetery alone. Or maybe Lucy's gone with her. She's a good friend like that. Regardless, I'm doing things differently now. Even after I return to L.A., I'll be back for the important stuff. Mare and I only have each other now, and I'm not going to abandon her like I did before.

We both climb from the car and pad up the porch steps, entering the house quietly so we don't wake a potentially

189

sleeping Lucy. But then I see that the back door is cracked, and I can make out her profile there on the porch swing. She's sitting in the dark, under a blanket of stars—and an old quilt of Mom's—and even though I know it would be better for us both if I went straight to my bedroom, her very presence is like a beacon, calling me, calling me home.

"I'm headed to bed. Early shift at work." It's Mare's turn to squeeze my elbow. "She likes hot chocolate."

I know what she's implying. Well, not even implying. Straight up saying in that Marilee way of hers. "I shouldn't." I say this without looking away from Lucy.

"Have you thought about what I said a few nights ago?"

I've tried not to, really, but of course, the wisdom in my sister's words has been locked in my brain for the last forty-eight hours. Still, I'm not any closer to knowing what to do with these feelings or thoughts.

So I simply shrug.

"If nothing else, will you check on her? She spent all day celebrating her uncle, and even though she probably won't say it, I think today's hard on her too."

I close my eyes. Of course. Lucy lost her own dad a long time ago, but that doesn't mean she's "more used to" the loss a day like today brings. Giving my sister a nod, I trudge into the kitchen and find the ingredients to make homemade hot cocoa.

Mare heads to bed while I work, and soon I've melted and whisked and waited until it's perfection. Pouring the cocoa into two mugs, I head for the back door and nudge it open with my foot.

Lucy's head jolts toward me. "Hey." Her eyes widen at what I'm carrying. "Did you make me something?"

"No, both of these are for me." I laugh when she sticks out her tongue, then gently hand off a purple-and-pink mug to her. "Mind if I join you for a minute?"

She shakes her head and shifts over a bit to make room for me, pulling the quilt toward her with her free hand. When I settle onto the swing—the wood creaking with my efforts—she flings the far edge of the blanket over my lap. The movement is so quick, so casual, that I know it's not calculated. She's not trying to get all cozy with me. She's just being considerate.

"Thanks," I say, angling my body so I'm facing her, one of my legs bent and resting on the bench, right up against her side. I start to move it, but then she looks up at me again, and I can't think of anything I want more than to be close to her. But right now isn't about that. Right now is about checking on her. Being her friend. "How are you doing today?"

Lucy purses her lips together and holds the mug between her hands. "Today was..." Her gaze finds the sky. For some reason, the light above us seems to reach farther tonight, like it's going on forever past the horizon. Maybe that's the thing about contemplating death and mortality and loss all day long. The expanse between this world and the next—the veil—doesn't seem quite as thick as normal.

Finally, Lucy finds her words. "Today was a lot of things. It was good to be with my family. That's always good. My uncle is kooky but a good man, and I love him. His goodness reminds me of Daddy—the little I remember about him, anyway." She takes a sip of the cocoa, hums as it flows down her throat. "I was so young when I lost him, that sometimes I wonder if I'm remembering him right at all. Or if I'm really just creating a version of him in my mind, you know? A version where he's all good, nothing bad, nothing annoying. I'm sure he wasn't perfect, and yet, I don't remember a single bad thing about him."

I'm silent, sipping on my own hot chocolate. Because in some ways, I wish my experience was like hers.

She looks over at me. "What are you thinking over there,

Flake?" Her nickname teases me, wrapping around my heart and squeezing.

I can't tell her. Can I? But she knew my dad. Knew the kind of man he was. A good man, when it all boiled down to it. One who would never have cheated on my mom or his taxes. One who supported his family with integrity, who helped out in the community, who despite his faults, did love us.

And yet, sometimes all *I* can think about is the bad.

What does that say about me?

"I'm more interested in what you're saying than in what I'm thinking."

"So that's how this is gonna go, hmm?" She just shakes her head at me, her finger tapping the porcelain surface of her mug. "Hardly seems fair. And here I thought we'd finally agreed to be friends."

Ugh, she's right. No matter what else Lucy is to me, I do want to leave Hallmark Beach with us being friends at least. And friends share—even when what's inside is ugly.

I sigh and force my gaze away from her. Up toward the sky, where I squint and stare at the patterns in the stars. When I see what I'm searching for, I lean toward Lucy. "Hey, look. You see? That's Ursa Major. The Great Bear."

"Really? I've never really seen a constellation before." Her hair brushes my shoulder as she tries to follow my line of sight. "Hmm. I'm not sure I'm seeing it."

I angle my body down a bit so I'm right up against her, can see things from her perspective. My finger traces the stars in the sky. "See it now?" My face turns toward her, and her hair tickles my nose.

"Maybe."

I drop my arm so my hand rests on my lap. "That's okay."

She sighs and lets her head fall back a little, and when it comes to rest against the edge of my shoulder, neither of us move away. We sit that way, drinking our hot chocolate, silently watching the stars for a while.

"I didn't know you were into astronomy."

"I'm not really. It was more Dad's thing." Probably a way he was able to "escape" Hallmark Beach without leaving the town limits. To dream of far-off places he'd forfeited by moving here. But I don't say that. Instead, I reflect. "He wanted both Mare and I to take up an interest in it too, but only I really did. I think..." My fingers tighten around the handle of my mug. "I think I was desperate to connect with him, you know?"

"Because you and your mom had cooking." She says this like it's a fact, like she's not even asking. Because she knows. She was there.

"Yeah. And he never really approved of that—"

"You don't think he liked that you cooked?"

"Oh, I know he didn't. He called it a waste of time." The memory of it vibrates in my mind. "Thought I should be using my time for a business or law internship or volunteering at the hospital or doing something that would eventually put me on the path to 'real success,' not something unstable. Cooking was too much like the arts for him. For most people, hard to eke out a living."

"Blake, that's awful. I'm sorry."

I shrug, and her head bobs a bit with the movement. Oops. "You know he always wanted me to get into sports—not because it would lead to a long-term career, but because it might get me a scholarship, connections I could use for the big career he had planned for me. That's the only reason I really played football, did track and baseball. I mean, sure, I enjoyed playing, but I was always itching to get back into the kitchen to experiment some more."

"You're really good at it. But I did like cheering for you from the football stands too."

The thought of that fires up my insides—though not as much as thinking about how much she enjoys my cooking. "Thanks. Either way, I'm grateful for your support." And I know I shouldn't, but I reach for her free hand and give it a friendly squeeze. But then, I just...don't pull away.

Neither does she.

I stare at our hands, an electric warmth pulsing through them, and clear my throat. What was I saying? Oh, yeah. "Anyway, as you know, he encouraged me to go to business school. To get my MBA. And I wanted to make him proud more than anything. But I think also...I kind of wanted to stick it to him. To show him that I could do something *I* loved—something that he didn't think had merit—and make it wildly successful."

"And that's why you push yourself so hard?"

"I guess so."

"But are you happy, Blake? Surely your dad wanted success for you because he wanted you to be happy. He had his faults, sure, but he wasn't a cruel man. He loved you guys."

Am I happy? "I guess I haven't really stopped to think much about happiness. The last decade of my life has been all about getting to the next thing, you know? Finishing one degree, then another. Apprenticing at the best restaurant I could. Becoming a manager so I could learn the ins and outs of the business. Putting together a business plan so I can reach the ultimate pinnacle—creating a successful restaurant. Maybe getting a cooking show. Dale said he knew some people, thought that could be a possibility." I close my eyes, suddenly tired at the thought of all I've done and all I still have to do. "But it'll all be worth it when I get there. When the dream is finally achieved."

Gently taking my empty mug from me, Lucy leans forward and sets it along with hers on the ground beside the swing. Then she turns to face me, one leg tucked under her, one dangling over the swing's edge. The moon and stars are streaming light onto her golden hair, and her blue eyes are reflecting their shine. "And *that* will make you happy?"

"You make me happy." That's what I *want* to say to her. The thought surprises me. Does being here with Lucy actually make me happier than the thought of achieving the dream I've had for more years than I can remember?

What would happen if I stopped striving? What if I just… stayed here in Hallmark Beach? Pursued something with Lucy? Gave up that "dream" of my own restaurant? Traded it in for something different?

Would I be happy then?

But Dad gave up his dreams for "happiness" and warned me against doing the same. Does that mean I'd have the same regrets?

My head starts to hurt. I blink the thoughts away. "Happy enough, I guess." Then I tilt my head. "What about you? What makes you happy?"

She tilts her head, and her ponytail swings to the side. "I'm not like you. I've never had some grand dream for my life. No steps to follow. I mean, I did intend to go to college, but then your parents died and…"

"You stayed for Mare."

Lucy shrugs. "And for me. I'm not sure I was going for the right reasons. I don't even know what I would have studied, you know? It just felt like I was stuck, like I should go do something more." Her fingers pick at a loose thread on the multi-patterned quilt. "Honestly, I've felt like that again lately. I mean, I'm doing my best to keep the restaurant going for Winona, but when she gets back, then what? I go back to being a waitress? But maybe that's okay. I don't know what else I'd do, anyway." She breathes out a sigh. "Maybe it's enough to just live my small-town life, love my people well, and enjoy the small quiet moments."

"Small quiet moments, huh?" That actually sounds nice. And I can't help but add, "Moments like this?"

She smiles, something soft and wistful and warm in it. "Just like this."

And suddenly, I wish that I was the kind of guy who *could* enjoy this moment here with her, without worrying about what comes next or what's expected of me or what I'd be giving up. Because Lucy deserves a guy like that—someone who will stay in the moment with her, soaking up every bit of sweetness and care she has to offer.

I want to be that guy.

I just don't know how.

LUCY

Ah. I definitely made the right decision in coming today.

Easing back into my lounge chair on the Seaside Spa's relaxation deck, I snuggle down into my white fluffy robe and sigh. "This is the life."

"Right?" April's in the seat beside me. Today, on Kelsey and Elisse's birthday, the sky's painted a vibrant blue, not a cloud marring its pristine surface.

On the other side of me, a spectacular view of Morro Bay opens up, the sparkling waters a deeper color than the world above but still shimmering like it holds a thousand winking secrets below its depths. A huge volcanic rock stands sentinel in the harbor, a guardian that makes this place both unique and beautiful.

My cousin shakes out her red hair and stretches her arms in a lazy way that reminds me of a cat. "That massage was probably one of the best experiences of my life."

"And you guys had tiny women." Across from us, Elisse cackles as she takes a sip of her champagne. "Imagine how Mare and I felt with our very brawny male massage therapists." She nudges Marilee, whose cheeks redden as she pushes her glasses up on her nose. "I'm going to have delicious bruises for daaaaays."

"Women can be strong too." Kelsey's quiet voice pipes up, a rare contradiction to her sister's more boisterous ways. "My massage therapist was small but mighty." Wincing, she rubs her shoulder and then tugs at one of the curls resting there.

"To strong women." Chloe raises a glass of her cucumber water. Of all of us, she looks the most at home in this fancy place, positively regal in her white robe, her blonde, perfectly highlighted hair flowing around her like a crown. This little birthday gathering wouldn't have been possible without her—she rented out the whole place and paid for every cent, claiming amidst our protests that it was her gift to us for being so kind when she first came to town and needed to throw a last-minute wedding for her brother.

I honestly think we made out like bandits in the bargain.

And hey, any excuse to try to forget my troubles for a day, right? To forget the pressure of the half-finished business plan waiting on my computer.

To forget the sweetness of that moment with Blake on the swing three nights ago. How I nearly begged him to stay—not just out there on the porch with me, but in Hallmark Beach.

To forget that wretched kiss from just over a week ago. The one I keep replaying in my mind. The one that I'm fairly certain will go down in history as the best kiss of my life despite its brevity and simplicity.

So, yeah. Thank the good Lord for distraction.

We all raise our glasses of whatever we are drinking—a bubbling Diet Coke in a fancy spa tumbler for me—and shout "hear hear" before taking sips and giggling. It's nice to be all together and to be celebrating. Since we're mostly all the same age (save April, who is two years younger and Chloe, who is a year older), I've celebrated every one of the twins' birthdays with them since I moved here. We were friends in high school, though not as close as we are now, when we naturally formed bonds because we all stayed in town after graduation.

Of course, the twins stayed because their family owns a local business. Loveland Winery is a staple around Hallmark Beach, producing some of the best wines in the whole state and employing lots of seasonal workers. They've also started hosting events on site, and there's talk of them building cabins on the property to have year-round guests as well—so long as Mrs. Loveland can get Mr. Loveland on board.

"What's the latest and greatest with everyone?" April says, her eyes bright despite the dark circles underneath. "I know I've been back for a few months, but I still feel so out of the loop." And it's no wonder. Other than me and Kelsey—her best friend from childhood—she really didn't keep in touch with any of us when she lived in San Francisco. She turns to Elisse. "You were working at Something Blue, right? But then you quit to work at the vineyard?"

"And I've convinced her to work with me again part time now that I'm running Something Blue." Chloe winks at Elisse, who rolls her eyes and pushes a strand of bobbed brown hair behind her ear.

"Yes, and by *convince*, she means she strong-armed me." She snatches up a food menu from the small circular table between her and Chloe and sends her a fake-as-all-get-out glare. "Don't let the pretty accent fool you. This one is a royal pain in the rear until she gets what she wants."

We all laugh, because if there's anything Chloe isn't, it's a pain. But Elisse likes to pretend everything annoys her, even if she'd die for any one of us. (And I have a sneaking suspicion she feels the same way about her long-time neighbor Landon Bennett, who's worked for her family for years. She never seems as ruthlessly alive as when she's verbally sparring with him. But don't dare say she's flirting, or she'll bite your head off and turn her wit on you instead.)

"For your information, I *didn't* get what I wanted." Chloe taps her manicured nail against her glass. "I wanted you to work for me full-time as an event planner, but you only agreed to be part-time coordinator for your family's property and a few others. Though I do plan to make full use of it." Her smiles shows she has no ill will toward anyone, least of all Elisse, whose loyalty to her family is one of the things we all love about her.

"Yeah, yeah." Elisse waves down our personal spa attendant, who is standing near the door into the white, wooden building where we all received our massages and are scheduled for facials after lunch. "I'm starving. Let's order."

The willowy woman in a beige shirt tucked into her black pants rushes over with a notepad, and we all spend a few minutes perusing the menu and placing our orders. I almost never branch out but decide to try a plate of sushi when Chloe gushes over how good it was the last time she was here.

Elisse raises an eyebrow at her sister when she orders a double cheeseburger, onion rings, and an Oreo milkshake.

"What? You only turn twenty-nine once," Kelsey says.

"That's not true," Marilee pipes up. "My mom turned twenty-nine like five times before finally admitting to us that she was really in her thirties."

Laughter comes easily now, and I wonder why I've spent so much time working when I could have been surrounded by my people. Because *this* is what life's about.

The attendant scurries away to give our orders to the kitchen, and we break into conversation about everything going on in our lives. About how Kelsey feels stuck in her job as assistant manager at The Purple Seashell, how she keeps thinking Aunt Janine will promote her to manager, but that

Janine is waiting to hear whether my older cousin Garrett—her only child from her terribly abusive, former marriage—is going to come home and run it so she can retire.

About how April's enjoying being back at the bookstore, because there's something reassuring in the familiar.

About how Chloe's itching for Freddy to ask her to marry him but doesn't think he will until their families both get more comfortable with the new relationship status—and each other.

The food's delivered and everything smells amazing, from April's pepperoni flatbread to Chloe's Caesar salad and my sushi.

Then my beloved friends turn their appraising eyes my direction, and I know I'm in trouble.

"Sooooo." And of course that's Elisse's antagonistic voice filled with perverse pleasure at my squirming. "How are things, Luce?"

"Fine." I slide my chopsticks from their wrapper and, unpracticed as I am, take a moment to orient my fingers. I'm like a baby with a fork for the first time. One chopstick slides from my hand, and I huff.

"Really? You seem...frustrated about something." Elisse cackles, and a few other friends giggle.

Ignoring them, I finally get a hold of the chopsticks correctly and lift a spicy tuna roll to my lips. The rice, seaweed, fish, and sesame seeds make an interesting dance in my mouth. I feel way more sophisticated than I am when the freshness of the tuna, the tanginess of the rice, and the spicy sauce dip and balance each other out.

After allowing myself to enjoy the bite and then swallow, I face my accusers with a lifted chin. I've gotta give them something true, or they'll never leave me alone. "If you must know, work has been all consuming lately."

They listen as I bemoan the restaurant's lackluster performance, my own attempts at making things better—that darn business plan, for one—and how I feel bad taking any time off or away. Thankfully, Tiny's holding down the fort on his own today, and I trust that he's going to do great even if we never did get back around to talking about what special he's going to offer each day this week.

When I finish, I pop another tuna roll into my mouth and chew.

"And that's all?" Oh no, not Kelsey too. She's not quite as teasing as her twin, but the way her voice lilts up at the end is all kinds of sunshine and hope. Whereas I don't mind giving Elisse a little grief, I hate to disappoint where Kels is concerned. "We were kind of hoping things might be happening on the guy front."

"I think Thomas Montrose might like me." And where in the world did *that* come from? I mean, sure, it's the truth. The sweet guy stops by the Robin now and again just to chat, to "make sure all is well," and I think it's nice.

My friends all glance at each other with shifty eyes and questioning looks.

"Well, yeah, that's been obvious for a while." Elisse waves her hand through the air. "What, do you like him back or something?"

"I don't know." I shrug a shoulder. Maybe I can actually get them off the scent of Blake. The idea of reliving our kiss—of having to tell them about his very sweet, very noble "rejection" —makes my stomach twist. Or maybe my gut just doesn't like this sushi. I push my half-full plate aside and grab my Diet Coke instead. "He's nice enough."

Chloe purses her lips. "I thought—"

"Maybe I *should* give him a chance." I mean, I don't want to, but my friends don't need to know that. Although, perhaps I really should. Maybe I'll end up with someone like Thomas.

After all, he's a good guy. Honest. A self-made businessman. And he loves Hallmark Beach just like I do. To my knowledge, *he* doesn't ever plan to leave. Not that I can say that out loud without raising suspicion. So I go for the catch-all that will describe Thomas's basic appeal. "There's nothing *wrong* with him."

"A ringing endorsement if ever I heard one." April shakes her head at me, then laughs almost hysterically. "There's literally zero chemistry between the two of you."

"Maybe chemistry isn't all it's cracked up to be." Oh no. Now my lower lip is actually shaking. *Stop it. Stop. It.* But my lip doesn't listen, and now my whole chin is joining in the fun. Argh.

I turn my head away from my friends, allow my gaze to take in the people strolling the boardwalk below where we sit on our raised decking. I don't know any of them. They're all in their own worlds, Air Pods in or head down and walking somewhere with purpose.

I wouldn't fit in here. I wouldn't belong. The only place I belong is Hallmark Beach. It's the only true home I've ever known, where the people are a comfort and a balm to my spirit —except in these moments when they flay me open with their directness. But even then, I know it's because they love and care about me.

My fingers slide around my torso, the soft robe calming my shaking hands.

And a tear leaves my eye and makes a trek down my cheek.

Before I know it, Mare has moved to my chair and is squishing me so she can sit beside me. April's reaching her hand across the expanse between us, squeezing my arm. Chloe and Kelsey plant themselves on the bottom half of my lounge chair, tipping the whole thing slightly their way.

And then Elisse squats between me and my view of the

ocean. She takes my cheeks between her hands gently. "Lucy," she says, the tease all gone. "What's going on?" Her words are sweet and soft and so very un-Elisse. At least on the surface. Under-the-surface Elisse is exactly this—standing between me and all the ways I try to hide the truth from my friends—and from myself.

These friends of mine make me face the lemons of life. Maybe it's not possible to ignore the pain, to just simply make lemonade like Mama said. But if there *are* lemons, I can trust that these girls will sit here and peel each one, biting into them and tasting their bitterness right along with me.

Mama might not be here, but these girls are. They're my family, and they aren't going anywhere.

Elisse releases my face and sits back on her haunches, waiting patiently. She's not budging.

I inhale sharply, release slowly. "I did a really stupid thing."

"We all do stupid things," Mare murmurs as she leans her head on my shoulder, and I wonder if she's thinking of Donny.

But there's a difference between being fooled by a con artist and willingly walking into a situation, knowing exactly what you're getting into—and doing it anyway.

"I..." I pinch the bridge of my nose. "I let Blake kiss me."

And that thought is all it takes for more tears to finally release.

Though they're not saying anything, I can practically hear my friends' concern, the questions they have (one of which is whether they need to throat punch Marilee's brother from this existence). Someone hands me a napkin, and I use it to dab away the wetness cascading down my cheeks.

And I tell them everything.

When I'm finished, spent emotionally and physically from the reliving of it all, I zero in on the pressure of their hands holding me, stroking my ankle, squeezing my elbow. They're anchoring me here, letting me be myself. Accepting me. "Thank you," I manage to whisper. "Thank you guys for loving me, even when I'm a mess."

"Are you kidding, Lucy?" That's April, my feisty cousin. "Have you met me?"

We all laugh, and it breaks some of the tension.

"Can I tell you something?" Elisse is all seriousness again, and it makes me sit up straighter. I nod. "First, I think you're taking too much on yourself with the restaurant. It's way beyond your job description, and ultimately, it's Winona's job to make sure her restaurant is flourishing." At my mouth opening to protest, Elisse holds up her hand to stop me. "I mean, feel free to continue with the business plan if you want to. But don't let the success or failure of it define whether *you* are a success or failure."

I inhale a trembling breath. "I just feel like I've never really achieved anything before. I'm surrounded by all of you with these fabulous and huge dreams, and...I don't know. I just feel inadequate. Like I should be doing more." Oh, that hurt to admit. There's a hollowness in my stomach that feels raw, cut. "Helping out Winona kind of felt like something bigger. A bigger purpose, I guess. But I'm failing at it."

"Trust me, you don't have to have big dreams to achieve something, Lucy." That's Chloe, and I know she understands more than most. "And you did something for me that nobody else ever did. You saw deeper. You saw me. And you welcomed me into your town, into your life without reserve. I don't think you understand how rare that is."

My other friends nod along, squeeze, hum.

"I agree with Chloe," Kelsey says. "But I do wonder..." She bites her lip, as if afraid to say the wrong thing. She doesn't want to hurt me, but maybe I need to hear what she has to say.

"What?" I ask.

"Well, if you really feel the way you do about Blake, then why are you letting him go so easily?"

My mouth flops open. "I'm not. He's the one who said he can't be with me."

"That's not true. From what you've told us, he just said he couldn't stay in Hallmark Beach."

I tug at the belt on my robe. "Kind of the same thing." Because he knows I'd never leave.

"Kels is right," Elisse prods. "Blake clearly has feelings for you too, but he knows he's leaving like he did before. Only this time, it seems he's got his head on straight and refuses to be someone who leads you on."

"All right, I changed my mind about him." April sighs dreamily. "He *would* make a good book boyfriend."

The others laugh, but my insides are roiling. Am I so used to being left that I just allow it to happen? Why don't I fight back? Why don't I ever go after what I want?

Maybe because I've never been given the choice before. Maybe because I don't even know what I want—or I'm too afraid to admit it.

The idea has me seriously feeling nauseous.

Or, ugh. Maybe that's the food after all.

twenty-one

BLAKE

Another spout of creativity took hold Monday morning—right after my small quiet moments with Lucy—and since then, I've lived, breathed, and (not) slept all things grilled cheese sandwiches.

I push a hand through my hair and slump against the back wall of my food truck, my eyes working to stay open while a final sandwich cooks on the grill top. The last three days—at least, I think it's been three days—have had my creativity in hyperdrive, and I've produced five new recipes that have gone on the menu.

Five new recipes I'm convinced will inspire rave reviews from critics once I implement them at the new restaurant.

A pang hits me in the temple, and I reach up to rub the spot. I really need to go home tonight at a decent hour instead of staying up until two a.m. experimenting in this tiny kitchen. I may only be thirty, but I've been abusing my body this week, spending hours of extra time on my feet, tensing with anticipation when I taste a sandwich that isn't quite right.

I've also been holding myself in place instead of running

next door to the Robin and feeding the experiment to Lucy so she can help diagnose what's wrong with it.

Reaching for my spatula, I flip the sandwich, let it cook a bit longer, then place it in the waiting basket filled with chips and a pickle. I turn, ding the bell, and call out "Painter!" before ducking back inside the truck. I start to shutter the window.

"Hey, Blake," a voice calls out.

Ducking down, I find Thomas there, collecting the sandwich. We haven't chatted for a while, except over text messages to go over a few details of the upcoming festival—which, believe it or not, is in two weeks from yesterday. "Hey, Thomas," I say, trying to hold back a fierce yawn that's itching to overtake me. "How's it going, man? You grabbing Chad's food for him?" The owner of Rainbow Ice was my last customer, but I don't see him anywhere.

"I'm good, and yeah, I was sitting at one of the tables while he waited for his order, but something came up inside. He asked me to grab this for him." Thomas shifts his sandwich basket from hand to hand, as if it's too hot to handle. The bottom of his bright blue Hawaiian shirt blows with a gust of wind that's picked up. "I actually was waiting for you to finish up so we could chat. Do you have a minute? I'll run this back to Chad and then...?"

The guy's now shifting his weight from one foot to the other, and his normal genial smile isn't present. My eyebrows go up. "Everything okay? My permits are still good through the end of the summer, right?"

Not that I know I'll be here that long. Dale and I haven't talked since last Friday and no decisions have been made, but his words about coming home early still reverberate in my mind.

"Oh, yeah, nothing like that." Thomas waits, eyes wide. "So...?"

"Sure. Let me close things down here, and I'll meet you at the Rainbow Ice tables in a few."

"Great." Turning like he's a soldier on a mission, the guy practically sprints away.

I shake my head and finish lowering the window shade, then flip off the stove and start to tidy up. My phone rings, and it's like Dale's heard my thoughts because his name appears on the screen. I hit speakerphone so I can keep working while I chat. "Blake here."

"Blake, good, glad I caught you." Dale sounds like he just hiked Mount Olympus. "Are you sitting down?"

"Should I be?" My stomach twists. Is something wrong with the restaurant deal?

And why is there a bit of relief at the idea?

"Kidding, kidding. But I do have some news for you. Excellent news."

"Wow." Trying to sound enthusiastic, I gather some spare disposable baskets and stack them. "What is it?"

"Remember how I mentioned my friend at a local network here?"

"Like TV network?" Of course, the second the words leave my mouth, I know I sound like an idiot.

Dale chuckles. "Yes, TV network. Anyway, they had a celebrity chef lined up to do a spot next Tuesday on the morning show, but he had to cancel due to a family emergency. I slipped my friend your name and resume a while back, and he said he'd keep you in mind for things like this." My business partner pauses. Meanwhile, my insides feel hotter than the stove, which is still putting off heat. "He wants you to fill in."

Whoa. My hands scramble for a rag in the sink, and I hastily wipe crumbs off the counter and into the small trash can I keep in the truck. I force my brain into business mode. Next Tuesday? That's not much time to come up with a recipe, to prepare. To drive to L.A., I'd have to close the truck for a few days...

Of course, I'd be back in plenty of time for the festival. That's the only commitment I actually have.

Still, my mind is spinning. "What exactly would it entail?"

"It's just a five-minute spot. You'd be showing fans how to make a dish for Fourth of July or their summer picnics. Of course, it's the perfect opportunity to show off a grilled cheese recipe you don't mind sharing with everyone."

There's chatter in the background. Is Dale spending his Wednesday evening at one of his restaurants? Probably. The man's as much of a workaholic as I am.

"Blake, this is your chance. We can plug the upcoming restaurant—at least hint at it—and you can prove yourself to be the charming guy I know is under all that starch somewhere."

Ha. "But that's not really me. I don't...pander. I just cook."

"Yes, well, if you want our restaurant—*your* restaurant—to be a raving success, you'll pander your pants off." At that, Dale chortles. "And if the network likes you, if the audience likes you, then my buddy says there are more opportunities. They're actually looking for a chef to do a podcast, a regular TV spot, plus—and this would be later this fall—a thirty-minute segment all his own. You could eventually be this generation's Wolfgang Puck."

"Uh." I clear my throat and yank at the collar of my shirt, then unbutton the top button. "Don't you think that's a little far-reaching?"

"I think the sky's the limit. What about you, Blake? Don't you want this? Don't you ache for the success this will bring? I know it's probably overwhelming, but these are the ways we create a dining experience people can't live without. That people will pay loads of money for. They'll be making reservations to taste *your* food a whole year in advance. Isn't that what you want?"

"Yeah. Of course."

But is it? I can't help but think of something my mom said once: *"Good food should be accessible to everyone."*

I've been so busy creating recipes here—which *is* what I came to Hallmark Beach to focus on—so Dale and I haven't really hashed out the details of the restaurant. I know he wants it to be more upscale than I do. Maybe now is the time to bring up our differences of opinion.

But then there's a knock on the back door of the truck. Right. Thomas. I've kept him waiting. "Okay, so Tuesday?" The five-minute spot doesn't sound too hard. I can at least commit to that much if it'll help the restaurant. Besides, it sounds like Dale's already told him I'll do it.

"Yes. You'll need to get in Monday afternoon. You sublet your room in the apartment, right? You can stay with me."

Of course I can. Dale is a perpetual bachelor, married to his work, and he's got a mansion in Beverly Hills. "All right. Text me the details and I'll see you Monday."

"Excellent." And with that, the call ends.

Another knock sounds. "Coming," I call as I hurry over to open the door.

Thomas is waiting on the grass. "I thought maybe you forgot."

"No, I just got a business call." Taking the steps, I turn and close the door, then follow Thomas to an empty table outside Rainbow Ice. Many of the others are occupied by families and couples. From here, I can see through the alley to the beach, where the stars light the way to the busy boardwalk, the sand, the ocean. "Sorry to keep you waiting. What's up?" The conversation with Dale may have woken me up, zinging adrenaline through my whole body, but I'm just waiting for the inevitable crash and would prefer to be home when that happens.

Thomas drums his fingers on the white resin tabletop. Then he stills abruptly. "I'm just going to come out and ask, man to man." He huffs. "Are you and Lucy...together?"

I sit up straighter, wide awake now. "Why?"

The guy kind of shrinks at the sharpness of my tone. "Look, if you are, that's fine. Great. I'm...happy for you." He swallows. "But if you're not, then I'd like to ask her out. But I didn't want to step on any toes." His hands make fists, and he pounds them lightly on the table. "So. Is there something between you that I should be aware of?"

Oh man. I want to punch this guy. To stand up, beat my chest, and scream that Lucy is mine and he'd better stay away. My insides tighten and shrivel. My lungs constrict. What is happening to me? Why do I feel on the verge of something like a panic attack?

Thomas is a good guy. Honestly, what man that I know in L.A. would even bother to ask before encroaching on another guy's relationship? He may be a bit odd, kind of a misfit who tries too hard, but at his core, Thomas Montrose is an upstanding citizen. He's well established. As far as I know, the citizens of Hallmark Beach like and respect him.

And he's just the kind of guy who would treat Lucy well.

I should say no. That there's nothing between us.

But I can't. Instead I sit there, staring the man down. If I were Superman with his laser vision, Thomas would be a heaping pile of ash right now (a bit gory, but that's the direction my thoughts have turned).

And in my silence, Thomas sighs, nods. Holds out his hand. "I thought as much. But I had to be sure."

What? I didn't say anything. But according to the flat line that Thomas's grim lips are making, my silence said something.

I let him grip my hand, shake it, and let go, then watch him walk away, hands in his pockets, head bent.

I blink. That wasn't right of me. I should have told him the truth—but the truth stares me right back in the face.

I don't want any other man to have Lucy Reynolds. To take care of her. To spend small quiet moments with her.

Because I love her.

Or, at least, I could, if I let myself.

But there's all the stuff Dale just told me. The restaurant, my career, in motion. Things swirling and moving. The pressures, building and mounting.

I can't stay here, can't let things fall apart there. I've worked too hard to reach my dreams to just...give them up.

But somewhere along the way, Lucy became part of that dream. And I don't know how to reconcile the two parts. Maybe, though...maybe it's possible to have both. Somehow. Maybe I could take whatever time I have left here in Hallmark Beach and spend it with Lucy.

Spend them seeing if this thing between us could grow. If we could figure something out.

Because I have the sneaking suspicion that my sister was right about regrets. Of course, I'll never know for sure what Dad thought in those last minutes of his life flashing before his eyes. But I do know that if I never explore what this is with Lucy, I will probably regret *that* all of my life—no matter how successful my life ends up being.

And I have to find Lucy *now* and tell her how I feel before I lose the nerve.

twenty-two

LUCY

I feel like death.

Death that's been dead for a while. A looooong while. Death just lying here, next to the toilet, festering and nasty.

Turns out, my stomach does not like spicy tuna rolls. Or at least, ones that must have had bacteria of some sort on them. Because for the last six hours, my stomach hasn't felt right.

And for the last two, it's been expelling every bit of everything I've eaten or drunk today. Maybe yesterday too, if that's possible.

Ugh. Okay, Lord, take me now.

I press my forehead against the cool tile of the hallway bathroom floor. If someone were to walk past, they might assume I was simply doing yoga, because I'm killing the child's pose here with my knees tucked under my body, my arms splayed out in front of me.

But nobody else *is* here right now. Blake's probably still working, and Marilee is watching Ryder because Jordan is running an overnight campout.

And that's good, because I wouldn't want either one of them seeing me like this.

My stomach rumbles and heaves again, and I sit up—my vision swimming before me—and force my hair back before hurling into the toilet. Seriously. How is there anything left?

I can't help the tears that come as I ease myself back and lean my head against the wall opposite the toilet. Food poisoning is seriously the pits.

When I first got home from the spa day, I knew something was off, so I lay down on the couch and fell asleep. But the sleep was fitful—full of memories from today, the well-meaning words of my friends—and I woke up with my stomach feeling just as knotted and jumbled as my heart.

And in between rounds of barfing, Kelsey's words bang around in my brain: *"If you really feel the way you do about Blake, then why are you letting him go so easily?"*

I want to laugh (but that would hurt), because nothing feels easy at this moment.

And then, as I sit there in the dim light with tears streaming down my cheeks, I hear the front door creak open. It has to be Blake. Oh no. He can't see me like this.

Then again, I don't have the energy or strength to shut the bathroom door, even though it's only two feet away.

"Lucy?" he calls from down the hall, where I hear his keys clatter into the metal bowl on the foyer table. "You here?"

I manage to groan, though I half suspect it sounds like a dying cat, and when he appears in the doorway—his shirt-sleeves rolled to his elbows, his khaki pants sporting a tiny grease stain—my tears flow faster.

And it's not because he's seeing me like this.

It's because I'm...relieved.

Not what I expected to feel at all. But I do. Relief that someone more capable than me (at the moment, anyway) is here to take charge.

To take care of me.

His features flicker with concern. "What's wrong?" He lowers himself beside me and presses the back of his hand against my forehead. Ahhh, it feels even cooler than the tile. "Baby, you're burning up."

Did he just call me...?

Aaaaand my body chooses that moment to vomit again. All over Blake's shirt.

How mortifying.

"I'm so sorry," I sob, and lie down so my head is once again on the floor.

"Shhh, it's okay."

I feel his hand stroke my back, and the touch is so tender I want to die. (I'm sensing a kind of morbid theme going on in my brain tonight. Guess that's what being sick brings out in me.)

But I can't believe he's still here, honestly. My head throbs.

He rustles around for a moment, and I hear something swoosh onto the floor near the door. Peeking up, I see his balled-up shirt lying there. Then, with gentle hands and a "Come here, Sunshine," he's easing me up, pulling me between his legs, and leaning my head against his chest, which now sports a white T-shirt that must have been underneath the dress shirt. The cotton is soft and worn against my cheek, and it smells like butter and sage. Like home.

"When did you start feeling sick?" he murmurs.

"A few hours ago. I had sushi at the twins' birthday and..." My stomach rumbles again. I shut my eyes and manage to stop the room from spinning around me.

"Have you had any fluids since this started?"

I shake my head. "I don't think I could keep anything down."

"Will you try for me? It's important to stay hydrated."

I whimper at the idea but nod anyway. For him.

"Good girl," he says as he smooths my hair, which probably

has puke in it. Sweet macaroni, if this isn't enough to scare away the guy I've finally admitted to wanting, I don't know what will. "I'll be right back, okay?"

No. I don't want to be alone again. I slide my hand from his chest to his taut waist, wrapping myself around him like a pretzel.

He chuckles. "I just need to go get you some meds and Gatorade, okay?"

I shake my head. "Don't leave."

Blake kisses the top of my head. "I'm not going to leave you, Sunshine." His words feel more meaningful than they probably should. He's not talking about forever. He's talking about right now. Because I'm sick.

And yet, my stupid heart chooses to find some semblance of hope in his phrasing anyway.

"I promise I'll be right back," he continues.

"Okay," I manage.

"Good girl," he says again, and I lean forward so he can stand up.

While he's gone, I throw up again. Twice. Somehow, I manage to stand on shaky legs in front of the bathroom mirror. *Must brush teeth.* Reaching for my toothbrush, I close my eyes against the rising nausea. This was probably not one of my better ideas.

Opening my eyes again, I take a good look at myself. Holy cow. I forgot that I stripped down to my spaghetti strap shirt and put on my comfy pajama shorts. My hair's a rat's nest, my makeup long gone—literal tear tracks mapping their way down my cheeks—and I look pale and worn out, like I imagine a new mom might, but without the glow of motherhood to back her up.

Blake appears behind me. "What are you doing?"

"I look terrible." That's not what I meant to say, but my

brain is so muddled, and my stomach hurts, and I just hate feeling weak like this.

I start to cry again.

"Aw, Sunshine. It's gonna be okay. I've got you." Before I know what's happening, Blake scoops me up and holds me against his chest as we leave the bathroom and make our way to the couch, where I can see he's made a little nest for me of blankets and pillows. There's an old emesis basin sitting on the coffee table, along with some water, some grape Gatorade, and the ugly pink of a Pepto-Bismol bottle.

With slow movements, he lowers me onto the couch and leans down beside me. Pulling a blanket over me—I'm suddenly shaking—he smooths back my hair and looks me in the eyes. "And you don't look terrible. Even sick, you are the most breathtaking woman I have ever seen." Blake pauses, tilts his head. "And when you are all better, we're going to have a talk about what that means, okay?"

I shiver and tuck my chin under a quilt my Aunt Bea made. "Okay." Bossy Blake is back, and I couldn't love it more, even when he makes me take the medicine—and I vomit it up—and drink fluids until I can hold them down.

All through the night, he takes care of me until my stomach finally settles and I can sleep.

I wake up once in the middle of the night, squinting through the dark to find him sitting on the opposite end of the couch, my feet on his lap, his fingers resting on my toes, where I vaguely remember him giving me a massage at some point. His head is leaned back against the couch cushions, and a little snore rumbles in the back of his throat.

He kept his promise. He didn't leave.

And foolish though it might be, my heart dares to keep on hoping. To keep holding onto his words: *"When you are all better, we're going to have a talk about what that means."*

twenty-three

BLAKE

Tonight, it's go big or go home—because I'm telling Lucy how I feel.

If I can manage to get her alone, that is.

But at the moment, it feels like the whole town is here on the beach outside of The Purple Seashell, where Chloe is throwing the festival planning committee (and their families and possibly all their friends too) a "soiree" to say thank you for all of our hard work. That feels like too fancy a word for the cookout and volleyball game going on right now, but I guess when you're from a European country, everything's fancy.

You'd think that my feelings for my sister's best friend would have been abundantly clear two nights ago when I came home and had the privilege of being the one to literally care for Lucy, but I haven't said the words yet. Mostly because I wanted her to be fully recovered from her food poisoning, which—given the way she's chowing down on a burger with Marilee at a table not too far from where I'm in line to grab a drink—she thankfully is.

But also, the last twenty-four hours, I've hardly been home again. In addition to running the food truck like normal (though

I shut down early tonight, obviously), Dale and I have been texting and calling back and forth about the upcoming TV spot on Tuesday.

Still, now that Lucy is better and *here*, I'm not losing my nerve. And I'm not wasting another minute.

Literally.

Abandoning the line, I beeline for her table, and when she glances up, her eyes widen. "Flake. Hi." Is it my imagination, or does she run her tongue over the teeth underneath her upper lip?

"Hey, ladies." I speak to both of them, but my eyes are only for Lucy. I'm sure my sister will forgive me once she realizes I urgently need to talk to Lucy.

But then Jordan comes running up with a volleyball, punching my arm. "Dude, there you are. We need your help." He gestures back to the sand volleyball pit, where Elisse, Kelsey, and a handful of other women are facing off against Frederick, Landon, and, I assume, Jordan. "The girls are slaughtering us."

I glance back at Lucy, who's got an amused look on her face. But when I open my mouth to protest, she takes a swig of her Diet Coke and nudges my sister. "Should we go join in the fun, Mare?"

Marilee shakes her head, her bun bobbing. "Oh no, I'll just watch."

"Aw, come on, Lee." Jordan winks at her. "You'll help even out the sides."

"How dare you talk to my friend like that," Lucy says in mock anger. She stands up and pulls Marilee to her feet, and my eyes can't help but linger for a moment on her powerful legs in those jean shorts again. Her high ponytail swings over her shoulders that are both delicate and toned at the same time.

Marilee, for her part, is laughing, good-naturedly accepting Jordan's teasing. "Fine, fine. I'll play."

"Let's show them who's boss," Lucy says as she starts to drag Mare away. Then she looks back at me and Jordan. "Coming, boys?"

There's a glint in her eyes, the way she's beckoning me—commanding me—with a single glance that makes her just about the sexiest woman I've ever seen. No way I'm turning down that challenge. I crack my knuckles. "Guess it's up to me to take you down."

"Oh, you think so?" Now Lucy's rounding, stepping right back up to me, and we're toe to toe in the sand. It reminds me of when she cornered me in my food truck a month ago—back when we were enemies.

How much has changed.

There's always been a charge between us, but now it's crackling like lightning that knows it's about to be released. The energy is palpable, exciting.

Filled with possibility.

And I crave it. I want to pour it into my veins and explode. Lucy does that to me.

I lower my face so it's within a few inches of hers. "I *know* so."

She lifts on her tiptoes and places her hands against my chest—and a bunch of tiny explosions begin. I can hardly stand another moment without kissing this woman. The words I've wanted to speak to her for the last two days nearly fall from my loose lips.

Her own lips nearly skim the shell of my ear as she whispers, "I'd like to see you try to take me down."

And that's it. No way can I go stand on a volleyball court and pretend like all I want is to flirt with her from afar. I want so much more with Lucy.

My hands fall to her waist, and it's my turn to whisper something to her. "Challenge accepted." And with that, I press the tiniest of kisses to her earlobe.

She gasps, and the sound only reassures me that this is good, and right, and real.

Even though I'm fully present in this moment with her, I sense the gaze of others, starting with Jordan and Marilee. One glance at them shows they're frozen, watching us with wide eyes.

Grinning, I grab Lucy's hand. "You guys are going to have to excuse us for a minute. We'll be right back." Though I actually hope not.

Before they can say anything, I tug Lucy away, toward the cliffs abutting the beach just north of the inn.

"Blake," she hisses. But she keeps trailing me.

I stop and turn, taking the opportunity to not just grasp her hand, but entwine every other finger of mine with hers. "Sunshine, if you don't want to come with me, I understand. But I need to talk to you. So...please?"

She bites that lip I'm dying to kiss again, and nods. Behind her, the sun is sitting on the horizon, preparing for another glorious sunset. The Hallmark Beach gossips are probably watching, having a field day with the way we're sneaking away. But I don't care about them.

I only care about her.

What a strange and new sensation. If I'm not careful, I'd give up everything for this woman. I can't quite do that—after all, I'm still the logical Blake I've always been, and I still have Dad's words in my ear. But no longer can I pretend like those dreams of nebulous "success" are enough either.

I want to see if it's possible to have both.

Want to see if Lucy is willing to try.

Finally, we reach the sandstone cliffs, where we'd find a

perfect overlook for the coming sunset if we climbed to the top. But I don't want to be up there for the world to see—both the crowd gathered on the beach and anyone who happens to be at the marina just north of here.

I want a world that's made up of just me and Lucy.

So I steer us straight for an outcropping in the reddish brown rocks, where the sun's rays only peek between, where the sand is dark and cool, where the air is damp. When we get there, tucked away from everyone else, even the sound of the ocean is muffled as I turn Lucy to face me, pressing her gently back against the wall.

There's enough light that I still see every one of her perfect features. The bumps in her hair from where she threw it up in a rubber band. The slight upturn of her nose. The freckle at the corner of her mouth. The way she's biting her lip, like she wants to speak but isn't sure what to say.

And the questions in those eyes that I once thought were icy blue but have since come to think of as Lucy Blue. Wholly, utterly belonging to her and only her.

Inhaling a breath, I place one hand next to her head and step closer. "Hi."

"H-hi." The word skitters out in that adorable Southern accent—the one that becomes stronger when her emotions are heightened, whether anger or otherwise—and her nose scrunches. "What are we doin', Blake?"

"We"—I pause—"are standing here."

She snorts. Atta girl. "I mean..."

"I know what you mean. And *I* meant what *I* said." With my free hand, I slowly move my finger along the strap of her tank top, mesmerized by the soft skin of her shoulder. "We're standing on the precipice of something, Sunshine. Something that started a long time ago. Something I fought. Something I'm still not..." I frown, blink.

Am I doing the right thing here? Because I don't have a plan. Not really. I only have a hope. But I don't want to hurt Lucy, to promise something I can't deliver.

"Hey." She lifts her hand to cover mine. "I never thanked you for the other night. For taking such good care of me."

Is she kidding? "What other option did I have?"

She flinches, and I realize how that might have sounded. "That's not what I meant." I blow out a shaky breath. "I meant...Lucy, no matter what I've done to convince myself otherwise, I can't help but be drawn to you." Crap. I'm ruining this. I groan. "And I realize that sounds like Mr. Darcy saying how much he wishes he didn't like Elizabeth Bennet—"

She raises her eyebrows in amusement.

"What?" I chuckle. "I have a sister. She forced me to watch my share of romcoms and Jane Austen."

Tilting her head, she's biting back a laugh herself. "You may proceed."

"Don't know if I should," I tease. Only Lucy can make me feel better about how utterly bad I am about sharing my feelings. "Next thing you know, I'll be saying ten things I hate about you." Shaking my head, I turn her hand around and grasp it, lowering our clasped fingers toward my chest. "But in all seriousness, Lucy, my stupidity in staying away from you—back twelve years ago, and this whole last month—has nothing to do with *you*. With your quality. With you not being good enough. Honestly, you're *too* good for me. You always have been. I don't deserve..."

Her eyes have gone misty, and she squeezes my hand. An encouragement to keep going. She's not running away screaming—or laughing—so that's something, I guess.

Here goes nothing. "I don't deserve you, and yet, I want you. I want this. I want to see if there's something here that can last." My heart's going crazy in my chest, and I'm sure she can feel the wild beating going on inside. "If we can ever want the same things."

Lucy's tongue flicks across her bottom lip, and I can practically see the gears moving in her brain. She presses her eyes closed, then open again. "I'm not going to lie, Blake. That really scares me."

"It scares me too. In a lot of ways, it would just be easier..."

"To walk away. To pretend like..."

I feel a tug on one of my belt loops, so I acquiesce to her call, closing the distance between us. Now my whole left arm—from palm to elbow—presses against the rock wall, and our bodies are flush against each other. Leaving her hand pressed against my chest, I fit my right hand underneath her jaw, my index finger curled there, tilting her face slightly upward. My thumb softly rests against the point of her chin. "Like we don't..." I lift the pad of my thumb, letting it glide across her mouth.

She shudders. "Like we aren't..."

My head sinks down, closer to hers, and I can't think, can only breathe and smell and feel Lucy—all of her. Physically, emotionally. She's all here with me, and I'm all here with her. "Like I'm not crazy." The tip of my nose skims hers, then slides down the side and along her cheekbone, where my mouth hovers over that freckle. "About." I press a soft kiss there, and her breath vibrates out.

In response, her hands both find their way to my waist, and her fingers tuck themselves under my shirt, grazing the skin just above my belt.

I finally move my mouth along her cheek, kissing my way to her ear as her fingers dig into my skin. And when I kiss a ring around her ear, I can feel both of us near the boundary we've always set for our emotions, about to break with wanting. The slow burn has us both in flames.

Pulling back, I look her in the eyes. There's a haziness there, a drunkenness I recognize in myself. "You," I finally say.

Then I'm plunging in, kissing her with all the pent-up passion I've held back for so long. My hands cup the back of her head and I'm angling my mouth deeper, and she's gripping my back, arching toward me, giving as much as I am. Then I'm tugging the rubber band from her hair so I can sink my fingers into it, plunging and stroking like I wanted to do that night in the kitchen while I nip her bottom lip and kiss her neck and revel in the glory that is Lucy.

"Blake," she groans as she moves her hands up my chest and around my neck, leaning back and letting the rocks hold us both up. I suddenly worry that it's too rough for her, so I flip us around and now the rocks are against my back and Lucy is leaning into me, reaching up on her tiptoes to kiss the stubble on my jawline.

I can't help but release the deep rumble in my chest when she lets me slide my hands along the curve of her waist as she tugs my head down and nibbles the lobe of my ear. How did I get this lucky, to be the guy that this goddess of a woman—this perfect girl next door, with the temper and the goodness and the loyalty and the forgiving nature of a saint—would allow me to touch her?

It's utterly unreal, but I want to spend every hour of my life showing her how grateful I am.

"Lucy." I say her name again and again, as I kiss her eyebrows, her eyelids, her nose, each corner of her mouth. Then I give her lips the softest kiss I can manage. "Lucy."

She must hear the difference in my tone—that there's something I need to say—and her eyes flutter open. "Hmm?" she says in the sweetest way, like she's just waking up from a dream.

Me too, Sunshine. Me too.

"Lucy, I don't know what happens from here." I pull her against my chest and stroke my hand down her arm. "But I want to find out."

"I do too," she whispers. Then we're still for a while, and finally she speaks again. "And I know you're still leaving at the end of the summer. That scares me. But we have some time to figure this out, right?" Her hold around my torso tightens.

Maybe I should tell her that there's a small chance I'm leaving earlier than planned. But nothing is set in stone, and I don't want to ruin this moment with *what ifs*. Once I know anything for sure, I'll tell her. "Right."

She looks up and pulls me in again for more kissing. I happily comply.

Finally, when we're both exhausted and breathing hard, I gently push us away from the rock wall and hold her at a distance—much to Lucy's whimpering protest, which makes me smile.

"We should probably get back out there before our friends send a search party."

"Let them."

I curl a strand of her hair around my index finger. "I don't know about you, but I kind of want to keep this in a little bubble for a while. To keep you this way all to myself."

"Good, so we're agreed. More kissing." She takes a step closer, and I chuckle.

"I do like that idea. But..."

She sighs. "I know. We should probably pace ourselves." Then she points at me. "But I don't have to like it."

"Believe me. If it were up to me, we'd never leave this spot. But since we are..." I loop my fingers through hers. "There's a question I've been wanting to ask you for a long time. Like, about twelve years."

She tucks away a smile. "Oh, yeah? And what's that?"

"Would you like to go on a date with me? Tomorrow, maybe?"

"Boo. I have to work tomorrow until late." She smiles. "But what about Sunday? I'm off then."

It stinks to have to wait, but it gives me more time to figure out the perfect plan for her. "Sunday works."

"Can you afford to close up shop that day?"

She doesn't know yet that I've pretty much gotten all the data I need now. That I don't have to keep the food truck running every day. But I don't want to go into that just yet. "Definitely."

Her smile turns shy. "I can't wait."

My heart shifts inside me, and I want to give her the world. Still, I can't promise her that just yet. But I can give her a date. A really good date.

I kiss her knuckles. "I can't either, Sunshine. I can't either."

twenty-four

Fear has never quite felt like this before.

Because this is the best first date I've ever been on.

I allow myself to stare at Blake from the passenger seat of his dad's sports car. There's something carefree and wild in the way he's sitting with the window rolled down, his elbow propped on the sill. He's wearing shorts, a T-shirt, sandals, and sunglasses. Wind whips through his hair as he drives Highway 1 down the California coastline, his fingers tapping on the steering wheel along with the Tim McGraw song on the radio.

I've never seen him so relaxed. So at home. Ever since our kiss—kisses—on Friday night, I've wondered if the magic would disappear. If he would. If I was too much, or if now that he'd gotten me out of his system (twelve years is a long time to wait for a kiss—what if he built it up in his mind and it wasn't as great for him as it was for me?), he'd change his mind about this date.

But from the moment he picked me up at my bedroom door four hours ago, we've laughed together, chatted about nonsense, and had a great time. First, we stopped at the local gas station and snagged a variety of road trip snacks (peanut butter M&Ms

and sour gummy worms for me, Red Vines for him). Then we grabbed lunch at this hole-in-the-wall Mexican place a few towns up the highway that had the best guacamole I've ever tasted. We spent the whole meal trying to dissect what made this green stuff so good, so we can try recreating it at home.

After that, a farmer's market—with everything from home-made jams to fruits and veggies, clothing, arts, and crafts—was the perfect place to slow down and peruse while holding hands. And only holding hands. Blake hasn't attempted to kiss me or show any more physical affection since Friday.

I both love and hate it.

Love it because he clearly wants more than just the physical with me. Hate it...for obvious reasons. Kissing this man exceeded all of my expectations, and I want nothing more than to revisit his lips for Round 2. (Or Round 3, technically, if we're counting that first kiss in the kitchen.)

Maybe today I'll get my chance.

He hasn't told me where we are going—just teasingly told me to have patience—but at this point, I'd go anywhere with him.

Which again, comes back to the whole fear thing.

I don't usually let fear control me or my emotions, and I think it's because I don't dwell on the negatives of life or the *what ifs*. I've learned to accept the bad with the good—like with my mom being gone. It's as if with her, I keep low expectations so that if she does surprise me, I just feel happy.

You don't have anything to lose when you keep low expectations.

But with Blake, I've somehow allowed myself to *expect*, to hope probably more than I should. It's ridiculous, I know—and possibly stupid, given the fact I know he's leaving at the end of summer—but I am already extremely attached to this idea of *us*.

Sweet macaroni, I have a whole heap to lose.

He finally must realize I'm staring at him, because he turns his head slightly. "What?" he says through a smile.

"You're just kind of hot, that's all." I take a sip of my Diet Coke and turn my attention to the scenery, which is all rounding curves, and seaside cliffs, and brilliant blue skies, and a stretching majestic ocean.

"Is that right?" Blake reaches across the center console and grabs for my hand. "Right back at ya."

We sit like that for a while as the country music station (which I picked) plays song after song. Despite my tone-deafness, I can't help but hum along.

"What got you into country music?" he asks.

"I'm from Texas. Duh." I laugh but snuggle into my seat. This vehicle may be old, but Mr. Moffitt kept it in premium condition. It's sturdy and comfortable, and I can't help but think how it reminds me of Blake. How different it is from the junker that Mama and I took on so many summer road trips. The one that rattled and bumped whenever we went over fifty on the freeway, that we prayed more than once would make it to our next stop.

The memories put me in a more sober mood.

"Sunshine? You still with me?" He squeezes my hand, then lets go to turn the volume on the radio knob down.

"Sorry." Greedily, I reclaim his hand in mine. "I was just thinking about the road trips I used to take with Mama."

"Tell me."

His invitation is soft, not at all demanding, and so I tell him about the wonder of ice cream at ten a.m. About seeing a herd of elk standing in the street and stopping for hours just to stare and watch them pass. About songs sung at the top of our lungs, endless talks about boys...wringing every ounce of happiness from every day that we could.

"There was never any time to be sad, even if we missed

Daddy." I sigh. "The year before the trips began was the worst of my life. Mama couldn't get out of bed. She didn't want to. If I hadn't fed her, made sure she drank water, brushed her hair..."

"I'm sorry, Lucy. That's a lot for anyone to handle, much less a young girl."

"I didn't feel so young." And for the first time, I allow myself to go back there, to ache for that girl whose carefree childhood was stolen from her in many ways. To dip in my toe and get a sense of how deep the sadness really runs. I have a feeling if I ever fell in, I might drown.

I shiver and draw strength from Blake's steady presence. From his hand in mine.

"No wonder you care so much about The Green Robin. About Winona having that same kind of experience with her own daughter as you had with your mom." He brings my hand to his lips and, eyes still on the road, kisses my fingertips. "I don't think I've ever known someone as loyal as you, Lucy Reynolds. You'd do anything for your friends."

His praise warms me through. "I'd be nothing without them."

"I envy you that." Blake puts on his turn signal and takes the exit ramp, crossing under a bridge and heading west toward the ocean.

"What do you mean?"

He pulls into a tiny parking lot with a gorgeous view of the Pacific just beyond and a trail that leads down toward a beach. Blake puts the truck in Park and turns to face me. He pushes his sunglasses up his forehead, which makes his hair stick up in a few places. It makes him look vulnerable. "Other than Dale, I'm not sure I have any true friends back in L.A."

"Why is that?"

He frowns. "First, school was my life, and the food truck business on the side. Then, there was the apprenticeship, and that was all I thought about. And finally, it was the restaurant where I worked."

"What about your co-workers? And surely you dated some." I try to say it casually, but on the inside, I have to mentally put away the claws at the thought of any other woman dating my man.

Not that he's *mine*. We haven't put a name to any of this. Then again, that kiss the other night—it felt like a declaration. A claiming of sorts. It was for me, anyway.

"I mean, yeah, my co-workers were great, and I got to know them to a certain extent. But I was the boss, so that always kind of put me at a different level. Not higher or anything like that. Just...I don't know. They respected me, and we were friendly, but not friends." He studies my hand in his and rubs his thumb over mine. "And as for relationships...there were a few."

Retract, claws. Retract!

"But nothing significant. I didn't have time. Or rather, I didn't make the time." Then his gaze connects with mine, and it is so piercing that I suck in a breath at the intensity written there. "I guess what I'm saying is, there was nobody back in L.A. that made me realize there's more to life than chasing success. Nobody that compelled me to get out of my routine. To consider doing things differently."

Nobody back in L.A. But maybe somebody in Hallmark Beach?

I want to ask the question, but before I can, he's releasing my hand. "Come on. Let's explore."

Huh? But as I climb from the car and close the door behind me, I understand. Before us, just down the stairs leading from the parking lot, spreads the most beautiful beach I've ever seen. The sun is halfway down the sky now, and instead of sand, the ground is littered with stones of all shapes, sizes...and colors.

Oh, the colors.

Yellows, greens, blues, reds. The rocks are smooth and glistening, and I'll bet anything that once they were jagged and dry. The ocean, over time, has beat against them, has sanded them down into something lovely, and now they decorate the landscape—proof that difficulty can sometimes produce things of beauty.

That just because you started one place doesn't mean that's where you'll stay.

And I can't help but think how this beach is a perfect representation of me and Blake. Of us, together.

I only hope our story has an ending as beautiful as this beach.

twenty-five

Today has been utterly perfect.

As I add wood to the fire I built on Firestone Beach, I turn my focus back to Lucy, who is wandering just a little ways down the beach, looking for a stone. What kind of stone? She doesn't know. When we first started exploring the beach a few hours ago, she just said she'd know the perfect stone when she saw it. We wandered the beach, climbed the waterfall, took a dip in the ocean, and have spent the whole time here alone, with bouts of stone searching.

And still, no perfect rock.

But the fact Lucy's still looking is something I love about her. She's got the sunniest disposition. I used to think it was a bit inauthentic, but now I just think it's Lucy. Her glass-half-full mentality balances out the daily dose of reality I'm constantly taking...and it's kind of nice to see things from her point of view. To come here today and not really have a plan beyond being with her. Nothing to "accomplish." No goals other than getting to know her better.

Of course, the whole day's been a practice in the art of self-control, especially given the way she looks right now. Even from afar and in the waning sunlight, her details are clear to me. Her hair is hanging damp down her back, and she's still wearing her swimsuit top with low-slung cutoff shorts and nothing on her feet as she carefully steps over the stones and occasionally squats to examine them more closely.

I strike a match and set fire to the kindling I've placed in the ring of rocks I spent the last thirty minutes arranging while Lucy combed the beach, her adorable off-key singing drifting back toward me. We are the only two here, something I didn't plan for but don't hate. Sure, I could have taken her on a date in Hallmark Beach, but there are lots of prying eyes—a fact that became all too clear the second we stepped from the rock outcropping at the party on Friday night.

So. Many. Looks.

We didn't even hold hands as we left, but many an old dude shot me a thumbs up, while some of the older women—*I'm looking at you, Alberta Jenkins*—flashed me frowns of disapproval. Thankfully, Jordan and Marilee didn't say a word to me, just let us join their volleyball game.

But I'm sure they noticed the way I couldn't keep my eyes off of Lucy.

Kind of like now.

She must notice my staring, because her head pops up and she breaks into a huge grin, waves. Standing, she walks back toward me, empty handed. "No luck."

"I admire your persistence."

"Some might call it futile, but I *will* find the perfect stone. Just you wait."

"I have no doubt you'll do whatever you put your mind to." Even if it's something as impossible as finding perfection.

Grinning up at me, she folds her arms around her body. That's when I notice that she's got goosebumps all down her skin. The setting sun and the breeze off the ocean feel amazing to me, but Lucy's clearly cold.

"Geez, Sunshine. Come sit by the fire I built you." I pop open a red camping chair and set it near the fire—though not too close. "Here. I have a sweatshirt too if you need one."

"Thank you, kind sir." Yet instead of sitting down, she just steps closer to me. Glances up with those big, innocent eyes—ones rimmed with mischief. "But I was kind of hoping you'd warm me up instead."

If ever a guy needed an invitation, this is it. But while I've been dying to kiss Lucy all day, I also don't want her to think that's all I'm interested in. I'm on a date with her because I like her. Because I can see a possible future with her. Not just because she's beautiful.

She's more.

Still, I also don't want to friend zone her. I—

"Flake," she says, a teasing lilt to her voice. "You're over-thinking this. Just hold me for a minute, okay?"

She's right. I'm overthinking, just like I always do. Not everything has to be planned or precisely calculated. "Come here."

Then I pull her into my arms, and she fits so well. Together we stand there, watching the sun disappear behind the horizon. Darkness descends around us, but the fire keeps us warm and brings light to our world. The trees down the shoreline are tall, dark spires in the sky. The ocean ebbs and flows, delivering a calming hush to my heart and mind.

Or maybe that's just Lucy. Even though I can't see a clear path forward between us, being in her presence makes every-thing clear. She teaches me how to just *be*. How to stay still and stop striving so hard. To be content in the little moments.

That's no small feat.

"I could stay like this forever," she murmurs.

I nuzzle my nose into her hair, breathe in the hints of vanilla somehow still clinging to her despite our earlier dip in the water. "I was just thinking the same thing."

"How did you find this place, anyway?" She burrows deeper into my arms, and I rest my chin on her head.

I blink, trying to remember the first time I was ever here. "I was in high school, I know that. Got into a fight with Dad over something. I think I said I didn't want to try out for football, and he thought I'd be throwing away an opportunity for a scholarship." I sigh at the memory. "Everything was an opportunity to him."

"An opportunity for what?"

"To get out of Hallmark Beach."

She stiffens in my arms. "Oh."

Keeping hold of her, I pull slightly away so I can see her. So she can see me, even if it's dark out. I like to think that doesn't stop her from seeing what's in my eyes. "Lucy..." How can I make her understand? "Did I ever tell you about the time when I was eleven and my dad took me to New York City?"

Shaking her head, she eyes the chair I set up for her. "Come tell me."

When she plops into the chair, I pull another out of its case and set it up right beside hers. I also dig in my bag and grab out one of my Bruins-blue UCLA sweatshirts. I hand it to her, and she eagerly dons it. The sight of her drowning in *my* clothing...I almost can't handle the way it makes my chest ache in all the best ways.

The fire pops and crackles, encouraging me just like she does as she turns in her seat and reaches for my hands. "What happened in New York?"

Please let me communicate this well. I swallow hard, grit in my throat. "We went there to visit my dad's old college room-mate, Steve. He and my dad were best buds. Steve was actually the one who originally suggested they vacation in Hallmark Beach after graduating from Stanford with their MBAs."

"And that's when your parents met."

"Yeah, exactly."

"And then what?"

"Well," I rub the back of my neck. "My dad fell head over heels for my mom, but she told him flat out that she'd never move from Hallmark Beach. That it was her home, where all of her friends—like your Aunt Bea—were, and that as much as she loved him, she couldn't see herself surviving life in New York, where he was headed at the end of the summer. See, he and Steve both had job offers there at a huge investment firm."

"And he gave it up for her."

"He did." I look away, into the flames. Each one sparks, grows, and gives way for the next. A circle of life, in a way. "And I always thought he was okay with that. But when I was eleven and we took that trip—and we saw the lavish life that Steve led...I mean, Lucy, he had a butler, was the CEO at the firm where he'd started, had all this mad respect from the people who worked for him, box seats at the theater, the fanciest cars. And I just saw it in my dad's eyes."

"What did you see, Blake?" Her hand tugs at mine, and I turn my attention back to her face. Her eyebrows knit together, like she's trying to piece together the puzzle.

"Regret." I sigh. "And determination."

"Determination for what?"

"For me to do what he hadn't. To choose differently than he did. To have the kind of life and respect and success that Steve had. To him, Steve had it made. Had an easy life. Of course, I'm sure that wasn't true. But to Dad..." I shrug. "So yeah. I was eleven years old when he first told me that I should make sure I'm well established before falling for someone." I cough. "That

I should stay far away from small-town girls who would only hold me back."

And that's when she slips her hands away. When her gaze leaves me. When she slouches down into my sweatshirt like she wants to disappear. "Oh." Her voice sounds so small, and suddenly I'm desperate to make her understand.

"Look at me." My voice is low and tumbling. "Sunshine. Please."

Finally, her gaze lifts again.

"Those were *his* words, Lucy. Not mine."

"But you believed them."

"*Believed.* Past tense." I scoot forward, trace a path down her cheek with my index finger. The firelight flares in her eyes. "I'll admit, the drive to make my dad proud has always been strong. Even when we didn't agree on the what—my cooking—I saw his point. And I also saw how bitter he was. I didn't want that. To resent my wife, my family..." I choke out the words. "So I just found it easier to pursue the things that would ensure I didn't become like him."

"You mean, that if you didn't pursue love, you'd have nothing to regret because you wouldn't have chosen it over your dreams?"

This woman. Somehow, she made sense out of my mind's muddle. I cup her face with my palm. "Exactly."

She leans into my touch. "So what's changed?"

I want to tell her that everything's changed. That I can give up L.A., that I can find peace here with her. But a part of me is still hesitant. What if this is exactly how Dad felt about Mom when he made the decision to give up everything for her?

But I can't tell Lucy that. Not while I'm still working out in my own head what all of this means. What's at stake. Because my dreams of the restaurant aren't just about me. They're about Dale too. He's invested time and money. Things are in motion

—and I can't just back out of all that, can I? Especially when I'm not sure I want to. Or have to.

Maybe there's still a chance that Lucy would be willing to come with me.

"All I know, Lucy Reynolds, is that the small-town girl in front of me hasn't held me back. She's given me a gift. She's opened my eyes to a world of small quiet moments. Of optimism. Of flavor and color. A world where perfect stones exist. Where I can be myself, where I can be a food truck chef, a brother, a friend, and that's enough."

"It *is* enough, Blake." A tear streaks down her cheek. "You're enough. You've always been enough."

"And you're everything." I lean in and softly kiss away her salty tears. "Everything I didn't think I could have."

And maybe still can't. Because you're leaving—and what if she doesn't want to come with you?

There goes my subconscious again, ruining the moment.

But as Lucy climbs from her chair and onto mine with me, slinging her arms around my neck and her legs over my lap and settling her head against my chest, we watch the fire dance... and my mind is pacified again.

Maybe, somehow, this thing between us will defy all odds. I don't know how, and right now, I don't have the energy to figure it out.

All I'm sure of is Lucy. And in this moment, Lucy is all I *need* to be sure of.

twenty-six

LUCY

Finally. It's done.

I sit back in Winona's desk chair and press a hand to my chest, cock my head. Allow myself to feel.

Is it possible? I think I do feel lighter. Like I can breathe. Because The Green Robin business plan is complete.

Well, it's ready for Blake's perusal, anyway. He offered to take a look weeks ago, but I wanted it as perfect as possible first. And while I don't think it's a masterpiece by any means, it's the best I'm capable of doing on my own.

And that's enough.

Elisse's words from last week drift back to me: *"You're taking way too much on yourself with the restaurant."* Ever since she said that, I've been processing why keeping the restaurant thriving has felt so important. Whether it's more about Winona...or me.

And when I decided to remove the burden of proving something to myself—and to the whole town—then I was able to do it from a purely selfless place. The pressure went away. And now, I can do my best for my friend and know that it's enough.

I smile, and my stomach gurgles. Patting it, I close the laptop lid and stand, stretching. "Time to celebrate with some good food," I say aloud to myself. And who wants to celebrate alone?

I know just where to go.

Heading to The Green Robin's kitchen, I find Tiny cleaning up from a decently successful night. "You save me anything good?" I peek over his massive shoulder to find him wrapping up a few roast beef sandwiches.

Grunting, he turns and pushes them into my hand. "Knew you'd be hungry when you finally emerged."

I laugh and press a kiss to his scruffy cheek. "Thank you, Tiny."

He rubs the spot I kissed, and I swear the guy actually blushes. Then he turns me by the shoulders and gives me a little push out the door. "Get outta here."

"Night!" I yell as I scurry out of the kitchen toward the front.

Jenny and Jake are holding onto broom handles and flirting in the dining room. They straighten when they see me and wave. "Night, Boss!"

For once, I don't bristle at the title. Maybe because I know I won't be the boss for much longer—just a month until Winona and her daughter return. Or maybe I've just realized that I'm not solely responsible for the rise or fall of this place. It's a team effort, and like my friends said, whether it succeeds or fails doesn't have any bearing on my own identity.

As I head out the door and down the front steps, I can't help but frown at the darkened food truck sitting on the edge of the Robin's property. Blake is back in L.A. for the night—a single, measly night—and I miss him already. When he was dropping me off at my bedroom door last night after our date, he told me about this quick jaunt he has to take up to L.A. for some meetings and restaurant business.

I hated the reminder that there's another life waiting for him. Away from me.

How am I ever going to survive it when he leaves for good? I mean, at least I still have a little over month before that happens. Maybe things will be different between us by then. Maybe we will somehow discover the answer during that time. All I know is that last night's date set a new tone to our relationship.

And yes, I'm calling it a relationship. I know Blake hasn't promised me anything, but the look in his eyes when he said *"You're everything"*?

I'm pretty sure that man is as gone for me as I am for him.

Still don't know where that leaves us once he has to move back to Los Angeles, but we have weeks to figure it out. In the meantime, I have to tell his sister about us. I'm sure my best friend suspects something is up—what with our behavior at the beach party three nights ago—but I didn't want to say anything until after our date.

I cross Main Street, but it's mostly deserted at this hour. The only place still open is The Black Hole, where the occasional hyped-up tourist scurries inside for some dancing.

As for me, I head for The Blackberry Muffin just south of the bar.

When I get there, I go around to the back and knock on the door that leads into the kitchen. Marilee pops it open, and her eyes widen in surprise. "Hey!" Not surprisingly, her purple apron is splattered with flour, and there's frosting on the tip of her nose. "What are you doing here?"

"Just came to chat." I hold up the bag of sandwiches. "And I figured you hadn't taken the time to eat."

"I've been busy." Even though her shoulders are drooping,

there's a brightness to her eyes, which can only mean one thing —she's decorating cakes. I already knew this, because she told me she'd be working late, and she doesn't ever bake the normal stuff at this hour. Marla Thompkins, the owner, doesn't want the specialty orders to interfere with Marilee's normal duties during the day, so she's limited the number of orders Marilee can take.

Marilee's turned away a lot of customers.

"Business is good, huh?" I pop through the door and shut it with my foot, then deposit the food in the only free space on the large yellow island made of swirly slabs of granite. The rest is taken up by Marilee's tools of the trade: bowls, flour, sugar, food coloring, spatulas, and a three-tiered cake that's frosted white and half decorated with iced roses. A piping bag with a bit of red icing is lying on its side next to the cake. "Wow, that's looking great." And as one who's been the happy recipient of Marilee's baking before, I'm sure it tastes even better.

"You think?" She's worrying her bottom lip, and her hair starts to fall from the bun shoved on top of her head like an afterthought. "I'm not sure I like how it's turning out."

"Here, take a break and eat with me." I slide onto one of the three black stools sitting under the island's lip. "Then you can let it percolate."

"Okay." She agrees so easily, and that's when I notice the bags under her eyes. The slowness of her smile.

The woman is running herself ragged.

"Mare, you look like you're about to pass out. I'm not sure burning the candles at both ends is good for you."

"Look who's talking, lady. You've been working just as hard."

"But that's temporary." I toss her a sandwich. "How long do you think you can keep taking cake orders and doing your normal job too?"

She rubs between her eyes, just above the bridge of her glasses. "I don't want to stop decorating cakes." Then she sighs. "But maybe you're right."

"That's not what I'm saying. Why don't you quit your job and start your own business? You're talented enough, and clearly there's a demand for it."

Marilee frowns and doesn't answer me. She needs time. Silently, we each unwrap a sandwich and take a bite. Mmm. The tangy mayo jives so well with the crisp lettuce and the savory beef. Maybe could use a touch of mustard…

And that makes me think once again of Blake. Is this how it's going to be from now on? Sweet macaroni, I'm ridiculous. But I still can't help a small smile from creeping across my face.

"What?" Marilee studies me, her tired eyes still observant.

"Nothing."

"I thought you came to chat."

"But we were chatting about *you*, not me."

"You're not going to tell me why you really came over here tonight?"

Ha. The irony. "I'll tell you if you tell me what *you're* thinking."

She chews, and something beeps over the oven. Maybe the clock. Finally, she sighs. "While I'd like to start my own business, I can't."

"Because of the debt?"

"Yeah. And because…Lucy, I've already made a mess of my life. This job…I don't have anything else."

"Thanks a lot." I stick out my tongue. "I'm sure Blake and Jordan and all of our other friends would love knowing that you consider us *nothing*."

Despite my teasing, she grabs my arm, her eyes wide with regret. "You know that's not what I meant. You all mean the world to me. But baking helps me feel close to my mom. And what if I give up the only job in this town that allows me to bake for a living to pursue something that might not pay the bills? That might utterly fail?"

I pat her hand. "If that happened—and I'm sure that it wouldn't—then we would all be there for you. We'd help you get back on your feet."

"I'm sure you'd do what you could."

"You don't sound sure."

She smiles, but it's wobbly. "I can't rely on you all to fix my messes, friend. Blake's got his own thing going on, and even though I know he'd help pay off the debts, I would never let him. And Jordan's got enough on his plate trying to run his own business and juggle being a good dad to Ryder, who misses his mom more every day." Then she swallows. "And someday, you're all going to have your own families. Even Jordan will get married, and you know that whoever he marries is not going to be okay with him helping out his old pal Marilee."

I don't say what I'm thinking—that if Jordan were to marry anyone, it would *be* Marilee. The guy's clearly crazy for her, and she's the only one who doesn't see it. "All of that may be true, but you know we will never be too busy for you."

"Not intentionally. But it won't be the same if you don't live here anymore."

The words are ice to my heart. "What? Who says I'm going anywhere?"

She blanches. "I guess I just assumed."

Wha—? Oh. "You mean because..."

And that makes her laugh, which is a lovely sound. If only it didn't come at my expense. "Because I assume you and my brother are an item after the way you snuck off to make out like high schoolers on Friday night. And snuck out of the house yesterday morning and were gone all day."

"I thought you were asleep."

"I could hear the flirting through the walls." She shakes her head at me. "Was that what you were coming over here to chat about?"

"Yes! I didn't want you hearing it from someone else. Or to feel like I was keeping things from you." I tilt my head. Now for the question of the hour. "Do you...mind?"

"Why would I mind two of my favorite people finding love together?"

"Oh. Well, I don't know about *love*." Or do I?

Marilee rolls her eyes. "Girl, I've seen the way you look at him. The way he looks at you. And I'd love nothing more than for you to be legally my sister someday—even though you're already the sister of my heart."

Ugh, this woman. I bring it in for a fierce hug around her neck before pulling back. I rub the edge of my sandwich wrapper between my fingers. "I'm scared, Mare. What you said about me not living here anymore...well, we haven't even discussed that at all. Like, I don't know where his head is at. What if he just plans to leave again, no matter what?"

"Are you thinking he'll change his mind or something?" Mare pushes her glasses up her nose. "You knew from the beginning he was leaving at the end of the summer. Is it really fair to assume he'll change all his plans? This is his dream, Lucy." Her tone is soft, her eyes filled with love. In only the way that Mare can, she speaks truth without being harsh.

"I know, but...does he just think *I'll* up and move away from the only place that's ever felt like home? Because that doesn't seem fair either."

"Maybe he's just thinking you'll do long distance for a bit."

"Yeah. Maybe." But long distance is only a temporary solution. We both know that. And I'm not a planner by any means, but I *am* excellent at keeping those low expectations. At creating situations that will result in the least amount of hurt later.

Is it who I am, or a learned behavior after the upheavals in my childhood and teenage years? Either way, I'm not sure I like this particular personality trait.

"It sounds like you guys need to have a really open discussion about all of this," Marilee says.

"You're right." I know she is. "But what if we find out we really can't work it out? That we want different things? Because that's terrifying." The idea that I've finally found the man of my dreams...and might lose him in one fell swoop.

"Better to find out now that you want different things than after you've been married for six years." Her words are soft, but sure. "And, yes, it's scary to take a chance on love. But Lucy Reynolds, you're one of the bravest people I know."

There she goes again with the irony. "I don't feel very brave."

"That's the thing about bravery. You're scared...and do what scares you anyway."

Okay, then. Looks like I'm having a conversation with Blake about the future.

And soon, before I lose my nerve.

twenty-seven

I'm not one to play hooky from work. Don't think I've done it a day in my life.

Until now.

It's eleven a.m. on a Wednesday, and I'm still in my gym shorts and a T-shirt—basically what I wore to bed. Since I returned from Los Angeles last night, Lucy and I have been up this morning cooking and bantering and kissing. Making up for lost time.

Because the whole time I was gone, all I could think about was getting home to her.

The radio's on low in the kitchen while I stack the last of the breakfast dishes—sticky with pancake syrup and egg yolk—in the sink. Turning, I find a pajama-clad Lucy at my elbow, our empty coffee mugs in her hand. She hip bumps me and I step out of the way, but only just enough for her to slide her body in front of mine.

She places the mugs in the sink, and I lean forward to trap her there, my hands on either side of her, her back against my chest.

This should be absolute heaven. After all, I missed Lucy something fierce while I was in Los Angeles.

But while I've tried to push the events of my visit to the city out of my brain this morning—even for a little while—I can't forget one little fact.

Lucy and I need to talk.

Ugh. Can't I just stay here in this bubble with her and deny my responsibilities, deny that a world outside of this one even exists?

I lean in and place a kiss on her shoulder, then nuzzle my nose against her neck. After being apart the last two days, I can't *not* touch her. When it comes to Lucy Reynolds, I'm a weak man.

Lucy leans her head to the side, giving me enough access to press my lips to her skin. Her tiny sigh of pleasure stokes the heat inside of me, and I nip my way up her long, graceful neck. Then she turns to face me, slipping one hand around me, her fingers flirting with the back of my shirt collar.

Yeah, we can talk later.

I kiss her, long and full.

She grabs fistfuls of my shirt and tugs me close, and I lose myself in the wonder of Lucy, pouring every ounce of the care I have for her into the kiss.

And maybe she can sense my rising anxiety over the conversation she doesn't know is coming, because she pulls back. Frowns. "Everything okay?"

"Yeah, of course." I hate the worry lines creasing her forehead, so I place a kiss there. This is the perfect opening to bring up what I need to say, but..."I just missed you."

Coward.

Later. I'll tell her later.

And I will. I just hate to ruin...this. Not that I'm worried she won't understand. She knows how important the restaurant is to me. And now that we are together, I have full confidence we can make anything work, if we both really want it to.

And I know I do.

Her responding smile is brilliant. "The feeling is mutual." Then she cocks her head. "I know we aren't really working this morning, but I was wondering if you maybe had time to look over that business plan?"

That's right. She mentioned over breakfast that she'd finally finished The Green Robin's plan.

I place my nose against hers. My hands find her waist, thumbs skating across the tiny strip of skin between her soft pink pajama pants and her white tank top. "Do we have to?" I say in a low, husky voice—the one that always seems to increase the throbbing of that very kissable vein in her neck.

"No." She draws a finger down my chest, ending at my stomach—which, yes, I fully admit to clenching so she can feel my abs beneath my shirt. "But you *did* promise."

She's right. I did. "What will you give me for the effort?"

Lucy goes up on her tiptoes, places her lips beside my ear. "I think I can make it worth your while."

I yank back and grab her hand, pulling her toward the couch. "Well, what are we waiting for?"

Laughing, she tugs away. "Cool down, Romeo." Grabbing her laptop off the island, she moves to the couch.

I follow suit, jumping over the back of the couch to land next to her—who even am I?—and take the computer from her lap, moving it to mine. She looks at me, amusement in her eyes, and I open the lid to find a password-protected screen saver: a photo of Lucy, Mare, and all of their friends at Chloe's brother's wedding.

My food truck is in the background. I'm somewhere in this photo. I like to think that, even when we were enemies, Lucy was thinking of me.

My chest a bit tighter, I gently tug her thumb toward the upper rightmost key on the keyboard so her thumbprint can unlock the screen. The business plan is open and ready for perusal. I start to read. I would have done it before now, but Dale kept me pretty busy yesterday, and then I was driving home as fast as I could to Lucy.

It's a few moments before I realize I just thought of Hallmark Beach as *home*.

And I don't really know what to do with that, because L.A. is calling.

And sooner than planned.

The television spot went well—so well that I was offered a twice weekly spot starting the week after next. Not only that, but Dale and I had a long chat yesterday about what still has to happen with the restaurant. He needs me up there to make some decisions—and I'll need to be there to film the TV spots. And since the recipes are ready, there's no real reason to stay until August like I planned.

No reason but Lucy.

But Dale wouldn't understand that any better than Dad would if he was here. Either way, it means the timeline has officially been moved up. I'm leaving the day after the festival.

In one week.

And I have no idea how Lucy is going to react.

Clearing my throat, I toss my arm around Lucy's shoulders and keep reading the business plan. Meanwhile, she snuggles into my chest and I feel her eyes aimed upward. I glance down at her, and my lips quirk. "What?"

"Nothing," she whispers.

Hmm. She's thinking about something. But what?

Focus, Blake.

Right. The business plan. I spend the next thirty minutes reading over it in detail, and I'm impressed. Lucy doesn't know all the right business lingo necessarily, but her ideas are fresh and really good. When I reach the end, I look at her again.

"Well?" she asks.

"It's got really good potential."

She frowns. "You think it's terrible."

"No, I don't." I laugh and move a strand of her hair behind her ear. "It was a compliment."

"I'd hate to hear your critique then," Lucy teases. She pokes me in the side. "But I want to make it better. So hit me with your ideas."

We spend the next hour or so brainstorming ways to improve her plan—things like streamlining the menu to save money, ordering supplies on a weekly basis instead of monthly, using her staff a bit differently, making use of social media to promote and market, and updating the Robin's website to accept online to-go orders.

By the end, she's facing me cross-legged on the couch, bouncing up and down. "Thank you, thank you! These are really great ideas, and all things I am sure Winona will go for." Then she stills. "It's no wonder you got Dale to give you money for your restaurant."

Then that look comes over her again—the one that says she's deep in thought.

I set the laptop on the coffee table and turn to face her, placing my right arm along the back of the couch, my hand just within reach of Lucy. I play with her earlobe. "Okay, what's up? You've gone quiet."

"Can't a girl be quiet and mysterious once in a while?" She smiles, but it doesn't reach her eyes.

"Sunshine."

"I'm sorry." Her smile wobbles. "It's just...I guess I don't like thinking about your restaurant, because it's going to take you away from me. But also, it's your dream, right? So I should be happy for you. And I am. But..." She bites her lip, and I want to kiss away her worry. "I mean, I see how happy you are cooking in your food truck. And I know I gave you a hard time about being here at first, but you've fit right in."

"It surprised me too. I only came here at first to take time away to work and create more recipes. And because Mare is here, and I wanted to make things right with her."

"Which you've done."

"Thankfully she's a very forgiving person." I'm quiet for a bit, thinking. "But Hallmark Beach was only ever supposed to be a stop along the way."

Her breath shudders in. Out. "I know that. But can you tell me..." Then she shakes her head. "Never mind. I don't want to bring us down."

"You never could do that, Sunshine." I lean in and kiss her soft on the mouth. "I want to know everything you're thinking and feeling. Even if it's sad. That's part of you, and that means it's something I want to know."

"You're kind of unreal, you know that, Blake?"

"Right back at you."

"Okay, so what is it about opening your own restaurant that satisfies the dream you have for your life in a way that your food truck business doesn't? Is it just the prestige that will go with it? The accolades? The success?"

The questions squeeze my lungs. They're so deep. And penetrating.

And yet, so simple.

Then she follows them up with the ultimate gut punch. "After what you told me about New York, what your dad said... I guess I'm wondering if the restaurant is really *your* dream—or his."

Oh, wow. Okay.

"It's complicated." I play with a loose strand of her hair. It's velvety and fine between my thumb and forefinger and soothes my frayed nerves. "For so long, it's all I thought about. The singular goal I planned my life around. Especially after my parents died. I've never even considered another path. Not until..."

You.

Her fingers find my knee and rub circles into the fabric of my pants. Ugh. If only we had more time together. More time to figure this out. More time to un-complicate the complicated...

"I know that cooking makes you happy. I see it whenever you're in the middle of grilling up something or thinking of a new recipe. You're lighter, you know? Like Mare when she's baking. But it also sounds like the restaurant business is a rough one. You said you barely had time for relationships, and you weren't even running your own restaurant then. So when you go back to L.A., well...where does that leave us?"

Hot dang, her questions hurt. They're ones I've asked myself but chose to ignore in favor of seeing where things went with Lucy. But is that fair to her? Maybe it's not.

My head spins with the implications.

"Do you think you could ever be happy..." Lucy takes in a deep breath. "Staying here? Running the food truck?"

In this moment? I want to say yes. But I can't be hasty. I have to analyze. To think, away from her and all the things she makes me feel.

She plows on. "It's just, I've been wondering about...the future. And that's probably really presumptuous of me, because what kind of girl acts like a few kisses means there's a future there, right? But still, I don't know where this is going, and it's driving me a little bit crazy." Her luminous eyes blink up at me. "Am I crazy, Blake?"

"Maybe."

She smacks my chest, and that makes me chuckle.

Then I take her face gently between my hands. "But it's not presumptuous at all. I see a future with you too. And I guess a question to ask you right back—do you think you could ever be happy living somewhere other than Hallmark Beach?"

Are we really having this conversation? My heart thuds in my chest.

She licks her lips. "I'm not sure. It's been my refuge—my home—for a long time, even before I ever moved here. The idea of leaving it is kind of like a knife to my chest." Sitting back, she takes my hands from her face and holds them in her lap instead. "Especially for someone who might end up being too busy for me. I...I don't want to end up like my mom. Devastated by love."

Love? Does she love me? No, that's not what she's saying. She's saying *if* she came to love me...

Still, my neck heats with the thought. My stomach swirls.

"Sunshine, the very last thing I ever would want to do is devastate you. To hurt you." And I can't avoid it any longer. It's time to tell her the thing about my conversation with Dale. "This is really hard, but there's something I need to tell you."

Lucy straightens ever so slightly. "That sounds ominous." She's trying to joke, but when I don't joke back, she frowns. "Wait, what? What's wrong?"

"Uh." I swallow hard. *Just spit it out, man.* "Dale and I decided that...that is, I'm needed...he...well, I'm going back to Los Angeles in a week. The day after the festival." I pause. "Not just for a quick trip this time. For good."

She blinks at me several times in rapid succession. "What? No, you're leaving at the end of July, not the beginning. In a month." Her fingers pull away one at a time, and I feel their loss. She hugs herself, her shoulders sinking down. I want to pull her back to me, but I know we need to face this.

Sighing, I run a hand through my hair. "That was the original plan, but Dale needs me back sooner. One of the reasons I went down there was to film a cooking spot on a morning news show. They liked me and want me to keep doing it. Dale thinks it might lead to my own show down the line."

"And that's what you want? To be a celebrity chef?"

"Not necessarily. But it'll be great exposure for the restaurant."

"Oh." And I see it—her withdrawing from me. Her eyes are shuttering, her lips becoming flat, her cheeks deflating. Like every bit of negative emotion she's feeling is being wiped from her memory, from her core, and she's becoming a robot. Hiding from me.

Then she flicks on a smile. "Well, that's great. I'm proud of you." She leaps up from her spot on the couch. "I guess you're going to be really busy the rest of this week, then." Her feet start to back up, like she's going to run and race to her room. Away from me. "We should probably just—"

"Lucy." I hop up and catch her around the waist, pull her to me. But instead of snuggling into my arms, she pushes against my chest without a word. I release her. "Please don't—"

A flicker of despair. "I can't do this, Blake."

I stiffen. "Do what?"

"*This.*" She points between us. "A week? You know that's not enough time to figure anything out. The pressure that puts on us...it's just too much."

"There doesn't have to be pressure, Lucy. Not from me. We'll spend the week together, continue to get to know ourselves in this context, and then I'll go. We'll call every night, text every day, and I'll come back and visit when I can—"

"And that's the key phrase. *When you can.*" She sniffs and looks away. "What happens when the rest of the world becomes way more interesting than this one, or you just get too bogged down in the details of that life, there? You said yourself that opening a restaurant is a time-consuming business."

"It is, but you're important too, Lucy. You're a priority to me, and I want to see what this could be."

"You seem to have it all planned out, but the thing you're not realizing is that it'll happen slowly. You'll get busy. And you won't mean for it to, but our relationship will slowly become less of a priority." She takes another step backward. "I'm just being realistic. Long distance doesn't work—not when one person is determined to go off and live this big life and wants something so very opposite of the homebody who is just happy to have a quiet, simple one."

The one who is left behind.

She doesn't say that last part, but she doesn't have to.

Now I get it. She's thinking about how her mom left, supposedly for a summer, and never came back again except for random visits. She all but abandoned her daughter, and like Lucy said...it happened slowly.

She doesn't want that pain again. And I get it. But she's not being fair. I'm standing here, trying to commit to her, to this, and she's acting like it's nothing. "Lucy," I say softly, reaching for her hand. But she doesn't give it to me. I sigh, frustration clinging to the edges. "I'm not your mom. This isn't the same."

"Isn't it, though?"

"No. It's not."

"Even if it's not, it's clear to see that we want different things. And that's not just something one of us can compromise on."

Is that the crux of it, then? As much as I care for her—as much as I want to make this work—is it really so impossible? She wants to be here. I have to be in Los Angeles.

I *want* to be in Los Angeles.

Don't I? It's what I've wanted for so long. Can I really even consider giving it up to be here with her? What if things didn't work out between us? *Would* I still be happy here, running my food truck business, living near my sister?

I rub my forehead. "I need time to think."

"Time's up, Blake. You made sure of that when you decided to leave earlier than planned without talking to me about it first." She cocks her head. "I really do wish you well, and I'm not mad, okay? Just sad. But let's part as friends this time." She's whispering now. "I don't think I could bear to be your enemy again."

And then, she's slipping from the room, leaving me with a hollow ache I don't know what to do with. So I do the only thing I can.

I head to the kitchen...and start to cook.

Maybe Dad was right.

Love *is* a distraction. Because the last four days without Lucy in them have been miserable, and despite several calls with Dale, I can't think about much else than her.

"Earth to Blake."

I snap my head around from where I'm standing in front of a dart board, holding several darts in my hand. Jordan's next to a refrigerator in his garage, which he's transformed into the ultimate "man cave"—boasting a black couch and TV, pool table, and speakers hooked up in the corners.

"What's up?" I ask.

"You want something to drink?" With the fridge door propped open, Jordan holds up a Dr. Pepper in one hand and a Diet Coke in the other.

"Sure, I'll take the Dr. Pepper." Lucy would tease me about that choice—to her, Diet Coke is the be all and end all of sodas.

Aw, man. Even here, at a last-minute guys' night, I can't escape the thought of her.

Jordan flicks a look at Frederick and Landon, who are engaged in a competitive game of pool. "How about you guys?"

Landon's got on his standard outfit of jeans, a black T-shirt, and his faithful Stetson, while Frederick has long ditched the black suits I hear he used to wear when he was Chloe's body-guard for gym shorts and a tee.

They both wave him off, too focused on their game. Landon's taunting Frederick, and Frederick is all narrowed vision and concentration.

Shrugging, Jordan shuts the fridge and carries the drinks to me. He hands me the Dr. Pepper and takes the Diet Coke for himself, popping the top and taking a swig before setting it on a cocktail table near the dart board.

"Thanks, man." I chug my own soda, letting the carbonation burn a trail down my throat. "And thanks for inviting me over. I definitely needed the distraction."

"I'm sure you've got a lot to do before leaving in a few days." Jordan picks up a few red darts from the table. "You gonna be busy tomorrow with all the festival prep?" He squares up with the dart board, eases his arm back, and launches one. His dart lands on one of the outside rings.

"Not really. I already bought all the supplies for the burgers and organized all the inventory, and Tiny and I are going to tag-team cooking burgers the day of since his trip to visit his nephew got postponed. As for the rest, Thomas is taking care of the brownies, and Lucy's doing everything else. Chips, drinks, recruiting volunteers to run the food tent, that sort of thing. I think she's been helping Chloe with a bunch of other non-food related stuff too." Or so I've heard through the grapevine of Marilee.

"Makes me glad I'm only in charge of the volleyball tournament." Jordan sinks another dart into the board, this one closer to center.

Behind us, the sound of a ball clacking against another rings through the air. Frederick calls Landon a dodgy bloke, and Landon laughs.

Glancing back at them, Jordan smiles and rolls his eyes. Then he brings his gaze back to the board. Adjusts his ball cap before throwing his last dart. Just left of center.

But he doesn't gloat, merely looks at me. "Your turn."

Grunting, I move into position and throw. My first dart misses the board altogether. Disgusted with myself, I take another drink of my soda. Shake it off. Try again. Same thing.

"Something bothering you?" Jordan asks. Grabbing up his soda again, he sits on the back of the couch next to me, legs crossed at the ankles. "I find I can never hit the board when I've got something else on my mind." His voice is so casual, but I'm no dummy.

I give him serious side eye. "Marilee told you about me and Lucy, didn't she?"

"She may have mentioned it." He holds up his hands. "But that's not why I invited you over. We were already getting together. You're not the only one who needed a distraction."

I turn toward him, forgetting the darts for a moment. "Why? What's wrong with you?"

He laughs. "You don't beat around the bush, do you?" Then he rubs the back of his neck. "Nah, it's just Ryder. He's had a lot of trouble sleeping lately. It's been about six months since his mom passed. He's been wetting the bed again every night, wanting to sleep with me. That kind of thing."

I blow out a breath. "Dang. That's rough."

"Yeah."

"You and his mom..." I clear my throat. "Was her passing hard on you?"

He shrugs. "I mean, yeah, of course. But we were never together. That is, we were never a couple. I'd like to say it was complicated, but it really wasn't. I didn't have feelings for her beyond..." His cheeks turn red. "But she was a good co-parent. A good mom to Ryder. Seeing how it's affected him has been really hard."

I study him, this solid guy who clearly stepped up to the plate when Ryder came along, doing right by him and his mom. From what I know of him, he's smart. His business is always booming, and it seems like his schedule is full. I think back to what he told me that day on the boardwalk, about why he came back to Hallmark Beach when he could have gone anywhere after business school: *"Guess you could say that everything I wanted was in this little town. It's home."*

The thought slams me straight in the heart.

I cough. "I think...I think I want to stay in Hallmark Beach."

Jordan's eyebrows go up, disappearing beneath the brim of his hat. "Yeah?" He takes the change of subject in stride. "That would be awesome. But you don't sound too sure. What about the restaurant?"

"I know. That's the problem. I *should* want that, right? It's an amazing opportunity. Plus, I've already committed to it."

"I don't think there is a right or wrong answer, necessarily. And an opportunity can be amazing and wrong at the same time."

Whoa. My brain buzzes with the implications.

Jordan continues. "Have you signed paperwork?"

"No. My business partner wants me to sign it later this week once I'm back. His lawyer's been drawing everything up."

"Then you haven't actually committed. Though I understand wanting your word to be your bond and all that." He takes another swig of Diet Coke. "Or is there more to it?"

"There's more." I sigh, glance back at Frederick and Landon. Much as I like them, I don't really know them yet. But Jordan's more than just a solid guy. He's my sister's friend. Mine too.

Imagine that. I have a friend. Huh.

I blink, rolling the dart between my thumb and forefinger. "You knew my dad. He had certain ideas about success. And I don't think—well, I *know* he wouldn't have considered a food truck business in a small town to be 'success.' But a booming restaurant in Los Angeles that brings in stars and reviews and celebrity chef status? That would be something."

Still holding onto his drink, Jordan folds his arms over his chest, nodding along.

"So while I think my heart wants to be here, I'm not sure my head will allow it. The thought of giving up my dad's dream for me—because if I'm honest, that's what the restaurant is—doesn't really compute." I pause. "Especially if I give it up for Lucy. My dad led with his heart, and then his head was never happy with him later. I guess I just need to figure out which to listen to."

"I get that, man. And I don't have all the answers by any means. Believe me, I'm still warring daily with my heart and my head." He shifts, and I wonder once again what's going on deeper inside of him—maybe as it regards my sister. Jordan moves on before I can think too much about that. "But I guess you just have to ask yourself what success means to you. Not your dad. You."

"Isn't there only the one kind?" I joke, but there's a serious question there too.

"No way. Success is how you define it. Take Freddy, for instance. He was a world-class bodyguard to royalty, and now he's a cellar rat at a vineyard."

"And loving it!" the Kentonian yells.

Guess they're listening after all. I roll my eyes. Jordan shakes his head and grins, waits until the pool sticks start moving again and Landon and Frederick start arguing about some rule or other before he continues speaking. "I know for a fact that Freddy moved here for Chloe and doesn't regret it. But he also left the service because he wanted to do something different. He was clinging to someone else's definition of success for a long time and ultimately decided that it was his life to live."

My lungs contract. How well I can relate.

Jordan stands and claps me on the shoulder. "And as much as I know you want to honor your dad, he's not here anymore. This is your life, dude. You've got to be the one to decide what kind of success you care about."

Just like in those romance movies Mom and Mare made me watch with them, a series of clips—a montage, if you will—race through my head.

A late night at home, feeding my sister and Lucy new recipes. Me in my truck, flipping sandwiches, Lucy expectantly at my elbow, waiting to try something new.

Sitting on a porch swing, stargazing and enjoying quiet moments with the most beautiful woman in the world.

Kissing Lucy at the cliffside. Kissing Lucy in my kitchen. Looking for perfection with Lucy on the beach.

It's all suddenly so clear, like a fog lifting from my eyes. If *I* was to die in a car accident tonight like my parents did, *these* are the clips of my life that would flash before my eyes.

And I would have no regrets.

Turning, I fire my last dart at the board. It hits the dead center.

I know what I have to do.

twenty-eight

Blake is leaving in three days.

I try my best not to think about it, to stuff away the negative emotions, but I can't, no matter what I'm doing.

When I'm talking to Winona on the phone, showing off the new business plan and hearing that she loves it—I'm thinking about Blake.

When I'm helping Chloe with last-minute festival details because she's got a lot on her plate and I've suddenly got lots of free time—I'm thinking about Blake.

Even now, when I'm playing poker with my family on July third, and everyone else is laughing and having a grand old time, and Uncle Burt and April and Scarlett are having a root beer chugging contest, and Aunt Bea is serving up a whole heap of spaghetti—I may be smiling on the outside, but on the inside, I'm miserable.

Because, you guessed it, I'm thinking about Blake.

The whole kitchen reverberates with noise, but I'm inspecting my Diet Coke, drawing my thumb through the condensation, trying to feel something other than this misery.

But I know it's better this way. Might not feel that way in

the moment, but better this brief cavernous ache in my chest *now* than the slow death of my hope over time.

It's just like when Mama left. Said she'd be back in a few months, and look. Thirteen years later, where is she?

Not. Here.

The same thing would have happened with Blake. He might not think it's the same, but the similarities line up pretty darn well. I'm just allowing the inevitable to happen—only much sooner than it would have otherwise.

As I glance around this room at some of the people I love best, those who have claimed me even though I didn't have to be theirs to claim, the tears well up and I can't hold them in any longer. Grabbing my phone, I dash from the room while everyone is occupied, heading up the stairs to what used to be my bedroom. Once upon a time, it was my cousin Jeff's, but then it became mine. Now, it's Scarlett's, and I hope she won't mind me being in here.

The furniture is all the same, but the decor has changed. No longer are the walls lined with posters of Tim McGraw and the Zac Brown Band, but rainbows and unicorns appropriate for a seven-year-old girl. My chest loosens a bit as I let my tears fall and roam the room, my fingers slipping over the edge of the white wooden dresser, the bookcase painted purple. April has, not surprisingly, stuffed the shelves fuller than they ever were when I lived in here, and my index finger skims the spines, stopping on a large book of fairytales.

I kind of want to hide it away so Scarlett doesn't grow up believing that fairytales are real life.

Somehow, I forgot.

Because for a moment, I thought that I was a princess. That Blake was my prince. And that somehow, we'd found our happily ever after.

Instead, I'm just a small-town girl who fell in love with a guy she shouldn't have.

"Why did I have to love him?" I whisper to no one in particular. At least I never was so foolish as to confess it out loud to Blake.

I step away from the bookcase and head for the window, where I find a fabulous view of the backyard. There's a huge tree growing tall and strong there. It's been here as long as I can remember, deep roots in the ground of Hallmark Beach, just like me. Wrapping my arms around myself, I press my forehead to the window, feel the waning warmth of the day seep into my skin.

In this moment, I just want my mama.

The realization startles me. I've tried really hard not to need her. Mama gets overwhelmed easily by life, so I never wanted to be a bother, for her to stay away because I'm too much.

But yeah. Right now, I do need her.

With trembling hands, I take my phone from the back pocket of my jeans and lower myself onto Scarlett's bed, which is covered in a fairy princess comforter. Because of course it is.

I blink at the phone and finally swipe to unlock it. Then, before I can stop myself, I dial.

The phone rings. And rings. And rings.

And goes to voicemail.

"Hi there, darling, you've reached Patti Reynolds Kotula. I'm off gallivantin', so you just leave a message and I'll get back to you when I can, all right? Hugs and kisses." Before the message cuts off, there's a low murmur—Kevin saying something in the background—and a giggle from Mama.

I click off, toss my phone to the end of the bed, and stare numbly at a picture of a green-haired fairy watering a flower with her red wand.

"Knock, knock."

I glance up to find Aunt Bea standing in the doorway. Her gray hair is pulled back in a ponytail just like mine, and she's wearing jeans and a T-shirt, just like me, along with a long-sleeved flannel shirt.

"Oh, hi," I say. "Sorry, I shouldn't be in here."

"Stop it, honey." She steps inside and closes the door behind her. "This will always be your room, no matter who's livin' in it."

My lip trembles.

She sits beside me on the bed, pats my thigh. "You seemed distracted at dinner. Sad."

Understatement of the year. "Sorry. I didn't mean to be."

"Never apologize for feeling something, or for expressing it." Aunt Bea clicks her tongue at me. "You know, you've always been such a light to us all, but that doesn't mean you have to be sunny all the time. Embracing the negative emotions along with the good makes the good all the better."

I guess I can see that. Using the tips of my fingers, I swipe tears from my lashes.

"So what's making my Lucy so sad tonight?"

Her Lucy. Oh, man. The tears start up again. *Thanks a lot, Aunt Bea.* I shrug and try for a grin. "What else? Boy troubles."

"The same boy who made you sad all those years ago, I reckon."

My gaze kicks up to her knowing one. I never talked to my aunt about Blake back then. "How did you...?"

"Please." She taps the side of her temple. "I have eyes, child. And it doesn't take a rocket scientist to see you love him. That you've always loved him." She tilts her chin down. "But that's not the problem, is it?"

I shake my head and start to sob. She pulls me into her embrace and lets me cry into her shoulder, whispering, "Shh,

shh, there, there" over and over again. Finally, I'm ready to tell her, and it all spills out. Every last detail, right up until the second before she walked in after I tried—and failed—to get a hold of Mama.

She sighs and wipes my tears with her shirt sleeves, which are softer than they look. "Lucy, I'm so sorry for what you've been through."

I shake my head, which is fuzzy in the way that only crying so many tears can make it. "I'm hardly the first person to experience heartbreak in the world."

"I'm not talking about Blake—although I am sorry for that too. I'll always be sorry when you're hurting."

"Then what are you talking about?"

She sighs. "Your uncle and I did our best to give you a home. But I know it's never been enough. You needed your Mama, and she wasn't here."

"Oh, Aunt Bea, that's not—"

"Hush, child, I'm talking." She smiles at me, so I know she's not mad. Then continues. "Your mama, she wasn't well. No mother who would leave such a sweet daughter behind could be well." As if she knows I'm about to protest, Bea holds up her hand. "I'm not trying to speak ill of her. I know she suffered terribly when Bill died. I can't imagine what I'd do if I ever lost Burt. Still, I'll admit that I've had a harsh word or two with the good Lord about your mother and the way she left."

"Really? You never said."

"I didn't want you to ever feel like you were a burden. Because you're not, Lucy. You're a blessing, and I'm sorry for your mama that she's missed out on seeing up close and personal what a beautiful woman you've become."

Oh, sweet macaroni. There she goes again. "Stop making me cry, Aunt Bea." I laugh.

But her face is just as serious as the time she told my uncle in no uncertain terms would she ever give up quilting, no matter how bad the arthritis in her hands gets. "We wanted to give you a home, but I worry that in creating a haven for you, we also created a prison."

"This home isn't a prison."

"Not just this home. This town too. It's become your sanctuary, which is a wonderful thing. A good thing. But once you were here, you never left again. You used to love traveling when you were little, but when was the last time you went farther than Morro Bay?"

Hold on, now. "I was going to go away to college, but then Marilee's parents died."

"I know, darling, and you're such a good friend to stay. But let's be honest. You never really wanted to leave. You only felt like you should. You were relieved when you had an excuse to stay."

Ouch. Guess the truth hurts. "So? What's wrong with loving your home so much you always want to be there? That you can't fathom leaving it?"

"There's a difference between loving it and using it as a place to hide."

I stand, head for the window again, holding fast to the image of that grand tree anchored there. But in studying it closer, I see signs that all is not well. Pieces of bark flecking off. It's listing to one side. There are patches where no leaves grow.

No. No, no. "That tree...what's wrong with it?"

"What?" My aunt joins me at the window. She taps the glass softly. "Ah, yes. I've been meaning to have it taken out. It's not been getting enough nutrients, I guess. It's just been existing there, looking all right, even though under the surface, the roots were dying. Took a while to see the problem, and by then, it was too late to treat it." Her hand goes to my hair, stroking it like only a mom can. "Your uncle doesn't want to take it out. It's sentimental to him, you see. But sometimes you have to get rid of the dead things so you can plant new life."

I turn to her, my eyes wet again—surprise, surprise. "But what if the soil's just...ruined? What if the new tree never grows as tall?" My questions come quickly, but the understanding in her eyes tells me she knows we are no longer talking about a tree. "What if this tree, right here, right now, with all of its issues, is the best thing that's ever going to exist? If you chop it down, expecting new life, and the new life doesn't come, or it doesn't look the way you think it will...then what? You're just left with broken hope."

"Or," she grasps my hand and squeezes it tight, "the new tree will exceed your expectations. But if you don't risk chopping down the old, you will never experience the life and growth that comes with the new. And, Lucy, what is a life of fear and hiding? Take the risk, my dear. Dream the dream. Just think of what a beautiful sight could be waiting for us this time next year if we do."

She pats my hand, then glances at the tree once more. "I think I know what's moved to the top of my to-do list." Aunt Bea winks at me. "How about you?"

My heart is galloping in my chest, my palms sweaty as I lean in to kiss my aunt's cheek. She smells like garlic and tomato sauce—and if a person can smell of wisdom, well, she smells like that too. "I guess maybe it's time to chop down some trees."

"That's my girl."

Her words warm my chest all the way out of the room, down the stairs, and out the front door, where I start to hightail it home, praying that Blake is somewhere to be found.

Praying that I'm not too late.

I was, indeed, too late.

By the time I got home last night, Blake's car was nowhere to be found. I waited up until three a.m., and he never came home. Mare was asleep, but I texted her to ask if she knew where he was. I never heard back from her, and when I went into her room this morning, found her phone charging on the bedside table but no Marilee. She must have left for the festival without it—not surprising, given how tired she's been lately.

I've kept my eye open for her all day, but between every Hallmark Beach resident and the thousands of tourists who have flocked here for the Fourth of July Festival, I don't have much hope of finding her. For hours, I've been rushing back and forth between the food booths down on the beach and the Robin, where we decided it would be easiest for Tiny and his small but mighty team to grill the burgers and place them into containers to keep them warm.

Blake was supposed to be helping out, but I haven't seen him either. It's possible that he ducks out every time he sees me coming, but it seems odd I wouldn't have even caught a glimpse of him.

"Heads up!"

I see the shadow of a volleyball overhead and duck instinctively, dropping the box of hamburger buns on the boardwalk at my feet. Thankfully, the ball hits the sand instead of me, and April jogs up to retrieve it. "Sorry about that, cuz. You okay?"

"Yeah, of course. What are you doing?" I stare at her red, white, and blue tie-dyed shirt, where a white number badge is pinned. "You hate volleyball."

"Ugh, I know, but Scarlett loves it. She begged me to do the parent-kid game."

Aw, April. "You're a good mama."

"It's just volleyball."

I squeeze her elbow. "It's more than that." Because moms *should* sacrifice for their kids. They *should* stick it out, even if something isn't their favorite.

And the next time I talk to mine, I'm going to have a very honest conversation with her about the fact that she didn't do those things—and how it hurt. Not looking forward to that, honestly. But maybe it'll mend something in our relationship. And even if it doesn't make us closer, I think it'll heal something inside of me. It's a way to clear away the dead things, to make room for something new.

It's a place to start chopping, anyway.

Sticking out her tongue like she doesn't believe me, April leans in and whispers loudly. "We are not doing well. But at least Scar is having fun."

Then she grabs the ball and runs off, leaving me shaking my head as I pick up the box and resume my trek to the massive food tent. There's a line wrapped around it and clear down the beach toward The Purple Seashell, where a small musical stage has been constructed and currently a band of college students are rocking out to a fast-paced version of "God Bless America." The sound carries across the whole beach, combining with the cacophony of other beach noises—gulls crying, waves churning, people laughing. Meanwhile, four different volleyball games are going on, stretching to the southern part of the beach.

Every square inch of sand seems to be taken up by people— those I know, and those I don't. But not one of them is the guy I'm aching to see.

"Lucy, hey!" Someone calls to me from the open white tent, and I shift the box up with my knee and wind my way through the crowd until I find an empty spot on the table.

Thomas approaches me, disposable serving gloves on his

hands, an apron around his waist. "Thanks for bringing those. I can go get the next round of supplies so you're not having to hoof it back and forth."

Behind him, there's a string of older women that we recruited to help serve the burgers, chips, sodas, and other snacks, including the mountain of espresso brownies Thomas cooked up. In the end, we decided to make food easy on ourselves by creating a combo deal—ten bucks for the whole meal.

Despite the ocean breeze and the fact it's not even eighty degrees in summer, it feels oppressive under the canvas tent. "Oh, I don't mind." I remove the rubber band from my hair and fluff the tangled strands out, combing my fingers through them. "It's been good to move around a bit. Get my exercise in and all that." And have a chance to look for Blake...

Thomas nods. "Gotcha. It's just that I know Blake was supposed to be helping us, but with having to go back to Los Angeles yesterday—"

"Wait, what?" My hand jerks, and the rubber band snaps, broken.

"Yeah, he called me and Tiny yesterday and asked if we'd be okay without him. We both found a few extra people to volunteer, so it wasn't a big deal." He squints at me. "I thought you knew. Aren't you guys..."

I let my hair fall around my shoulders, and now it's like I'm walking on fire coals in here. "Oh, right. Los Angeles. Yeah, I knew he was leaving."

Just not yet.

And before he can say anything else, I turn on my heel and race out of there, my chest heaving with the exertion and the news I just heard.

Because he didn't even say good-bye.

But can I blame him, after the way I walked out at the first sign of conflict? He wanted to make things work between us. Wanted to show me that he wasn't like my mom. That he *did* want me.

And I doubted him. I doubted us.

What do I do now?

I have to go find him. Track him down in Los Angeles—even though I've never driven there, wouldn't even know where to look. Tell him I'm sorry. That I want a new adventure, and it's with him.

Wherever he is.

"Lucy, help!"

I turn this time to find Chloe racing toward me with a walkie talkie. The woman is in honest-to-goodness heeled sandals, white linen pants, and a red tank top that ties at the collarbone. Somehow she's missing the same sheen of sweat I feel coating my brow. And she's a woman on a mission. "Right now, I have to deal with the boatmen who were hired to launch our fireworks tonight, but there's also an issue with the sound equipment on the stage, and I can't seem to locate Dallas Loveland, who owns all of it." Her voice miraculously remains calm. If I were her, I'd be screaming, but Chloe is a professional. Still, I'm guessing under that royal exterior, she's stressed, so I raise my hand and salute her.

"I'm on it."

"You're an absolute gem, Lucy. Thank you." Then she clips northward, presumably toward The Purple Seashell's private beach, where the fireworks will be held in just a few hours.

Okay, no worries. I will just locate Dallas—or one of his many sisters or brothers—and solve this problem for Chloe before jumping in my car and heading for L.A. Though first I need to get Blake's address from Marilee, because of course, I never got it from him. No problem. I'll just look for her while I'm searching for Dallas.

Ha. Apparently, I really am an optimist, because it's much harder to find someone in this crowd than I thought. I do manage a glimpse of Marilee while I'm searching for Dallas, but by the time I find him, she's long gone. I huff out my frustration. At this rate, I'll get to Blake by Christmas.

As I'm weaving and looking, I realize I can't abandon my post anyway. The food line has gotten utterly ridiculous, so I sigh and head back to the tent, asking Thomas where I can pop in. He gives me brownie duty and sprints off to the kitchen for more chips, and I spend the next several hours greeting festival goers, handing out crumbling, delicious-smelling chocolate goodies, and pretending like my thoughts are right here in Hallmark Beach.

They're not, though. They're with him.

The sun sinks farther down the horizon line, and the sky's now streaked with reds and yellows. People start to move toward the northern tip of the beach, and I can see them carrying blankets with them to set up and watch the fireworks display. We finally close the food tent at eight, and I trudge alone—along with a crowd of people—toward The Purple Seashell beach, rubbing the back of my stiff neck. My entire body drags, and I know already that it wouldn't be smart to drive the four hours south to Los Angeles tonight.

But first thing in the morning? You bet your boots.

"Lucy!"

I want to duck my head and hide, because who needs something from me now? But then I see it's Marilee waving at me from the spot where she's sitting with Jordan and Ryder. Ryder is in Jordan's lap rubbing his eyes and yawning in between bites of brownie.

Mare says something to Jordan, then hops up, brushes off

her shorts, and walks toward where I stand, too tired to take another step. "I've been looking for you all day," she says as she leans in for a hug. "Well, in between playing volleyball and eating and keeping Ryder entertained."

First April, then Mare? "You played volleyball too?"

She smiled, something sad in it. "Ryder wanted to play in the parent-kid game, but Jordan was busy running the whole thing. He started to cry because his mom couldn't be here"—her eyes fill with tears—"and so I offered, even though I'm obviously not his parent."

If that isn't the sweetest thing. "Wish I could have seen that." My friend has such a heart of gold, especially where it concerns that little boy. "I've been looking for you too. I was wondering...do you have Blake's address? The one in L.A.?"

Her nose scrunches. "I think so. Why?"

I kick at the ground with my sandaled foot, and some sand falls under my toes. "He left town already—and I have to get him back."

Marilee's eyes widen. "You want him back?"

"I know I said I couldn't do this, but...Mare, I'm miserable. I made a mistake. And it might mean that I move away to L.A., and I hope you'll forgive me for that but I lo—"

She claps a hand over my mouth. "Don't you dare tell me before you tell him." Her eyes sparkle, even in the waning light of day. "And you're such a goose, Lucy. He didn't leave town. Well, he did. But just for the day. He's back." She points behind me. "And I think he's looking for you too."

"What?" I whip around so hard I almost fall over. And there, on the top of the cliffs, Blake's standing in shorts and a button-up, short-sleeve casual shirt that's whipping with the breeze. His hand is at his brow and he's scanning the crowd.

My whole body lights up the second our gazes collide. He

holds up a finger, as if telling me to wait right here. But I'm not waiting anymore. I shake my head...and start to run.

"Thanks, Mare," I toss over my shoulder.

"Love you!" she calls back as I rush up the sand, rounding the rocky outlay and climb, climb, climbing until I reach the top.

Until I reach him.

When I'm only a few feet away, my steps slow, and my vision narrows until it's filled only with Blake. The breeze sends his scent my way, and I'm enveloped, bathing in the citrusy notes of his cologne. The intensity of his blue gaze heats me slowly, and I find that I'm completely fine being scorched by him.

Is he a mirage? Is this a dream?

But no. He's here and so am I, standing right on the edge of the cliff, together in the dark. The only light now is the stars above. Below us somewhere, thousands wait with bated breath for the firework show to begin.

Yet I only care about the fireworks sparking here, between us.

"I thought you left."

"I did." His eyes flit over my face, like he's drinking me in. I know the feeling. "But not for the reasons you might think." Then Blake's wrapping his big hand around my waist, lowering his head to mine so our foreheads are touching. "I decided that I didn't want to be like my dad, choosing to focus on regret and all the *what ifs* instead of embracing the gifts I've been given."

My hands reach for his upper arms, lying flat on top while my thumbs press into his biceps, soaking up his strength.

He keeps talking. "I know you'll be shocked, but I took some time to analyze my life."

"No. You?" I tease.

"Hush, woman." He kisses the tip of my nose, and I

shudder at the contact. I want more of him, always more. "I thought about which parts of my plans were actually something I wanted—not just what was expected of me. And I realized that what I want is to be proud of the work I do. To love what I do. And..." He exhales. Inhales. "To come home to a good woman that I love. Someone who makes all of my hard work matter in the first place."

I hear the hiss and whine of a firework as it careens from a boat out on the water up into the sky. There's a red flash and a burst of something beautiful overhead.

But I'm more concerned with what's happening here.

With how Blake tugs my hips against his, moves his mouth to my ear, and whispers, "And if you haven't figured it out yet, Sunshine, that someone is you." Then his lips are brushing against my ear before Blake pulls back to look at me. "I love you, Lucy. And I'll do whatever it takes to prove I'm not going anywhere. That I'm in this with you for the long haul."

The next firework sparks, ignites, and the light it gives off allows me to see the pleading—the utter hope—in Blake's gaze.

Oh, this man. How did he make me love him back when I was so determined not to?

"Say something, please." His hand tightens around my waist.

"Something." I finally let a smile flit across my lips.

"Sunshine," he growls, and the sound of it sends a thrill up my spine. "Put me out of my misery. I've told you what I want. What do *you* want?"

The question of the hour—the last twelve years, really. "What do I want? It's simple, really. You." I lift up on my tiptoes and press a kiss to his stubbly cheek. It's so unlike Blake to not shave, but I kind of like this undone look of his. "Flake, I've spent almost half my life loving you. Why would I stop now?"

He breathes out a disbelieving laugh before grabbing my face and kissing me. Another firework, then two, bursts in the sky, and the explosion rocks my whole body. Or maybe that's just Blake's kiss. His hands are everywhere. My hair, my cheeks, my ears, arms, waist, back, like he can't get enough. Our mouths move together, in sync as we bask in the glow of each other.

I don't care where we go or what we do for a living. Blake is enough.

"What?" he says, freezing, his mouth hovering over mine.

Oops. Did I say that out loud? But I shake myself. What does it matter? I'm done hiding my feelings away. "You're enough. I want an adventure with you. So…I'm moving to L.A. If that's okay with you."

"I don't think that's a good idea." He softly tugs on a strand of my hair. "I'd miss you if you left."

It's my turn to freeze. "What do you mean?"

He grins at me. "I spent the day in Los Angeles yesterday and all this morning because I was selling my recipes to Dale. Well, selling him the use of my recipes for the restaurant in exchange for a small stake in the business. I'll still be involved, but only from a distance and only as an investor. We'll hire another chef. Another manager. Dale was disappointed but understood my decision and respected it."

I blink. Sweet macaroni. Am I understanding what he's saying? For real? "You're giving up your recipes?"

"Not completely. Dale's just licensing them, and we agreed I'll not license them to anyone else—except I have the right to use them in my food truck here in Hallmark Beach."

Whaaaaat? I bounce on my tiptoes. "You're staying? Are you sure? What about your dream?" I sputter question after question, my brain working faster than my mouth.

He laughs. "Yes. Yes. And as for my dream"—Blake folds

me up in his embrace—"it was waiting for me back here in Hallmark Beach the whole time."

Then he kisses me with all the depth and love I feel right back for him. And as a slew of fireworks burst and flame in a raging, beautiful finale overhead, I know that my love story with Blake is just beginning.

Marilee

I sigh as the last vestiges of color disappear from the sky, leaving a smoky haze of firework dust behind in the dark night. Somewhere behind us all, up on the cliffs, I pray that Blake and Lucy are getting their happily ever after.

Some of us aren't so lucky. But if I can't have romance, at least I have this.

Ryder's sweet red head is mashed against my shirt, and his even breathing tells me that despite the fireworks, he's fallen asleep. I kiss his hair, which smells of sugar and little boy sweat.

"That was really something, huh?" Jordan's voice is low beside me.

All around us, people stand, gathering up their blankets and chatting about how great the festival was. I feel bad I couldn't do more to help out this year, but between my schedule at the bakery and helping Jordan out with Ryder... well, it's a wonder I didn't fall asleep right along with the kid.

"Lee."

"Hmm?" I turn to find Jordan watching me.

"You look exhausted."

His eyebrows are knit together, his worry lines popping. I want to press my finger right there between his eyes, smooth out his skin. He worries too much about me. About Ryder. About everyone but himself. Such a selfless guy. Such a good friend.

"I'm all right." And of course, I can't help the yawn that comes. I'm trying to hold as still as possible, to shake off the yawn, and my glasses slip down my nose with the slight movement. Darn things need to be tightened, but who has time to go one town over to get them fixed?

Jordan reaches over and, with a crooked smile, pushes my glasses up.

"Thanks." What would I do without him? He's the cool, steady cucumber to my flighty mess. My eyes drop to Ryder. "Guess you should get this goober home, huh?"

"Probably." He stands and reaches down to pull Ryder from my arms. For a moment, our noses are nearly touching, and I see some sort of emotion flit across his features. I've seen it before but can't put my finger on what it is. Of course, all of my friends tease me about Jordan liking me as more than a friend, but he's never said anything.

Which is good. Because I don't think of him that way.

I can't.

Not that he's not handsome. Goodness knows he is, with his boy-next-door chuckle, his muscled frame, and his tan skin. That blond hair that's much fuller and healthier than my own, which I keep up in a bun because it's just not worth the effort of doing it.

And besides all that, he's just a good guy. In fact, other than my brother, Jordan Carmichael is the best man I know.

But that's why I could never afford to think of him as more than a friend. He deserves the whole world—a woman who has the capacity to love him fully. Not someone like me.

Broken. Used up. Messy.

He takes Ryder gently from my arms and repositions him so he's tucked against his shoulder. I start to gather up the blanket, when someone behind us gives a grunt of disapproval.

Turning, I find Larry and Constance Comer staring at Jordan and Ryder. Larry's got his hand on Constance's back, and she's wearing a scowl on her weathered face. I've only interacted with Ryder's grandparents—his mom Georgia's parents—a few times, but in the past, they've always been nice enough. Not warm necessarily, but not baring their teeth like this either.

"You should not be keeping him out this late," Constance snaps. "He's clearly exhausted."

Jordan frowns. "It's a special occasion. I don't norm—"

"Little boys should be safely tucked away in their beds at this hour. And wasn't he scared of the fireworks last year? Georgia told us that he cried. I can't believe you'd bring him back here and subject him to this."

I take a step toward Jordan, as if he needs my support, but then Constance turns her eye to me and looks me up and down. Her scowl deepens. "Well. Hopefully he won't be too exhausted from this to enjoy our sleepover on Friday night." Then she flounces away, Larry hurrying after her. He glances back and lifts his shoulders as if to say, "I don't know why she's acting like this."

"That was weird." Jordan huffs and rubs a finger underneath his cap. Even though the boy's asleep, Ryder's arms have gone around Jordan's neck, and it's clear to see that even in sleep, he trusts his daddy to keep him safe.

I step toward them and place my hand on Ryder's back, rubbing it lightly. "I'm guessing it's just hard for her to be here without her daughter. The first year is always the worst, with every little anniversary reminding you of your loss."

"Aw, Lee." He nudges me with his foot. "You're so good at putting yourself in other people's shoes."

"I've literally been in their shoes. Though I can't imagine how hard it must be to lose a child." That's not true, though. Not that Donny thought the babies we lost counted, since I was only ever a few weeks along when I miscarried. I don't mean to lie to Jordan. The words were just out before I thought about them. He knows about a lot of my relationship with Donny—was here in town for the worst of it and held me up in the middle of it all—but I never told him about the losses.

But I don't feel like choosing this moment to tell Jordan about all of that, so I rush on. "Anyway, you didn't do anything wrong by bringing him here. He had a blast today."

"In large part because of you. Thank you again for playing volleyball with him. It meant the world."

"I know I'm not his mom." How many times have I wished...? Because if any of my children had lived, I would want them to be exactly like Ryder. Curious, mischievous, funloving like his daddy. And sweet. Kind. "But I'm glad I could be here for him. For both of you."

Then I smile up at him and thank God that I have been given a friend like Jordan Carmichael.

JORDAN

When Marilee looks at me like this—her eyes so wide and innocent, her smile as sweet as one of her cookies—it takes everything in me to not lean in and kiss her.

To not pretend that she *is* Ryder's mom.

That she's my wife.

That we're a family.

It's hard not to pretend that we're about to head to the same house instead of different ones. That together, we get to tuck Ryder into his bed, right before I get to tuck her into mine and hold her all night long, every night for the rest of our lives.

It takes everything I have in these moments to remember that, while Marilee Moffitt is *my* fantasy—everything I've wanted since I was a teenager—I'm not hers.

And I never will be.

Quick Author's Note

Eek! Can you believe that we are already two books in to the Hallmark Beach series? It feels like just yesterday that I dreamed up this little town, but it's actually been a few years...

And now, I'm addicted. I don't know about you, but I want to curl up and enjoy more Hallmark Beach stories. I want to see Marilee, April, Elisse, and Kelsey get their happy endings too!

(Although if you just aren't ready to leave Blake and Lucy yet, I understand. That's why I wrote you a bonus epilogue. Download it at kristincanary.com/BeachsideEnemy.)

But moving on...are you ready for Jordan and Marilee's story? I am seriously so stoked for this best friends to lovers story that may just have some of my favorite tropes thrown in. Marriage of convenience, forced proximity, and one bed, anyone?

If that sounds right up your alley, you can order Beachside Kisses With My Best Friend right now. It should release in late 2024.

AND FINALLY, turn the page to check out how to grab a

FREE PREQUEL to the California Dreamin' series, which you should definitely read while you wait for Jordan and Marilee's book.

This series is all about a San Diego friend group that, much like our Hallmark Beach crew, is total #friendshipgoals. This series also includes some of the best tropes and swoony book boyfriends you could ask for!

a free story for you

Enjoyed *Beachside Kisses With My Enemy*? Not ready to quit reading yet? If you sign up for my newsletter at kristincanary.com/freebook, you will automatically receive *Enamoring Her Amnesic Ex*, the love story of Connor's brother Kevin and his wife Lola (who you briefly met if you've read Book 1 in my California Dreamin' series, *Loving the Ladies' Man!*). This is just a gift from me to you as a thank you for choosing to hang out with me.

Enamoring Her Amnesic Ex:

Two years ago, he broke my heart—and now he's forgotten all about it.

When my sister goes into labor, what are the chances that the nearest hospital would be the one where my ex, Kevin Bryant, is a surgical resident?

You know—the man who decided being a doctor was more important than love and left me reeling. Hard.

But when we run into each other—quite literally—he falls, hits his head, and wakes up with amnesia.

And he still thinks we're together.

His brother Connor asks me to pretend we're dating, just for a little while, so we can ease Kevin into the truth.

But the real truth is that being around this strong, capable man again is making me remember things *I* would rather forget.

Yeah, hi, my name is Lola, and I'm clearly a glutton for punishment. Because here I am. Pretending with him. Taking care of him.

Kissing him.

Just waiting for the bubble to burst.

Because as soon as Kevin snaps out of this and remembers the past, there WILL be another heartbreak.

And all I'll have is the memories of what was.

Read on for a sneak peek of the California Dreamin' prequel novella, Enamoring Her Amnesic Ex...

Of all the hospitals in San Diego, my sister had to pick the one where *he* works.

Fine—if we're being technical, she didn't really have a choice. Her water breaking in the frozen foods aisle of her grocery store wasn't exactly Theresa's plan.

But come on, universe. Did the closest hospital have to be *his*? I feel I have a right to be upset by this, but since I can't be mad at Theresa, here I am with the biggest bouquet of flowers I can afford (hint: it's not THAT big) obscuring my face as I slink down the brightly lit hallways. And you'd better believe that anytime I see a tall doctor with brown hair, I hug the wall like it's wool and I'm static, baby.

But I'm not letting a potential encounter with my ex stop me from meeting my newest niece. Because family trumps everything—even if being in the place where Dr. Kevin Bryant is a surgical resident is giving me sweaty pits and an itchy nose. Or hey, maybe that's the flowers shoved in my face.

Wiggling my nose like that girl from *Bewitched*, I book it in my jeweled wedges down the hall, almost to the magical door where Theresa and Jake await with their new bundle of joy.

And then, I hear it—that voice I'd know anywhere, even though it was only part of my life for five months.

And yeah, they might have been the most intense and wonderful five months of my life, but phantom whiplash still hits me when I think about them. Because all the intensity, all the wonder, came to an abrupt halt when Kevin figured out I didn't fit into the picture he had for his life.

Now, I can't help the yelp that comes from my mouth as I stop and peek through the flowers. My traitorous heart—which shouldn't care one fig about the man standing at the nurses' station after he broke my heart into a million pieces nearly two years ago—thumps a happy jig against my chest.

Down, girl.

Because he may have the same high brow, the same tousled dark hair, the same strong arms and lean body that suggest he still runs and lifts weights every morning like clockwork, but the harshness in his tone, the rigidness of his stance as he yells directives at the nurses and disappears behind a set of doors are proof that he's not the man I thought I knew.

My Kevin was sweet. A little uptight, yes, but considerate and generous. My Kevin would never treat people like that.

But maybe I just saw what I wanted to see back then.

"Lola?"

I turn to find my brother-in-law standing in the hall outside my destination door, his brown-gray eyebrows raised. Jake's eyes are a bit red, probably from crying—he's a freaking waterspout, I tell ya—and his clothing is rumpled, I assume from the long night at the hospital.

Striding forward, I raise on my tiptoes and brush a kiss against his cheek. "Congrats, Daddy."

"Thanks. How's Sami?"

After Theresa went into labor and Jake joined her at the hospital yesterday, they asked me to pick up my five-year-old niece Sami from kindergarten and keep her at my apartment overnight.

"Wonderful and precocious as always." In fact, the girl asked me a million questions about birth and babies that started making me sweat. Thankfully, I was able to distract her with a Disney movie and pizza night. This morning before grabbing the flower bouquet I'm now holding, I dropped Sami back at school, where Jake will pick her up this afternoon so she can officially meet her baby sister.

"That's my girl." A grin sweeps his face and he pushes glasses up the bridge of his nose. Then he scans the hallway. "By the way, why were you standing there like Harriet the Spy just a minute ago?"

Note: Sami is obsessed with Harriet the Spy, so it's completely adorable that Jake uses it as a reference point in conversation. Not so adorable is the fact he caught my strange behavior upon seeing Kevin.

"No reason." I straighten and tug at the hem of my aqua-colored blouse. "How are Theresa and Baby Girl? Did you guys come up with a name?"

"Not yet."

"All right, all right. You twisted my arm. I guess I don't mind."

"Mind what?"

"Sharing my name with her. Lola Warren's got a great ring to it, don't you think?" I wink and breeze past him. As I step inside the room, my sister's tired voice wades out from the other side of the privacy curtain—and an older voice responds.

Mom.

Ugh. Is it too late to escape? I turn on my heel, but Jake shakes his head. He juts his chin toward my sister's bed. "I need you to stay with her. Theresa's craving a breakfast burrito from Dos Brasas."

"Fine," I hiss out. "But I expect one too. As payment."

"Payment for spending time with your sister and adorable niece?"

I stick my tongue out—not so mature for a twenty-four-year-old, but when did I ever claim to be mature? "For forcing me to talk with my parents."

"She's already been on the phone for fifteen minutes." There's a bit of sympathy in Jake's voice now. He knows why this is hard for me. "I'm sure you won't have to talk long."

"Still, you'd better throw in a Diet Coke to revive my energy when you return."

He chuckles, pats my shoulder, and leaves.

Groaning inwardly, I brace myself for the inevitable. Then I throw on a happy face and walk around the curtain, ginormous bouquet in tow.

Theresa's blonde hair is a bit grungy, tossed up in a messy bun on the top of her head—stay-at-home mom style, as she'd say—and her face is devoid of makeup like always, but the tiny smile lines around her lips are on full display as she snuggles her infant daughter against her chest with one arm and holds up her phone with the opposite hand.

When she sees me, Theresa turns the screen my way. "Look who's here."

I wave at the grainy image of my parents, who are squeezed in front of their computer in Zambia, where they teach English to underserved communities. Apparently they do a lot of good in the village where they've lived for more than a decade.

I hope so, considering what it's cost them—what it's cost all of us.

Stuffing down the bitterness, I set the flowers on the windowsill of the small room. "Hi, Mom. Hi, Dad."

"Lola! So good to see you." My mom looks older every time I see her on-screen—her hair a little grayer, the wrinkles around her eyes a little more prominent—but maybe it's just the terrible Internet connection. I wouldn't know, since they haven't been back to visit since Sami was about six months old and I've never been to Africa.

"You too, Mom." I move to the head of the bed, and Theresa flips the phone back around so it's fixed on her youngest daughter, who is sleeping and breathing in and out with an adorable little mew. At 8 pounds, 6 ounces, she's bigger than Sami was, though her legs are scrunched up like a little frog. Theresa has dressed her in pink footy pajamas that are just about the cutest thing I've ever seen.

Bending down, I kiss her sweet downy cheek, then the top of Theresa's head. "Good job, Sis."

"She's pretty great, isn't she?" My sister yawns and nearly drops the phone. "Sorry. Long night."

"We won't keep you, dear." Mom clicks her tongue. "Oh, I just wish I was there to hold my grandbaby."

"You could come home, you know." The words are out before I can call them back. I know better. Nothing is going to change. At this point, why would it?

"Lo ..." Theresa warns.

Dad sighs deeply, taking his glasses off and rubbing his chin with a big meaty fist. "You know we would, Lola, but the people here need us."

We *need you.*

They're the words I've longed to say for eleven years since they left a thirteen-year-old me in the guardianship of my twenty-three-year-old barely married sister because their new life was "too unstable for children." But I don't say those words, because they're not true anymore. Nope. Theresa and I have learned to rely upon each other. We are all the family we need.

I force another smile. "I know."

After a few more pleasantries, my sister says goodbye and hangs up the phone. "That wasn't so bad, was it?"

"Torture." I tilt my head. "But worth it to meet this sweet girl."

Black-as-night curls stick out the bottom of Baby Girl's white cotton beanie with a pink satin bow. Apparently all Flanagan girls are born with dark hair that eventually falls out and comes back in nearly white blonde. At least, that's what happened with me, Theresa, and Sami. "Can I?"

"Of course."

My long hair falls forward over my shoulder as I gather the tiny bundle in my arms and get her situated. Her button nose and rosy lips remind me so much of her older sister, it's uncanny. "The Flanagan genes are strong with this one."

"Right?" Theresa pours a glass of water for herself from a pale pink jug. There's only enough to fill half her cup, and she downs it quickly. Then she relaxes against the bed. The room is small but thankfully private, and it smells like a mixture of baby formula and lemongrass. A large window lets in the morning light of another gorgeous mid-September day in San Diego.

As Baby Girl coos and inhales, I sigh in contentment. This is where I belong. With my family, who need me. I'll never regret choosing this life.

"So." Theresa studies me then tugs at the thin sheet covering her. "Did you see that job opportunity I sent you yesterday? You know, before I made a complete mess in Aisle 3." She hangs her head. "I'll never be able to show my face in my favorite grocery store again. Can you imagine the person who had to clean that up?"

"Oh, stop it. The staff will take one look at this sweetness and forget all about how she came hard and fast into the world." I run a fingertip along her forehead, tracing her cheeks, her nose. "Although maybe it wouldn't hurt to get them all gift cards as a thank-you. I'm definitely glad the manager acted quickly when she realized your contractions were coming so close together."

"Me too. And so grateful Jake made it just in time." Theresa, who is not the crier in the family, sniffles despite herself. "Find yourself a nice guy like him, Lo. It may have taken me a few years to see him as more than my nerdy lab partner, but now I find him the most handsome man alive. There's nothing sexier than watching him hold our daughters. Daughters. As in, more than one." Tears start streaming down her cheeks at an alarming rate. "Oh my gosh, I'm sorry. These postpartum hormones are something else."

I reach across to the counter and snag a few tissues, shoving them into her hand. "You definitely scored one of the good ones."

And once upon a time, I thought I'd done the same. From the moment I met Kevin at the diner where I still work—and accidentally served him a hamburger instead of his requested pastrami sandwich—things were like lightning between us. Hot and charged, yes, but deep too, leaving a lasting trench, a mark, on my heart.

Theresa blows her nose and then fixes her eyes on me again. "You didn't answer my question."

My nose scrunches. "What question?"

"The job opportunity. Did you look at it?"

"Oh." I kind of want to ask her which one she means, since she sends me several each week. But I'm not sure if she's in a teasing mood, given the sheen of tears still coating her eyeballs. "Um, no, haven't had a chance yet."

"Well, I think it's perfect for you. Assistant costume designer at a theater in Los Angeles." She straightens and I can tell she's about to go into teacher mode—I guess she can't help it after teaching science to middle schoolers for so many years.

"Now, I know it doesn't pay all that well, so you might have to have a second job, but you're basically working two jobs now anyway. And this way, you'd get paid for the theater work. No more of this volunteer stuff. Which would be fine, but you have a bachelor's degree in costume design, for goodness' sake. You should be paid for your genius."

Baby Girl rustles and makes a sound like a grunt. *I agree, girl. I agree.* "It does sound like a great opportunity." I let my words trail off.

"But?"

"But you know how I feel about moving. I'm not going to be some distant aunt who never sees her nieces."

"Lo, Los Angeles is only a few hours away."

"I know, but—"

"And"—I hate how big-sister bossiness pervades her tone—"if you're ever going to go to New York and design on Broadway, then this might be a good step in the right direction."

"New York isn't happening, Reese." I try to infuse a lightness to my tone, as if my statement doesn't prick my insides.

"But it's your dream."

"Was my dream. In middle school. But now that I know what it would require ... well, I'm just not willing to make that sacrifice."

I refuse to abandon the people I love like my parents did.

Like Kevin did.

Not for a million dollars—and not even for the chance to design costumes on the Great White Way.

As if I've somehow summoned her help, Baby Girl opens her big beautiful blue eyes—and starts to wail. It happens so suddenly that I jump, but Theresa just laughs and holds out her arms. "Saved by the cry of hunger."

Standing, I hand over the hangry monster who has replaced my sweet little niece. But as soon as Theresa has her suckling—

like a freaking boss, I might add—she turns her pointed gaze to me again. "Now, where were we? Oh, yeah. About to dissect the trauma our parents unwittingly unleashed on you by sticking you with me as a pseudo mom. Is that about right?

"I mean, when you put it like that ..." I tease.

Thankfully, I'm saved by yet another interruption when Jake waltzes through the door, a brown paper bag in hand and a soda. He wiggles them in the air and Theresa nearly leaps from the bed—but doesn't, of course, because I'm guessing Baby Girl would deafen us all if she unlatched. But when Jake places a foil-wrapped burrito the size of my forearm on the table in front of Theresa, she gives him the most solemn expression before saying, "I don't think I have ever loved you more than in this moment."

He turns amused eyes to me before handing me a burrito and the soda. "Do you feel the same?"

"Would it be weird if I said yes?" I grin. Living with him and Theresa for five years before living on campus at the University of San Diego for my undergrad gave Jake and me lots of time to perfect the brother-sister relationship. Even though I have my own apartment now, I still spend lots of my free time at their house, watching Sami and doing movie nights with my sis.

Theresa rips into her burrito, taking a bite and sighing with pleasure. The scent of sausage and cooked eggs makes my own stomach rumble, and I start to unwrap my burrito, which is warm in my hands.

"Do you have to work today?" Jake asks.

I freeze. Shoot, what time is it? My eyes land on the ancient clock above Theresa's head and the tension leaves my body. "Not for another hour." Which is good, because the lunch rush at Dom's waits for no one. Of course, I've told my boss that I might be switching shifts a lot in the next few weeks as Theresa might need me. And thankfully, the first costume fittings for *The Music Man* aren't until this weekend, so I don't have any set times I need to be at the theater until then.

Before I can even take a bite of my burrito, Theresa has inhaled hers, all while Baby Girl happily nurses. Jake is watching in awe of them both, and suddenly I feel like the thirdiest third wheel ever. I should be used to it by now—it's basically been happening since my parents foisted me on the newlyweds—but I still can't seem to escape the ick swirling in my stomach at the thought that I'm more an invasion than a help.

I stand, set the burrito on my chair, and grab the now-empty water jug from Theresa's side table. "I'll get you a refill."

"Oh, thank you. That would be great." My sister strokes Baby Girl's back. Both of them look like they're in a food coma.

Hustling from the room, I quickly find the kitchen area where the nurses stash little packets of crackers, containers of applesauce, and sandwiches for hungry mamas. There's an ice and water machine and I use both to refill the container to the brim. Once I set the lid on top, I take my time moseying back to the room. I stop to study a wall papered with children's artwork from the pediatric wing, smiling at the crooked lines and creative shapes.

"Lola?"

For the second time in an hour, someone is calling my name. But this time, it isn't my brother-in-law.

It's *him*.

And his voice in my ear is so unexpected that I shriek and jump, forgetting that there's a full container of water in my hands.

Liquid careens out of the top—guess I didn't secure that lid as well as I thought—and all over Kevin. As if that wasn't bad enough, I drop the jug, allowing what's left inside to spill out onto the floor beneath him.

Eyes wide, he's staring back at me with a look that likely mirrors my own. Along his strong jawline is a dusting of stubble, which is kind of a surprise given his propensity to shave every day. He always said doctors should present themselves as professionally as possible.

I lift a hand and give him the tiniest wave known to mankind. "Hi, Kevin."

"What ..." He looks down at his green scrubs, which are drenched. Then his gaze moves back to me. "What are you doing here?"

The once-bustling hallway is now strangely devoid of people, as if the universe knows this moment is embarrassing enough. "I didn't come here to see you, that's for sure." I cross my arms over my chest.

"That's not what ..." Kevin tugs at the badge on the pocket of his scrub pants. "Sorry. It's, um, good to see you."

"Sure it is."

Kevin shifts from one foot to the other. I'm shocked he's still standing here, to be honest. Maybe he's expecting me to go quietly like I did the last time we spoke. But I've got two years' worth of pent-up anger and hurt just begging to be unleashed on him. The only reason I'm keeping them in check? I don't want my sister's care to suffer. Not that a surgical resident would have anything to do with Theresa. But still.

Oh, yeah. And I guess I also maybe feel like he wouldn't care one way or the other. He was so clinical when he dumped me.

No feeling. No heartache.

It was so ... *easy* ... for him to let me go.

So sue me if I'm relishing his discomfort in this moment just a tad.

A pager on his belt goes off and visible relief finds the cracks in his face. "Well, I'd better go. I hope ..." He swallows. "I hope everything is okay."

Dang it. There's a sliver of the Kevin I knew—the one who understands what it is to lose someone and works desperately hard so others don't have to. I can't leave him thinking that there's something wrong with my family. Or me. "Theresa had a baby."

"Right. Of course. That's why you're in this wing."

"Yep." My smile hitches one corner of my mouth at his logical brain at work. "Why are you here though? Doing a rotation in OB?" While dating him, I acquired quite the medical vocabulary.

"Just covering a shift for a colleague." He checks his watch. "Speaking of."

"Right." I bite the inside of my cheek, because the idea of saying goodbye ... "Well."

"Well." His eyes connect with mine and spear me right there on site. I can't move, can't breathe. Their deep chocolate tones wash me in their sweetness, in the depths of what was. What could have been. If only ...

Then the connection is severed when he pivots quickly.

But instead of moving away, he slips in the puddle of water that—until this moment—I'd forgotten completely about.

Apparently he did too.

His head bangs against a medical cart behind him. Before I know what's happening, his eyes loll back into his head and close.

"Kevin?" I drop to my knees, and my jeans are soaked in an instant—not that I care. He looks really pale, though I don't see any blood and his breathing seems okay. I pat his cheek but he doesn't wake up. Turning my head toward the nurses' station down the hall, I cry out. "Help!"

A few people come running and they push me aside while I watch them take stock of the situation. They call for a bed and a woman in a white coat hurries over and examines him. It's all happening so quickly and my own breath is coming in short bursts. I clench my fists at my sides.

Finally, as they lift him onto a bed, his eyes flutter open.

"Thank you," I whisper as I step forward.

But the doctor gives me a side-eye. "Sorry, miss, you need to step back."

"Don't talk to my girlfriend like that," Kevin says before his eyes roll back into his head and he passes out again.

Did I miss the "ex" in ex-girlfriend? Maybe I'm the one who hit my head. And no, it's NOT wishful thinking, thank you very much.

The doctor and team start wheeling him away and I realize I'm biting my lip so hard that I taste blood. One of the nurses— a sweet older woman with a white poof of hair—puts her hand on my lower back. "We're taking him to the emergency department to get a full workup. Don't worry, we'll take good care of him."

And I do the only thing I can do. Because this is Kevin, and even though he is the absolute last person I wanted to see today, this is kind of all my fault and I owe it to him to make sure he's all right.

After shooting Jake a quick text, I follow the nurse down the hall.

Enamoring Her Amnesic Ex is ONLY available by signing up for my newsletter. Grab it here: kristincanary.com/freebook

Kristin is a wife and boy mom who functions best on peach tea and cookie dough ice cream. A desert dweller, she always has her eye on the next trip to a beach somewhere—and if she can't travel there in person, then you'd better believe she's going to write about it. Kristin is never fully satisfied with a movie, TV show, or book without a hefty dose of romance in it, and she's grateful to be living a true-life love story with her own crazy little family. Connect with her at KristinCanary.com.

 facebook.com/kristincanary

 instagram.com/kristincanaryauthor